DEADLY POLICY

A Silver Sleuths Mystery

Other Books by Mitzi Kelly

Classic Revenge

DEADLY POLICY
•
Mitzi Kelly

AVALON BOOKS
NEW YORK

4/12
Thomas
Bouregy

Kel

Published by Avalon Books,
an imprint of Thomas Bouregy & Co., Inc.
New York, NY

Library of Congress Cataloging-in-Publication Data

Kelly, Mitzi, 1958–
    Deadly policy : a Silver Sleuths mystery / Mitzi Kelly.
        p. cm.
    ISBN 978-0-8034-7473-4 (hardcover : alk. paper)   1. Older
people—Fiction.   2. Mothers and daughters—Fiction.
3. Insurance crimes—Fiction.   I. Title.
    PS3611.E454D43 2012
    813'.6—dc23

                                                    2011041516

PRINTED IN THE UNITED STATES OF AMERICA
ON ACID-FREE PAPER
BY RR DONNELLEY, HARRISONBURG, VIRGINIA

In memory of my grandmothers,
Mildred "Mimill" Jendrejeski and
Ella Marie "Nonnie" Michon.
I love them and will always miss them.
Age is only a number.

Acknowledgments

Whenever I'm given the opportunity to show my appreciation to the people in my life who I feel make the Silver Sleuths series possible, I'm almost overwhelmed. The considerable support I receive is incredible and something I will always treasure.

This project wouldn't be near as much fun to work on if it weren't for the laughs, patience, and love I receive from my husband, John, and my son, John Lewis. I am so blessed.

With deep appreciation, I would like to give thanks to my very special—*and I mean this in a good way*—family and friends. You've provided enough material to keep this series going for years!

I am very grateful to Jack Lopez, an exceptional friend with an uncanny eye for detail. I sincerely value our friendship. Thank you for your thoughtful assistance.

A very special thank-you to my editor, Lia Brown, for your patience and hard work. I appreciate your insightful comments and dedicated goal toward quality. It's a pleasure working with you, and I'm looking forward to our growing relationship.

With much gratitude, I would like to thank my agent, Susan Cohen. You have the extraordinary ability to know what I'm trying to say even when the words get in the way. You have taught me so much, and I can't fully express how much I appreciate your advice and support. I will forever be grateful for your encouragement and friendship. You are truly remarkable.

To the many others who have crossed my path and provided exciting glimpses into the human spirit, regardless of age, I thank you from the bottom of my heart!

Chapter One

Trish Anderson's eyes flew open. She listened carefully, her heart pounding in her chest, but everything was quiet. And very dark.

Slowly, she sat up. The light of the moon cast faint illumination through sheer, sage-colored curtains, letting her know that sunrise was still a long way off. She pulled the covers up to her chest and shivered, but it wasn't from the cold. Something was wrong. She just didn't know what that *something* could be. She strained to hear a noise, anything that would give her a hint as to why the hair at the back of her neck tingled, a sign she had learned not to ignore.

Trish didn't scare easily, a blessing since she lived alone in the big house, but there was no denying that lately she was more alert, more aware of sounds and her surroundings than she used to be. And she knew why.

Trish still hadn't recovered from the murder of her dear friend Susan Wiley. The crime had rocked the stately and peaceful neighborhood. And she and her two best friends, Millie Morrow and Edna Radcliff, had been instrumental in solving the crime. They'd had to face pure evil when they set out to prove Susan's murder had not been committed by her husband, as the local police had believed. Sam Wiley had since moved from the area, and the feeling of loss, and the knowledge that such violence can happen anywhere, at any time, was never far from Trish's thoughts. She waited several moments, listening for any strange noise, and then took a deep breath, willing herself to calm down. It must have been a bad dream, or the

central heat had kicked in, or someone's dog had barked. Regardless, all was quiet now.

"This is ridiculous," she muttered out loud. What was she
going to do, stay up for hours feeding her imagination by listening for a sound that *might* signal danger? *No*, she thought to
herself firmly. *No, I will not!*

Chastising herself for being such a chicken, Trish snuggled
back under the covers and closed her eyes.

But not for long.

A loud, pounding noise had her bolting upright again; the
sound was definitely not the heater kicking in.

Two options were available. She could dive back under the
covers and pray really hard that this *was* just a bad dream, or
she could play Ms. Courageous and venture outside the safety
of her bedroom to see who was banging at her door. She was
halfway under the covers when the doorbell rang, two long
peals followed by silence. Then the pounding started again.

One of the options was no longer viable. She flipped on the
bedside lamp and swung her legs over the side of the bed as
she cast a quick look at the clock. *Five thirty?* Who would be
knocking on her door at five thirty in the morning? It had to
be an emergency; there wasn't any other explanation.

Quickly, Trish slid her feet into her slippers and thrust her
arms into her robe. She didn't think she was in any danger,
because whoever was at her door obviously wasn't worried
about making his or her presence known. Nevertheless, she
made a fast detour into her bathroom, looking for some kind of
weapon . . . just in case. Grimacing, she reached for her hairbrush. It would have to do.

The pounding on the door started again. Shaking her head,
she pulled her robe tight and hurried down the hallway. "If
there are dents in my door, I'm going to be one angry lady," she
muttered.

Trish was almost to the door when the incessant pounding
stopped. Relieved, she sent up a thankful prayer and moved
close to look out the peephole. Nothing. She tilted her head and
closed one eye. Still nothing. Then it dawned on her. She had
neglected to turn on the porch light. She was reaching for the

switch, excusing her witless thinking as due to a lack of sleep, when she suddenly froze, small tendrils of fear crawling up her back at the rough scraping sound coming from the other side of the door.

Slowly, she took a step back, unconsciously raising her weapon as her eyes drifted downward toward another noise. Whoever was standing on her front porch was jiggling the door handle! Then, while her mind raced but her feet refused to move, she watched as the door swung open.

"Good morning," Millie Morrow said casually, pocketing the key she had used to open Trish's door. "I wasn't sure you heard me. Don't worry about brushing your hair. I've seen you worse. Got any coffee?"

Trish's mouth opened and she started to speak, but Millie just brushed past her and headed for the kitchen. Millie wasn't on fire, all her limbs appeared to be working fine, and she seemed perfectly able to talk. So what was the emergency? Unless, of course, she considered her friend's outfit. Millie had either dressed in a big hurry or she was preparing to try out for some type of team sport. She wore a white Dallas Cowboys cap over her short gray hair, a maroon Texas A&M University sweatshirt, black San Antonio Spurs sweat pants, and red tennis shoes.

"I couldn't sleep, either," Millie said over her shoulder. "I think we must be the only people awake on the whole block."

Trish's lips clamped shut and she slowly closed the door. Thrusting the hairbrush into the pocket of her robe, she tried to decide whether to strangle her eighty-year-old friend or laugh. The strangling idea was gaining momentum, though.

"I was sleeping just fine, but thanks for asking," Trish mumbled ungraciously as she walked into the kitchen and plopped down in a chair.

"Sarcasm doesn't suit you," Millie said, giving Trish a pointed look while she poured water into the coffeemaker.

"Who said I was being sarcastic?"

Millie stood on her toes, pulling coffee cups from the cabinet. "We need to talk."

Trish yawned. "And we couldn't do that at a decent hour, like normal people?"

"Normal is highly overrated. Besides, we were both up."

"Again, *I* was sleeping."

"Oh. Well, you're up now." Millie shrugged. "By the way, why are you wearing your robe inside out?"

Trish glanced at her sleeve. Why, indeed? Groaning, she laid her head on the table and closed her eyes, slowly counting to ten. "What do you want, Millie?"

"I'll get us some coffee first. I want you wide awake while we talk."

Trish opened one eye and peered at Millie suspiciously. This sounded serious. But knowing Millie, she could simply be worked up over the inane prizes in cereal boxes.

Trish and Millie had been close friends for over five years now, ever since Trish and her now ex-husband had moved into the old, established neighborhood in Grand River, a small suburb right outside of San Antonio, Texas. Trish had immediately fallen in love with the feisty widow's independent personality. Sure, she was stubborn, opinionated, and even eccentric by some standards, but Millie was also loyal to a fault. So, if she was upset about something, the least Trish could do was hear her out. After all, something must really be bothering Millie for her to come over so early. Well, not necessarily, Trish admitted wryly, but something *felt* different this time.

"Where's Edna? I'm sure you banged on her door, too, didn't you?" Trish asked, stifling a yawn, envious that Edna Radcliff, the third person in their friendship circle, was probably sound asleep in her bed down the street next to her wonderful husband, Joe. Thoughtful, always polite, with a tender spot for anyone less fortunate than herself, Edna brought a sense of calm whenever they were all together. Of course, Millie teased Edna unmercifully about her gentle character, but they had been friends for years, and Edna knew that if it ever came down to it, Millie would bust through any barrier to stand by her side. Getting Millie to admit it was another thing, though.

Carrying the coffee cups to the table, Millie sat down and placed one in front of Trish. "I wouldn't disturb Edna this early. She's probably still sleeping. She doesn't get up as early as we do."

Trish curled her fingers over the table's edge until her knuckles turned white to prevent her hands from doing something she might or might not regret.

"But I did leave a note on her door," Millie continued. "She'll probably be here before long."

Trish loosened her grip and prayed for patience. Millie stirred sugar into her cup, her lips pressed tightly. This wasn't like Millie at all. She was usually full steam ahead—as she had been earlier, pounding on the door.

The soft whooshing sound of the central heat kicking on seemed to shake Millie from her thoughts. "I'm so upset I can't think straight," she said, pulling off her glasses and squeezing the bridge of her nose.

Trish slowly set her cup down. Her mind conjured up, and then rejected, the many different scenarios that could cause the furrow between Millie's eyes. But one thought that couldn't be rejected easily was the idea that Millie may have been diagnosed with a serious health problem. From all appearances, she was fit, trim, and energetic almost to an irritating level. She had a sharp mind and a quick wit, and she didn't seem to have a problem remembering things. Still, there was no getting around the fact that Millie was also in her eighties.

Drawing in a deep breath and swallowing past the lump in her throat, Trish reached across the table and covered Millie's hand. "What is it, dear? You know I'm here for you."

"Of course I know that," Millie said, patting Trish's hand. "And I appreciate it, Trish. I really need to talk to somebody. And, let's face it, you're better than nobody."

Trish heard the smile in the other woman's voice and turned quickly to the coffeepot. Her vision blurred, and she blinked rapidly. Millie was being so brave. Of course, that's how she handled everything. It had gotten her into trouble more times than Trish cared to remember, but it was also one of the things that made her so lovable.

"Okay, let's talk. Tell me what's wrong." She placed Millie's cup in front of her and sat down, bracing herself for what Millie had to tell her.

Millie raised her cup and then put it back down without

taking a drink. Her eyes raised to Trish's, and she said in a quiet voice that trembled slightly, "Michelle's integrity is being questioned."

Trish leaned forward and clasped Millie's hands. "We can deal with this, Millie. You're not alone, and *what did you say*?"

"I know. It's shocking, isn't it?" Millie said, pulling her hands back. She threw her cap on the table and ran her hands through her hair. "I'm so angry I could spit bullets."

Trish stared at Millie. "*Michelle's . . . integrity . . . is . . . being . . . questioned?*"

"Yes. And the question now is, what are we going to do about it?"

Trish stood up very slowly and placed her hands on the table. "Millie Morrow, you crazy old bat, I thought you were dying!"

Millie's eyebrows shot up. "You're calling *me* crazy? Whatever gave you the idea I was dying?"

"Gee, I don't know," Trish said, her eyes narrowing. "Maybe it has something to do with waking me up at five thirty in the morning like a wild bear, or your remarks about being upset and needing to talk. Silly me, I should have guessed that it had something to do with Michelle's *integrity* being questioned!" Trish knew her voice was getting louder, but she couldn't help it. The relief at finding out that Millie was not dying from some horrible disease was strong enough to make Trish want to kill her best friend.

Millie stood then in a huff and glared right back at Trish. "So all that talk about us being in this together, and that's what friends are for, was nothing more than a bunch of hogwash, wasn't it?"

"You're the one spouting hogwash, Millie. I can't believe you did this to me." Turning her back, Trish picked up her cup and carried it over to the coffeepot.

"I didn't do anything to you! It's not my fault you jumped to conclusions. Why would you think I was dying, anyway? I'm in better health than you are!"

Trish snorted. "You're thirty-five years older than I am."

"And I'm thirty-five pounds lighter, fatso. You're going to die before I do," Millie said smugly.

Trish's mouth fell open. She had seen the twinkle in Millie's eyes, but she couldn't just let her get away with that remark. Before she could say anything, though, the doorbell rang. She gave Millie the most offended, angry look she could muster. Then she stuck her nose in the air, gathered her robe around her, and marched stiffly to the door. *Fatso, indeed!*

Millie had been teasing Trish unmercifully lately about the exercise machine she had sold a couple of months ago. Practically brand new, she had gotten a good price for it and had treated Millie and Edna to dinner at the Old San Francisco Steak House. Of course, Millie hadn't teased her *that* night, not while she was digging into her medium-rare filet mignon.

Trish already knew it was Edna at the door. All three of them seemed to have developed an almost uncanny sense of knowing when something important was happening, and they would eventually come together at one of their homes, drink gallons of coffee, and discuss the situation. Their strong bond of friendship had only intensified ever since they had worked together to clear their neighbor of killing his wife. There's nothing like a good old-fashioned murder to bring people closer together.

"Come on in, Edna," Trish said as soon as she opened the door. "You're about to witness a murder."

Edna's smile vanished, and her eyebrows rose. "What did you say?" she asked, following Trish into the kitchen.

"What did who say?" Millie had poured a cup of coffee for Edna and placed it on the table. She had also found the package of chocolate chip cookies.

Edna sat down with a concerned look on her face. "I think Trish is upset about something."

Millie waved a hand. "She's just upset that I'm not dying."

Trish shot Millie a look. "That's not true. If you died, I wouldn't have the pleasure of killing you."

"For heaven's sake, girls, what is going on?" Edna asked. "And what in the world are you wearing, Millie?" Edna looked like she was torn between laughing and frowning. She also looked perfect, as she normally did. Edna had a charming way of appearing as if she just stepped out of a salon. Even now, so early in the morning, her hair was impeccably styled, her face glowed with light makeup highlighting her features, and she wore a lavender sweatsuit. She looked ten years younger than her sixty-five years and most of that could be attributed to her attitude. Trish kept waiting for some of Edna's *attitude* to wear off on her, but so far no luck.

"According to Trish, nothing important is going on. And, if you must know, I had to dress in a hurry this morning. Don't be a snob. My outfit matches just fine."

Before Edna could explain that "themes" didn't necessarily match, Millie continued, "Thanks for coming over so early, by the way."

"Of course. Did you think I'd ignore the note you left on my door? Besides, I'm always up early. I'm not usually *out and about* so early, but your message sounded serious. I was worried."

"Well, it is serious," Millie said, "and I wanted my two best friends to help me figure out the best way to deal with this problem. I see now that was a mistake." Millie's voice had turned pitiful, and the pout on her lips had Trish rolling her eyes.

Edna's eyes widened, and she reached across the table to grab Millie's hand. Her voice was full of concern. "Oh, Millie, you're not—?"

"No, she's not!" Trish snapped. "And that's not why I'm upset. She scared me to death, as she evidently did to you too. There's a difference between a problem and a *problem*, but Millie doesn't seem to know the difference. Besides," Trish added, sucking in her stomach and thrusting her chest out, "she called me fat."

"Stop talking about me as if I'm in the other room."

Edna leaned back in her chair, a puzzled look on her face. "Maybe someone should explain."

Trish crossed her arms. "Go ahead, Millie. Tell Edna about this earth-shattering, life-and-death problem."

Millie scooted forward in her chair, the forlorn attitude completely gone. "Girls, Michelle needs our help," she said with a determined light in her eyes.

"Michelle? Your daughter Michelle?"

"No, Michelle Kwan, the Olympic ice-skater. She wants us to

show her how to improve her triple lutz. *Of course, my daughter Michelle!*"

Edna ignored the sarcasm, as she usually did when Millie was in a mood. She leaned forward, concern on her face. "What's wrong?"

"Well," Millie said, playing to her sympathetic audience, "I'm sure you've seen the news stories lately about all the stolen cars." When Trish and Edna both nodded, she continued. "The news angle is on the number of cars stolen and how soon it will be before this crafty car-theft ring will be caught and stopped."

Trish cocked her head. "Don't tell me someone believes Michelle moonlights as a car thief."

Edna gasped. "You've got to be kidding!"

"Now you can see why I'm so upset."

Well, yes, Trish conceded. Upset, yes, but to the point where she had to barge over before the sun was even out? Not so much. "Who has accused Michelle?"

"Well, nobody has the courage to accuse her outright. They're more subtle than that. They probably know I'd sue them for everything they're worth!"

"I don't think you can sue anyone, dear," Edna said. "Michelle is a grown woman. She'd have to do the suing."

"Who are we even talking about?" Trish asked. Millie had a way of talking around a story, leaving all the important details out. The fact that Edna would usually humor her did nothing to help Trish's patience.

"The head honchos at Security Insurance, where Michelle works. The great majority of the stolen cars have been insured by the local branch. She and her boss, Richard Kelp, were notified yesterday that there could be an internal investigation. According to Michelle, they were informed that the risk analysis the home office uses to come up with normal claim percentages is way off, so much so that they've hinted it could be fraud."

"Why, that's terrible!" Edna said. "How could they even think that?"

Millie slammed her hand down for emphasis. "Bingo! That's precisely why I'm upset!"

"Wait a minute," Trish said, leaning forward. "You said there *could* be an internal investigation. That doesn't mean they are going after Michelle. They're just investigating a strange coincidence. Why would you think they are targeting Michelle and not her boss, anyway?"

"It doesn't matter to me who they are going after," Millie said. "Michelle, Richard, the cleaning crew, or the garbage people! The fact is that Michelle is going to be in the middle of it." Then she looked at Trish and Edna. "We need to do something."

Trish was amused at Millie's dire tone. "But what can *we* possibly do?"

The next time Trish found herself asking such a stupid question, she thought, she hoped someone would bonk her over the head.

Chapter Two

The Grand River Police Department resembled a well-kept home instead of an official establishment, welcoming visitors with its white rock exterior and natural landscaping, but Trish still felt a knot of apprehension settle in her stomach when she pulled into the small parking area. Not because she had outstanding tickets or had robbed the neighborhood corner store. She and Edna had brought Millie with them.

It was no secret that Police Chief Henry Espinoza and Millie rubbed each other the wrong way, but Henry *was* the chief, after all, and common sense dictated that it would be wise to show him the respect his position deserved.

Trish parked the car. "Now, Millie—" But Millie was already out of the car and marching toward the front door.

Trish groaned and leaned her head on the steering wheel. "I'm going to kill that woman."

Laughing, Edna scrambled out of the backseat. "We better catch up with her before she gets arrested."

Trish sighed and reached for her purse. *And that would be a bad thing?*

The sterile atmosphere of the front room left no doubt that this was indeed a city office, and one with no budget. Several metal chairs with blue, thin-cushioned seats graced one wall, and in the corner, a large battleship-gray desk stood unoccupied. In fact, in the few times Trish had been in the police department, she couldn't ever remember anyone sitting there. But with the chief, three officers, and one detective making up the entire force, an information clerk probably wasn't necessary. A person could just walk on down the hallway and yell to get someone's attention.

Speaking of . . .

"Oh, dear," Edna whispered as she grabbed Trish's arm and pointed toward the end of the hallway. "There she is."

"Oh, dear, is right," Trish muttered. "Let's go save that poor man."

With Edna in tow, Trish hurried toward the commotion in the hallway, where a young officer was trying valiantly to prevent Millie from going any farther.

It didn't take a genius to figure out that Millie was dead set on getting to Henry's office. It almost appeared as if the two were boxing, Millie moving sideways and the officer, at least two feet taller than Millie, mimicking her movements in an effort to stop her, a frazzled look on his young face as he attempted to deal with the crazy woman.

"Please, ma'am," the officer coaxed, "I've tried to tell you that Chief Espinoza is busy right now. I can help you if you'll just tell me what the problem is."

Millie danced to the left. "And I'm telling you that he'll want to see me, young man. Henry and I are practically partners. You'll be lucky if you're not fired over this incident."

"Millie!" Trish exclaimed, but before she could get a grip on Millie's shoulder, the older woman ducked her head, faked a move to the right, and then quickly darted left, successfully scooting past the harried officer. Muhammad Ali would have been proud.

The officer threw his hands in the air and glared at Trish as though she were responsible for him losing the match. Smiling weakly, she sidled past him. "Uh . . . we're with the old lady."

She heard Edna apologizing in her sweet, comforting way at the same time that she saw Millie opening Henry's door, without bothering to knock. *Oh, oh, not again.* Henry frowned on unannounced visitors, a sentiment Millie obviously didn't much care about.

Trish reached the door to Henry's office in time to hear him say, "What—? Oh, it's you. I should have known. Millie

Morrow, don't ever barge into my office again!" He was standing with his hands placed on top of a large black metal desk, and he had a ferocious scowl on his face.

Henry was approximately six feet tall, with a solid, muscular build, and dark hair slightly streaked with gray. His brown eyes were sharp and intense, and at the moment, glaring at Millie, who had plopped down in one of the chairs facing his desk.

Swallowing, Trish gave Henry a small nod and, with an apologetic look on her face, sat in another chair that was placed in a corner. Henry's office was small, but she wanted to be as far away from him as possible.

That left the chair next to Millie for Edna, who smiled brightly and said, "Good morning, Henry."

"Oh, geez, it's the Three Musketeers." Sighing audibly, he sat down heavily in his chair. "What have you gotten yourselves into this time?"

"There's no cause to be rude, Henry," Millie snapped.

Trish bit her lip to keep from laughing out loud. *Isn't that a little like the pot calling the kettle black?*

"Henry," Edna said quickly before Millie could insult the chief again. "We're so sorry to intrude on your busy schedule—"

"He's not busy, Edna! He's just sitting here!"

"—but we have a problem we want to discuss with you," Edna continued, giving Millie a stern look. "I'm sure you're aware of the recent spike in stolen cars around San Antonio."

"I watch the news," Henry said carefully. Then he looked up, a smile crossing his face. "Wait a minute . . . if you're here to confess or something, you should have an attorney present."

"Very funny," Millie said in a wry tone. "When you're fired from this job, you can always find work as a comedian."

"Millie!" Edna exclaimed. "You need to apologize."

Millie sniffed. "When elephants fly."

Trish had to hold on to the strap of her purse very tightly to keep from swinging it at Millie. She looked at Henry. "What we're concerned about is that the majority of the cars stolen are insured by the company Millie's daughter works for. In fact, it's such a large number, their home office has run the odds, and they suspect fraud on the part of the local agency."

Henry leaned forward and placed his elbows on the desk. "That *is* strange," he admitted, "but what do you think I can do about it?"

"Do we have to tell you how to do everything, Henry?" Millie demanded. "Go do whatever it is cops do. You're the paid servant, not us!"

"I'm sure Millie didn't mean that the way it came out, Henry," Edna said quickly, her eyes darting between Henry and Millie.

"Yes, I did!"

Trish stood up and placed a warning hand on Millie's shoulder, trying to diffuse the situation. "Millie is upset because her daughter is caught in the middle of this. Please forgive her for the harsh remarks, but she wants to help and doesn't know where to turn." Millie sputtered and started to rise, but Trish squeezed her shoulder and pressed down. "Is there anything you can do?"

Henry glared at Millie for a few seconds longer, but then he sighed and leaned back in his chair. "Unfortunately, there's nothing I can do except keep my eyes and ears open for anything happening here in Grand River. I don't have any jurisdiction in San Antonio, and that's where the thefts are taking place. At least, so far. Besides, I'm sure it's purely coincidental that your daughter's insurance company has insured most of the cars. Wait and see, and I'll bet other agencies start taking a hit too."

This time Trish couldn't keep Millie in her chair. "That's it? *Wait and see?*"

Henry nodded. "I'm afraid so. Now, when—*and if*—this crime wave spreads to Grand River, that will be a different story."

Millie leaned forward and placed her hands on Henry's desk, giving him the most threatening look she could muster. "Look, Buster," she growled, "we've played this song and dance before. You didn't think we knew what we were talking about the last time we came to you for help, and do you remember how that turned out?"

Henry also rose to his feet, a thunderous look on his face, but Millie was on a roll. "We're getting a little tired of doing your job for you. I think we're going to start our own police department, and you'll be lucky if we hire you to sweep the floors! Come on, girls, we've got a crime to solve." And with that gracious remark, Millie pirouetted toward the door and stomped out of the office.

Any minute now, steam would start billowing from Henry's ears. Trish was pretty sure it was time to leave. "Thank you for your time, Henry," she said. "We'll let you get back to what you were doing."

"You mean *just sitting here*?" he said as they scooted out the door.

Millie was storming out the front entrance as Trish and Edna hurried down the hall. Trish nodded her head toward Millie and muttered, "We make a pact right here and now. If we ever have to come here again, and we make the stupid mistake of bringing Millie, then we taze her before she has a chance to open her mouth. Agreed?"

"Agreed!"

"I wonder what's keeping them?" Millie asked for the hundredth time as she craned her neck to look toward the door, but busy waiters and waitresses dressed in black-and-red uniforms kept blocking her view as they bustled from table to table in an effort to satisfy the hungry lunch crowd.

"We thought we would be at the police station longer than we were," Trish said pointedly. "Michelle and her boss aren't late; we're early."

"They'll be here soon, dear," Edna said patiently. "One of their clients might have come in just as they were leaving." Trish shot Edna a look. It was easy for Edna to sit there all sweet and understanding. After all, she had gotten a full, uninterrupted night's sleep.

Millie had wasted no time after her dramatic exit from the police department proclaiming that they were going to have to clear Michelle's name by themselves. They needed to gather as much information as they could, she had explained to her

friends, pointedly ignoring their hesitation at getting personally involved.

"There they are!" Millie said, waving her hand.

Michelle stood right inside the café next to a nice-looking
man, obviously searching the crowd for her mother. "I don't
think they can see you," Edna said. "Why don't you go over and
get them?"

"Nonsense." Millie pulled out her chair, climbed on top of
it, and started waving her arms wildly.

"For goodness' sake, Millie!" Edna said sharply. "Get off
that chair before you kill yourself!"

"Oh, stop being such a worrywart," Millie said once she
had gained her daughter's—and everyone else's—attention.
Then she nimbly climbed down off the chair, dusted the seat
off with her hand, and sat down, primly placing her napkin in
her lap. Trish buried her face in her menu to hide her grin
from the other patrons' incredulous stares.

Michelle approached the table with her boss close behind
her, a wide grin on his face. Michelle was used to her mother's
antics, but it didn't mean she didn't get embarrassed now and
then. And *now* was evidently one of those times, if the bright
red spots on her cheeks were any indication.

Millie's husband had died long before Trish moved into the
neighborhood, but from pictures she had seen, Michelle Matson resembled him more than she did her mother. Where Millie was under five feet tall, with a tiny frame and sparkling
blue eyes, Michelle was several inches taller, with a solid frame
and warm brown eyes. Their personalities differed also. Millie
was boisterous, exuberant, and stubborn, whereas her daughter was more reserved. Thank goodness.

"Richard, I'd like you to meet my mother's two best friends,
Trish Anderson and Edna Radcliff. They used to keep my
mom out of trouble, but now they're as bad as she is."

Millie frowned, "Hey, I'm sitting right here, you know."

"Nobody is as bad as your mother, Michelle," Edna said with
a wink as she held out her hand. "It's very nice to meet you."

"Same here," Richard said, his dark brown eyes crinkling

at the corners as he then shook Trish's hand. "You three are somewhat of a legend in Grand River, you know. All I can say is I'm glad you're friends."

Trish groaned. "Don't believe everything you hear. We did not leap over tall buildings and fly at the speed of sound to capture a killer. Honest."

For weeks after the murder of their friend had been solved, their little city had buzzed with the news that three of their own had been instrumental in its successful conclusion. Surprisingly, Henry and his detective, Larry Thompson, had been more than kind with their praise of the women's involvement, which had led to an almost constant barrage of questions from neighbors, an interview request from the *San Antonio Express-News*, and even an invitation to appear on one of the morning shows, all of which the women declined. The pain was still too raw for Sam, who had never really recovered, first from the loss of his wife and then the consequent arrest for her murder.

"No, as a matter of fact, my two friends here *fell* out of a building, and we drove around a lot at the speed of sound, but that's the extent of our superpowers," Edna grinned.

Richard laughed. "Well, I'm honored to meet you, just the same. Michelle thinks the world of you, and that's enough for me." Trish's interest was piqued when Richard pulled out Michelle's chair and she turned to give him a grateful smile. Could there be a blossoming romance going on here?

According to Millie, Michelle wanted no part of a relationship with anybody right now. Her focus was on raising her teenage kids and furthering her career. Her husband of twenty years, Tony Matson, had divorced her so that he could date other women, and Michelle had been devastated, not only at losing her husband but at the fact that she had become so dependent on Tony for everything: financial decisions, social decisions, and even family decisions.

That had been three years ago, and since then, Michelle had regained her self-respect and taken control of her life, and she hadn't looked back. Still, Richard was an attractive man, obviously a gentleman, and he seemed to sincerely appreciate

Michelle's service as an employee, going so far as to let her run his whole office.

The matchmaker in Trish rose up, and she couldn't push the thought of Michelle and Richard as a couple from her mind. Even though *she* had no desire to be tied to a man again after her own disastrous marriage, that didn't mean she wouldn't want Michelle to be happy with a loving, caring man. But first things first—the two of them had to be cleared of any involvement in the car thefts. Being suspected of a crime was no way to start a relationship.

Then another thought struck Trish, and she almost groaned out loud. If *she* was imagining how perfect a relationship would be between Michelle and Richard, was it a stretch to believe that the insurance investigators had reached the same conclusion? *Conspiracy to commit a crime* was not a small charge, and the suspicion alone could drive Richard out of business.

Millie startled them all when she clapped her hands together. "Now that all the nicety-nice chitchat is over, let's get down to business. We're not going to get any help from the local police, so we're on our own. You start, Richard," she said in her best police-officer tone while leaning across the table and staring him down. "Tell us everything you know about the car thefts and why you think your agency is being targeted. Don't leave anything out, regardless of how unimportant you think something may be. Edna, you take notes."

Richard coughed into his hand and stole a sideways look at Michelle. "Uh—"

Trish groaned and rolled her eyes. "For goodness' sake, Millie, they just got here! Let's at least order lunch, and then we can talk."

"I agree, Mom," Michelle said in a hushed voice. "Besides, I told you earlier that I'm not comfortable with you three getting involved in this. You're already jumping to conclusions. We don't know that our agency *is* being targeted. It may be just an unfortunate coincidence."

Millie shook her head. "You need to let us handle this, Michelle. We have experience, and we're offering our services free of charge. Now, we're wasting valuable time. You can eat and talk at the same time. Edna, where's your paper?"

"Uh . . . I'll see if I have any in my purse." Edna was clearly caught in the middle, a situation she normally didn't handle well. Always trying to make everybody happy usually resulted in making someone mad.

And Trish was getting mad. "Edna, put your purse down. We'll do this after we eat."

"Oh . . . okay," Edna said, putting her purse back on the ground.

Millie leaned back in her chair and crossed her arms over her chest. A power struggle was definitely brewing. "Edna," she said very slowly, "you need paper and a pen to take notes."

"Uh . . . of course," Edna said, reaching for her purse.

"Edna," Trish said, just as slowly, leaning back in her chair and mimicking Millie's posture, "we'll do this after we eat. Put your purse down." Out of the corner of her eye, Trish saw Michelle grinning, her nose buried in her menu, and Richard staring at them as if he were afraid an all-out brawl was going to break out.

Trish groaned silently. Millie had a way of bringing out the worst in her. "Excuse me," Edna said to the approaching waitress. "I think we're ready to order." The waitress waved a finger at her, the universal sign that meant she'd be right with them. Edna nodded and then leaned across the table. "Whether we discuss this situation *while* we eat or *after* we eat, we still need to eat! You two had better stop acting like children, or you can take your own darn notes. Now grow up and behave!" With that, Edna straightened in her seat, calmly placed her napkin in her lap, and turned to ask Michelle how her children were doing.

Millie and Trish stared at Edna, then at each other. There really was not much that could be said after that. Conversation flowed easily over the table, and soon the waitress came and took their order. Millie refrained from asking any "professional" questions until they had received their meals, eaten, and the plates had been cleared.

Edna patted her lips with her napkin, then, without a word,

she reached down, pulled a small notebook from her purse, and nodded at Millie. "Now we can talk."

Millie didn't hesitate. She leaned back in her chair again and adopted the same pose as she had before. "Okay, young man, from what I understand, you're in trouble. Big trouble. And you need some help. When did these car thefts start?"

Richard placed his napkin on the table. "It's hard to say when this trend actually began. In our business, you always have occasional car thefts. But after doing some internal analysis, we believe it started about two months ago, and it's just steadily gotten worse."

"Did you get that, Edna?"

Edna ducked her head and started writing. "Two months ago. Got it."

"So your agency has insured the majority of these stolen cars, correct?" Richard nodded and she continued. "Have you tried to find out if there is some kind of connection between the victims?"

"The police haven't mentioned anything, but I'm not sure they would tell us, anyway."

Millie gave an unladylike snort. "You're right on that point."

"Oh, no," Michelle suddenly whispered. She leaned forward in her chair and motioned to the side with her eyes. "Guess who just showed up," she said to Richard.

Everyone turned to look in the direction she had indicated. "Stop that! Act natural. Maybe she won't notice us," Michelle said.

"Who?" Millie asked. Everyone else had turned back around, but Millie was craning her neck and peering through the crowd.

"My ex-girlfriend," Richard said with a sigh.

"Now *there's* a case for you, Mom." Michelle offered playfully, while Richard shifted uncomfortably in his chair. "We may have a genuine stalker situation going on."

"Give me specifics," Millie said, still trying to figure out whom they were talking about.

"I'll take notes," Edna said helpfully.

"Michelle's teasing, you nincompoops!" Trish said in exasperation. "Millie, turn around before you get whiplash."

"Uh-oh," Richard said through lips that didn't move. "She's heading this way."

"Who?" Millie asked again.

Trish saw a woman heading toward them. She quickly picked up the dessert menu while simultaneously giving Millie a kick under the table. "Shh!"

"Ow! What was that for?" Millie exclaimed, reaching under the table to rub her shin.

Trish gritted her teeth. *One of these days—*

"Well, Richard, how nice to see you. Imagine running into you here, sweetie," the woman said, stopping beside Richard and placing her hand on his shoulder. "And, Michelle, how are you?"

"I'm fine, Barbara. How are you?" Michelle's voice was flat.

"I'm wonderful, thank you," she trilled, ignoring Michelle's tone. "Richard, are you going to introduce me?"

Trish saw the grimace cross Richard's face. "Barbara Ferguson, meet Millie Morrow, Edna Radcliff, and Trish Anderson."

Barbara reached across the table to shake hands. "It's very nice to meet all of you. I'm a close friend of Richard's," she said with a sugary-sweet smile. "Are you family?"

"Yes, we are, sweetie," Millie said casually, leaning forward to shake Barbara's hand. "And we protect our own."

Chapter Three

Stunned silence surrounded the table after Millie's remark. *Where did that come from?* Trish wondered.

Edna's mouth dropped open, Michelle's cheeks were turning red again, and poor Richard looked as if he had just swallowed a frog. And all the while Millie just sat there, oblivious to the tension her outlandish remark had created. With luck, Barbara would think that Millie was suffering from some form of dementia. Heaven knows, Trish often thought that exact same thing.

Barbara's eyes turned cold, and her smile froze in place. Even in anger, she was a beautiful woman, but somehow she didn't come across as *real*. At first glance, she looked to be in her midthirties, but her expert makeup application couldn't quite hide the tiny lines at her eyes and around her mouth. Probably more like forty-five. She had bleached-blond hair coiled up in a French knot, startling blue eyes, and a figure to die for. She was tall, about five foot seven, without heels, and had an air of self-confidence that was surely a front. From Trish's experience, nobody with real self-confidence had to work so hard to insinuate themselves into a conversation.

Edna broke the uncomfortable silence first. "That's a beautiful suit you're wearing, Barbara. The color is perfect on you."

It took a moment for Barbara to compose herself. With a barely visible motion of her head, she turned toward Edna. "Thank you. It's new," she said, her obvious vanity on full display as she smoothed her mauve-colored skirt. "I think it's important for a woman to stay on top of fashion."

Trish was glad that neither Millie nor Michelle had seen the quick, pointed look Barbara had given Michelle. Edna had, though, and her friendly smile vanished.

"Well, I need to run," Barbara said. "It was wonderful to see you again, Richard. Call me, won't you?" Then, with a general nod to everyone, she turned and walked away, her skin-tight skirt making every move noticeable.

Michelle shuddered and leaned forward. "That woman drives me nuts," she whispered.

Richard sighed. "I have to agree."

Millie frowned at him. "What did you ever see in her?"

"Mother! That's none of your business!"

"It's okay, Michelle," he said with a shake of his head. "Let's just say my judgment was at a low point. But Barbara is not only my ex-girlfriend; she's also a client. My company insures her car and her house, so I have to remain civil. But having her show up all the time is getting a little creepy."

"Well, we'll deal with that problem after we find out who is behind the car thefts. We can't spread ourselves too thin, you know."

Trish had just taken a sip of her iced tea, but she almost spewed it across the table. *Spreading themselves too thin?* It was doubtful they were going to jump up and circle the city looking for stolen cars, for goodness' sake.

"Okay, no point wasting daylight." Millie stood and reached for the check, which she handed to Richard. "We're doing this one pro bono, but you have to cover our expenses."

"Of course," Richard said seriously.

"Now, we're going to go brainstorm in private. We can't have our clients knowing all our secrets. Besides, the less you know, the safer you'll be if you're ever questioned. Go back to work and act natural. We'll contact you. Understand?"

Dumbfounded, Trish and Edna stared at each other. *Clients?*

Two hours and two pots of coffee later, the three women were nowhere closer to figuring out how to begin their investigation, who the criminals could be, or, as Millie kept saying, what their modus operandi was. There must be a new book, *Spying for Dummies*, that Millie was using as a reference.

The most important thing they had accomplished was to get Trish to understand why Millie was taking this so seriously. To believe they could solve a city-wide lawbreaking surge with no resources, no experience, and no *guns* was pushing the scope of reality a bit far, however.

Trish was going to have to burst her friend's balloon soon, but for now, she sensed it was better to let Millie rant and rave about protecting Michelle.

If Millie could scheme, she would feel productive, as if she were actually doing something, and as long as Millie's scheming remained in the safe confines of the kitchen, everything would be fine.

Edna put down her pen and rubbed her hand. The notebook was half full of the notes Millie had dictated, almost all of the ideas completely useless. "I think we've done enough for now."

"Hmm . . . you may be right," Millie said, glancing at the wall clock. "I'd say we've accomplished quite a lot today. Besides, Michelle is going to come over after work and set up e-mail on my computer. I better go dust it off."

Trish raised an eyebrow. *E-mail?* "You've had that computer for over a year now. Have you ever even turned it on?"

"Well, poop for brains, didn't you hear what I just said? Would I need to dust it if I had been using it?"

"Millie!" Edna exclaimed.

"Oh, stop being such a fuddy-dud."

"What do you need e-mail for?" Trish asked before Edna embarked on a course of vocabulary etiquette.

"Don't ask me," she shrugged. "Michelle said it would be more convenient, and I wouldn't have to worry about waiting for a decent hour to call someone."

Trish grinned. So she and Edna weren't the only ones honored to have Millie barge in over at all times.

After giving Millie their e-mail addresses so she could test her system, Edna stood and stretched. "Joe should be home by now. Call me if you need anything. Or," she added with a smile, "*e-mail* me."

"I haven't seen Joe in a while," Millie said as she followed Edna to the door. "What's he up to?"

"Oh, you know Joe. He's always working on something. He's building a cactus garden out back. It's really beautiful. You both need to come over soon and see it." Edna's husband of over forty-five years, Joe was still a striking man. He completely adored his wife and had more patience than God gave the saints in heaven. He had proved that countless times when he helped all three women out of tight spots during their first gig as detectives.

Of course, he had also threatened them with their very lives if they got involved in anything similar again.

Trish attached the financial statements she had been working on to an e-mail and forwarded them to her client. She glanced at the clock and recorded the time she had spent on this project. *How did it get so late so fast?* As much as she loved her work dealing with numbers and budgets, she was more than ready for a hot soak in the tub and then bed.

Yawning, she checked for incoming messages one last time, thankfully noting that Millie must have finally called it a night. Twenty-five test messages from *mmorrow007* had been more than a little frustrating. She had just slipped into her robe, pulled her hair up under a shower cap, and added fragrant bubble bath to the water when she heard a loud crash followed by the sound of squealing tires. *What in the world?*

She rushed down the hallway and hurried to the large window in the living room, pulling the curtains back just enough to peer outside. The streetlight at the corner cast just enough light to make out the road and the edges of several yards in front of dark, quiet homes. The moon peeked out occasionally through floating clouds, its light forcing the shadows from huge oak trees and mature shrubs to dance erratically for a few moments before softly disappearing into thick darkness.

Trish shivered. This was a quiet street, the residents retiring early behind the solace of their doors, comfortable in their belief that this was a secure, safe neighborhood, untouched by the perils and unrest of the big city. Nothing ever happened here.

Except that one of their neighbors had recently been murdered in her own home in broad daylight.

The smart thing to do would be to call the police and let them make a quick run down the street to ensure everything was as it should be. But then she would probably have to wait for them to arrive, and then wait for them to report that they hadn't seen anything amiss. She was much too tired to do all that waiting. She decided to take a quick look outside, just for her peace of mind. Otherwise, she wasn't going to get any sleep tonight. There had been a definite crash, but she couldn't really swear the sound had come from her own street. She'd verify that everything was okay in her immediate world and then put the incident out of her mind.

Trish squinted through the darkness from the safety of her porch. All was quiet except the gentle sound of branches thick with leaves swaying in the mild breeze. She couldn't see a thing outside the circle of light from her porch. But then the clouds parted, allowing the moonlight to reveal what had obviously caused the commotion.

"Oh, for goodness' sake!" Trish exclaimed. Across the street, she could see that Millie's garbage can had been crushed and pushed into her mailbox, which was now leaning sideways at an awkward angle. Trash had spewed out in the yard and in the street.

Terrific. Millie would be furious when she saw the damage to her trash can and mailbox. Trish debated whether she should go pick up the trash. It didn't appear as if anyone else had heard the crash, though, and if the garbage stayed out all night, every stray dog within a mile would be parked out in front of Millie's house having a picnic.

With a loud sigh, she pulled her robe tight and hurried across the street. She yanked at the ruined garbage can until it pulled away from the mailbox. It made a loud scraping noise, but she wasn't worried. If the original crash hadn't awakened the neighbors, then the ruckus she was making certainly wouldn't. Muttering under her breath, Trish started picking up the trash, at least what she could see of it.

Millie certainly ate a lot of fruit, Trish thought with a grimace as her bare hand closed around a banana peel for the third time. The thought had no sooner left her mind when she froze. The unmistakable sound of a shotgun being cocked right behind her was immediately followed by a beam of light.

"Hold it right there, buster!" a deep, gruff voice commanded. "The police are on the way."

Trish instantly recognized the camouflaged voice. She turned and faced the miniature Rambo. "Millie! For God's sake, put that gun down! And lower that flashlight!"

"Trish?" The voice was normal now, and deeply surprised. "What are you doing digging in my trash?"

Trish couldn't see a thing with the light blinding her. "If you've still got that gun aimed at me, I'm going to kick your tail end!"

"Oh," Millie said, as if she were holding nothing more than a squirt gun. Abruptly, the light shining from the flashlight veered up and down and sideways in a spasmodic dance of fitfulness as Millie struggled to heft the shotgun over her shoulder. "Don't worry. It's not loaded," she grunted.

"You just about gave me a heart attack!" Trish said, and she wasn't exaggerating. She could actually count the rapid beats of her heart pounding against her chest. "What are you doing carrying a shotgun?"

"Protecting my property, that's what! And, by the way, that's not much of a disguise you're wearing. I've seen that shower cap before. I knew it was you the minute you turned around."

Trish prayed for patience. "I am not wearing a disguise, you crazy old bat! I was doing you a favor. I heard a loud crash, and when I looked outside, your trash was all over the place. So I came over here—concerned friend that I am—and tried to pick it up so you wouldn't have to deal with it. I certainly didn't expect to get shot for my efforts, though!"

"I told you it wasn't loaded," Millie said. "Besides, I saw what happened."

"You did?" Trish dropped the banana peel in the can.

"Yep," Millie nodded. "I had just turned off the computer and happened to look outside when I saw headlights veering

Mitzi Kelly

straight for my driveway. I thought it was a runaway car," she said, her eyes getting big, "but after it hit my trash can, it backed up and rammed it again right into my mailbox!"

Trish was stunned. "Are you sure?"

"Of course, I'm sure! That's why I got my gun. I figured if the car came back, I was going to shoot out the tires. But when I got back to the window, I saw someone going through my trash. I thought you were the car—er, I mean, I thought you were the driver of the car."

"Thanks for clarifying," Trish said wryly. "Wait a minute! I thought you said the gun wasn't loaded."

"It's not," Millie grinned sheepishly. "I forgot to grab the shells."

Trish was trying hard not to grin, but the vision of Millie shooting out tires on a car was almost too much to imagine. You had to hand it to the lady, though. Millie sure didn't lack chutzpah. Trish cleared her throat and tamped down a laugh. "Probably some kids out for a joyride. We'll get Joe to look at the damage in the morning, but for now let's pick up this mess and call it a night."

"Wish I could have gotten the license plate number," Millie grunted as she bent over and picked up a milk jug, struggling to keep the shotgun balanced on her shoulder.

Trish rolled her eyes. "Let me do this, Millie. You're liable to fall over. Anyway, I wish you could have identified the car too. Darn kids are going to kill somebody."

When they had finished, Trish set the can at the corner of the driveway, where it rested somewhat steadily against the curb. Hopefully, the garbage men would still pick it up. "Okay, that's it," she said and sighed. "Lock your doors, and I'll see you in the morning."

Trish was halfway across the street when she heard her name. She turned and saw Millie standing on her front porch, the flashlight in one hand and the shotgun still balanced on her shoulder. America was safe with Millie at the helm.

"Thank you."

A smile crossed Trish's face, and a warm feeling spread through her as she looked at her outlandish, stubborn friend standing in the glow of light from the porch, her yellow "bear" slippers peeking out from under the full-length purple robe she wore—and a shotgun almost as tall as she was perched on her shoulder.

"You're welcome."

Trish felt as though she had just closed her eyes when she was awakened by the pounding on her front door. She wasn't afraid this time; she recognized the knock. She looked at the clock and groaned. Six A.M. She practically fell out of bed and slipped her arms into her robe.

Grumbling out loud, she made her way down the hallway and threw open the front door. "What *now*?" she demanded. The warm feeling from the night before was now replaced with smoldering frustration.

As usual, Millie ignored her mood. "Don't you ever answer your e-mail?"

Trish stared at her for a few seconds and then pushed the door closed, but Millie quickly stuck her foot in the doorway. Sighing, Trish turned and headed for the kitchen, with Millie right behind her. "Where are you going?"

"I'm going to make coffee. I presume you're going to want some."

"We don't have time for that!"

Trish stopped suddenly and Millie ran right into her. "*You don't want coffee?*"

"I've already had some. You go get dressed, and I'll make you a cup of coffee."

"Get dressed? What for?"

Millie placed her hands on her hips and sighed loudly. "You'd already know if you checked your e-mail! I had to call Edna this morning too. You both have to get with the program if we're going to be successful," she said seriously. "Michelle called and said she was going to the insurance office and asked if we could come over there as soon as possible. She didn't say why, but her voice was shaky. That was half an hour ago, and you're not even dressed yet!"

Get with the program? "First of all, Millie," Trish said with forced patience, "e-mail is not the same as a phone. You don't send me a message and then I get a warning bell. I have to turn on my computer and check for messages. It's not an immediate notification."

"Then why does everyone use e-mail?" Mille asked. "What a waste of time. I'm going back to using the phone."

Terrific. "Second, why would Michelle be going to the office so early?"

Millie shrugged. "She didn't say. Would you hurry, please?"

It was Trish's turn to shrug. "Okay, *okay!*"

Trish pulled up in front of Edna's house and lightly tapped the horn. The sun was just peeking up over the horizon, the rays of early-morning light falling gently on the rooftops. The front door opened, and Joe stuck his head out and waved. Edna, bless her heart, came out carrying coffee for all of them in travel cups.

"What did you tell Joe?" Millie asked as she took two of the cups while Edna scooted into the back seat.

"The truth," Edna said as she closed the door. "I told him we were going to see Michelle and then go to breakfast."

As if on cue, Trish's stomach grumbled. "Good idea."

"Bet you didn't tell him about the car thefts," Millie snickered.

Edna pursed her lips. "I may have forgotten to mention that."

"Well, I've got something you can tell him. Someone tried to kill me last night."

Edna gasped and almost dropped her travel mug. "*What?*"

"For heaven's sake, Millie!" Trish admonished. "Don't you dare scare Edna like that."

"Well, they could have."

"Would someone *please* tell me what happened?" Edna asked impatiently.

Millie turned toward Edna, her face lit up with excitement. "Last night someone intentionally rammed my garbage can into my mailbox."

Edna's eyebrows rose to her hairline. She turned to look

over her shoulder toward Millie's house. "Oh, my goodness!" she said when she saw the damage; then she quickly turned back to Millie. "You weren't hurt, were you?"

"She wasn't even outside when it happened," Trish said.

Edna looked confused. "Then why did you say someone tried to kill you?"

"Because, if I *had* been outside, I would be deader than a doorknob."

"But you *weren't* outside," Trish said. "It was just some kids joyriding who thought damaging someone's property would be fun. It was mean and inconsiderate, but it wasn't intentionally against you."

"You don't know that for sure," Millie said with a pout, crossing her arms over her chest.

Trish looked at Edna in the rearview mirror and rolled her eyes before pulling away from the curb. "*Drama*," she mouthed.

Edna quickly ducked her head and took a sip from her mug. It wouldn't do for Millie to see her grinning.

It was only a short drive to the insurance office. "I wonder why Michelle wanted us to come over here," Trish said as she turned the corner onto the street where the insurance agency was located.

Millie shrugged. "I don't know, but it sounded important. Maybe she thought of something that would help us crack the case."

"It's not a case," Edna said. "Well, it's not *our* case."

"Is so," Millie spouted.

"Oh, heaven help me," Trish groaned. "Would you two stop—"

"Hey! Look up ahead. What's going on?" Millie asked as she peered out the front windshield.

Whatever it was couldn't be good. Two police cars and an ambulance were parked in front of the insurance office with all of their emergency lights flashing. Trish slowly pulled into the parking lot, and Millie jumped out before she could even turn the engine off.

"Oh, please don't let anything have happened to Michelle," Edna prayed as she and Trish got out of the car.

Mitzi Kelly

"No, there's Michelle running up to Millie now."

Michelle looked frazzled. Her clothing was disheveled, she wore no makeup, and her hair was pulled back in a ponytail. She was wringing her hands as she talked to her mother and then gave her a quick hug. As Trish and Edna approached, concern etched deep on their faces, Michelle gave them a thin smile.

"Thank you for coming," she said. "I have to get back inside, but I'll talk to you in a little bit." She then turned and headed back to the commotion.

Millie's eyes were wide with excitement. It looked as though she could barely contain herself as she practically danced from one foot to the other.

"What's going on?" Trish asked.

"There was a dead body on the front step when Richard got here this morning."

Chapter Four

Trish drew a quick breath, almost choking. "*What?*"

"A dead body! Isn't that great?"

Edna looked like she was about to fall over. Trish swiftly placed her arm around her shoulders and stared at Millie. If it weren't for the police cars and the ambulance, Trish would have sworn this was some sort of horrible joke. It may be time to get Millie checked out by a professional—a whole swarm of them.

"Have you lost your mind?" Trish hissed.

Puzzled, Millie looked at Trish for a moment. Then her face cleared. "Oh! I'm not happy about the dead-body thing," she whispered as she drew Edna and Trish close. "No, that's just going to make more work for us. What I'm excited about is that because of this, Henry *has* to get involved now. This area is definitely under his jurisdiction."

Edna's eyes opened wide. "That is completely inappropriate, Millie. Just when I think you can't shock me any more than you already have, you say something completely outrageous."

Millie waved a hand. "So what's new? You're always shocked about something."

Trish looked at the scene. From where they stood, the front of the office was somewhat hidden by bordering shrubs and a flowering pink crepe myrtle. A group of officers, paramedics, and plainclothesmen stood to one side while a steady stream of activity centered at the front of the tan stucco building. Some of the officials were speaking into their radios, and some were entering and exiting the building.

Yellow caution tape had been wrapped around the entire front of the structure, and drivers on the busy street adjacent to the insurance office were rubbernecking to try and get a glimpse of the action. It was impossible to hear or see anything specific, but the atmosphere fairly crackled with tension as the sober-faced professionals went about their duties.

If Trish had not been with Millie last night and early this morning, she would have bet a ton of money that Millie had somehow found a dead body and placed it on the doorstep herself just to get Henry to look into the car thefts.

"What happened? Did Michelle tell you anything?" Edna asked.

"No, she couldn't talk. She just said she was glad we were here for moral support."

Trish chewed on her bottom lip. "Well, we need to see if we can do anything for her. And, Millie," she threatened, linking arms with her friend in an attempt to control her exuberance, "you'd better behave yourself!"

Edna hesitated. "I . . . I think I'll wait here."

"Chicken," Millie said.

"I am not chicken!" Edna exclaimed. "I just have more respect for this situation than you do. For goodness' sake, Millie, someone has died!"

"And you better get used to it," Millie ordered. "In our line of work, this is bound to happen. We can't have you running to hide every time a body shows up."

"This is not our line of work!" Trish practically shouted. But when she saw one of the officers raise his head and look in their direction, she lowered her voice. "Edna, if you're uncomfortable, go wait in the car. I just want to make sure Michelle is okay, and then we're leaving."

Millie tried unsuccessfully to free her arm. "We can't leave! There could be clues at the crime scene."

"And we'll hear about it if there are." Trish struggled to keep her grip on Millie's arm. No way was she letting her friend loose. "Do you really think the police are going to let us go snooping around while they're here? Now, stand still, or I'll bonk you on the head!"

"Look," Edna said. "There's Larry. I wonder if he knows we're here."

"Larry!" Millie shouted at the top of her voice.

Trish clenched her jaw. "I think he does now."

Larry was in the middle of a conversation with an officer, but he looked up and waved, his expression grim. Even though Larry Thompson was a member of the police department, or as Millie called it, "The Enemy," he had proved he was trustworthy and a good ally. He had been a new detective on the force when the ladies had been involved in clearing their friend of the murder charge, but Larry had been helpful and considerate, going out of his way to make Millie feel important.

Of course, now that the *importance* had gone to Millie's head, Trish intended to talk to Larry about knocking her down a peg or two. Millie's opinion that they were now experienced detectives and could hang a shingle on their door was going to land them in big trouble. Trish could feel it in her bones.

Larry patted the shoulder of the officer he was speaking with, and then, after a quick look at the scene around him, he made his way toward the ladies. Larry was tall and muscular, with rich brown eyes and black hair that looked as if he had run his hands through it several times this morning.

"Millie, wipe that grin off your face," Edna whispered.

Instantly, Millie's expression changed from excited anticipation to one of innocent curiosity. "Good morning, Larry," she said, a little too casually. "What brings you out so early?"

Larry's lips twitched, but his eyes remained serious. "I would have thought your daughter would have already talked to you."

"No, no," Millie said quickly, but when Larry raised an eyebrow, she continued. "Well, I mean, yes, of course I've talked to Michelle. We came by to take her to breakfast. We do it every Wednesday. At seven A.M. We go to that little café across the street. I usually have pancakes and Edna has—"

"Millie, you're digging a hole," Trish said, sotto voce.

"Oh, all right!" Millie snapped. "Michelle called early this morning and asked us to come by. It sounded like an emergency, so here we are. I haven't been able to talk to her yet, but she did tell me that there was a dead body on the front step when Richard got to the office. So, what's the scoop?" she asked eagerly. "Was it foul play, or did someone have a heart attack or something?"

"Or something," Larry confirmed with a deep sigh. "I need to get back there, but this is an official investigation right now. You ladies have to stay away until the area is cleared."

"But I want to see my daughter!" Millie demanded.

"I'm sure you can in just a little while," Larry soothed. "Why don't you go across the street to that café you go to all the time, and I'll tell her to meet you over there."

"What café?"

"Come on, Millie, let's let Larry do his job," Trish said, tugging lightly on her arm. "We'll find out what's going on soon enough. Thank you for coming to talk to us, Larry."

"Yes," Edna agreed as she grabbed Millie's other arm. "We appreciate it. And we'll keep Millie out of your hair. Don't you worry."

"I bet we find out who did it before you do!" Millie shouted over her shoulder as she was shepherded across the parking lot. "You should let us help you. We've already proved we're better than you are at this crime-solving stuff."

Trish and Edna both stared at her.

"Well, we have," Millie muttered defensively.

After what seemed like hours, Michelle pushed through the doors of the restaurant. She looked exhausted, and it was obvious she had been crying. She sank gratefully into the booth beside Millie and ordered coffee from the passing waitress. Thankfully, nobody seemed to notice that Michelle had just walked over from the excitement across the street. The general buzz of curiosity that had dominated the conversation floating around by the guests of the café had just begun to die down.

Millie wrapped her arm around her daughter. "Aren't you hungry, sweetheart? You need to eat."

Michelle shook her head. "No, I'm not hungry. What I want to do is go back home, crawl under the covers, and pretend all of this has been a really bad dream."

Edna nodded in sympathy. "I'm sure this has been very trying for you. We were told this wasn't from natural causes. Is that true?"

"Not unless a bullet through the head constitutes natural," Michelle said wryly.

All three women gasped. "I'm sorry," Michelle said quickly. "That came across as cruel. I'm just tired from all the questioning."

"Does anybody know who the victim was?" Trish asked.

Michelle nodded, and her eyes filled. "Unfortunately, it was one of our clients, Mrs. Blakely, a sweet woman who was recently widowed. She would often come by to pay her premium in person just to visit. Poor Richard is just beside himself."

Millie shook her head. "That's horrible! Was she killed at your office?"

"That's what is so strange. The police don't seem to think so. Evidently there's no blood at the scene." Michelle shuddered and paused a second, probably reliving the nightmare. "Richard came in very early this morning before the office opened to work on a quote for an entire fleet of cars for a new client. He didn't even see the body at first, because it was partially hidden in the bushes by the front door. Of course, when he did, he immediately called the police, and then he called me."

Everyone at the table fell silent as the waitress refilled their coffee cups. The popular café was crowded with morning business people ready to start their day, and the entire atmosphere was one of smiling faces and mouthwatering aromas. Now that the police cars and ambulance had finally left the insurance office, friendly chatter filled the area, and busy waitresses bustled back and forth to serve the clientele so they could be on their way.

If only they knew, Trish thought, as she surveyed the room and wished she were among the innocent patrons as they talked shop or planned the upcoming weekend or discussed their children's progress at school, totally unaware that a vicious crime had been discovered right across the street.

"Michelle, I don't think you should be working there right now," Millie said firmly. "At least not until everything returns to normal."

Michelle gave a tired smile and reached for her mother's hand. "Don't worry, Mom. I'll be fine. I just can't help but feel that we're in some kind of jinxed whirlwind right now. First the car thefts, and now this. I wonder how long Richard will be able to keep the doors open."

"Surely you're not going to work today, though, are you, dear?" Edna asked.

Michelle shook her head. "No. Richard has gone to give an official statement at the police station, and I'll do the same this afternoon. We put up a closed sign for now, and we'll open tomorrow. I just hope we can take down that awful crime-scene tape."

The waitress appeared to refill their coffee cups, but Michelle declined. "I need to go change clothes and head over to the station. I'll call you this evening after the kids have settled down and let you know if I find out anything, Mom." She leaned over and planted a kiss on Millie's cheek. "Thank you for coming down so quickly this morning," she said, with a look that encompassed them all. "Just knowing you were all there was a huge comfort to me."

Millie's eyes followed Michelle until she walked out the door. "A huge comfort, huh? Well, she hasn't seen anything yet."

Terrific.

Drastic circumstances call for drastic measures. Trish reached behind the boxes of raisins and dried fruit mix on the pantry shelf and pulled out her secret stash of Chips Ahoy cookies. She could resume her diet tomorrow, but right now her friends could use a little comfort food.

Edna finished pouring fresh coffee, and they all sat down to continue the argument that had begun on the way home.

"I'm really disappointed in you two," Millie said, stirring sugar into her coffee. "When you have a negative attitude, you get negative results. I would think you were both old enough to know that." Millie's nose was stuck so high in the air she would drown if the roof sprung a leak.

"This has nothing to do with negative thinking, Millie,"

Trish said. "You're being unrealistic, and I would think *you* were old enough to know that."

Edna leaned forward and placed her hand over Millie's. "This must be so difficult for you, but there is no way we are qualified to investigate who is stealing the cars and who murdered that poor woman. Surely you realize that."

Millie pulled her hand away and reached for a cookie. "If I remember right, you didn't think we could solve Susan Wiley's murder, either, but we did. We're good at this stuff. You just need some self-confidence."

"Millie, be reasonable," Trish said, then grimaced at the oxymoron. "We want to help Michelle, we really do, but the best thing we can do for her is give her moral support while the police do what they are trained to do. This will all be over soon. Michelle will be cleared of any suspicion regarding the car thefts, and whoever killed Mrs. Blakely will be sent to prison. You just have to be patient."

"Patient? You want me to be *patient* while someone tries to railroad my daughter? I don't think so! If you won't help me, I'll do this on my own." Millie's lips tightened. "I'm not going to sit idly by and watch my daughter's life be destroyed."

Maybe, with a little effort, Millie could be a little more dramatic, Trish thought sardonically. She was about to utter a retort when Edna interceded. "Nobody expects you to sit idly by, dear, and we're not deserting you. You're only assuming Michelle is being targeted, and you have no reason to believe her life is going to be destroyed. Innocent people become the victims of crime all the time, and the police know that. Outside of being there for Michelle while this whole mess unfolds, what exactly is it that you think we can do, anyway?"

Trish would have kicked sweet, calm Edna under the table if she could have reached her. The last thing they needed to do was give Millie an opportunity to think of a plan for how they could get involved.

Excitement lit up Millie's face. "That's the spirit!"

Edna quickly looked at Trish, then back at Millie. "Um . . . I wasn't exactly saying we should—"

"Remember our first case?" Millie asked, ignoring Edna's feeble attempt to clarify her comments. "All for one?" With a huge grin, she held her hand out.

Edna swallowed and tried to smile, but it came across more as a grimace. After a moment, she placed her hand on top of Millie's, and then they both looked at Trish.

"Our *first* case?" Trish asked. "You're kidding, right? That was pure luck, and you know it. We knew Sam and we knew Susan. We had a starting point. We were able to find out who Sam knew and who would be angry at him. This is different, Millie. San Antonio has a population of a gazillion people, and you think we're going to be able to find out which one of them likes to steal cars?"

Edna kept her eyes glued to the tabletop. Millie just stared back at her with raised eyebrows. Trish groaned. Oh, what the heck. What's the worst that could happen? They could placate Millie by discussing a few ideas, talking to Richard and Michelle and probably driving around town occasionally in search of stolen cars. And during the course of their activities, the police would probably solve both cases and life could return to normal. If it would help Millie to stop worrying so much about Michelle, it would be worth it.

With a deep sigh she placed her hand on top of her friend's. "And one for all."

Millie jumped up and gave first Trish and then Edna a hug. "I knew I could count on you! I'll get us some more coffee, and then we'll figure out where to start our investigation."

Trish scowled at Edna behind Millie's back. "This is all your fault," she whispered.

Edna bit her lip and leaned forward to whisper back, "I know. You can kill me when this is over."

"Count on it," Trish muttered.

Millie refilled their coffee cups and then sat back down. "First of all, we need to find out what Tony Matson's been up to."

Trish frowned. "Michelle's ex-husband? What does he have to do with any of this?"

"That's what we're going to find out. Personally, I think he's involved somehow."

Edna's mouth fell open. "Millie, you can't be serious! I know you don't like Tony, but accusing him of stealing cars is outrageous. Unless . . . you're not talking about . . . *the murder?*"

"Of course not! Well, I don't think so."

"Consider me officially withdrawing my hand from the Three Musketeers vow," Trish said.

"Just hear me out," Millie pressed. "Tony is a real jerk. Lately, he's been threatening Michelle with trying to get custody of the kids. He does that every month when he sends child support, but Michelle thinks he's starting to get serious about it."

"But the kids are teenagers, Millie. Don't they have the right to say whom they want to live with?" Edna asked.

"Yes," Millie conceded. "Tony's been a good father, and the kids love him. He was just a horrible husband. So imagine this . . . what if Tony set out to destroy Michelle's reputation? Even go so far as to have her implicated in a crime? He'd sure have some power behind him if he took Michelle to court."

Trish couldn't hide her astonishment. "So you believe that Tony has been running around San Antonio stealing cars that are insured by Michelle's company so she'd appear guilty, and then he can go to court and tell a judge his ex-wife is unfit to take care of the kids? Get real, Millie. That's absurd!"

"You're the one who wanted a starting point. Now you have one!"

Chapter Five

I am really not comfortable about this," Edna said as they pulled into the parking lot of the police station.

"Do you think if you say it one more time you'll feel any better about it?" Millie said.

Millie had a point. Edna had repeated that same statement five times in the last fifteen minutes, but Trish really couldn't criticize her. She felt the same way; it was not a good idea to approach Henry again so soon.

She parked the car, and immediately Millie reached for the door handle. "Wait just a doggone minute!" Trish shouted.

Millie jumped. "What's wrong?"

"Nothing's wrong . . . *yet*. And I'm trying to make sure it remains that way. We are not going to burst in there and interrupt Henry. We are going to stay in the front room and politely ask if he's available to see us. We need to show some respect, or we're not going to get any in return. Do you understand?"

Millie's eyes opened wide in a display of pure innocence. "Why, of course."

Trish caught Edna's eye in the rearview mirror. Edna shrugged, as if to say, "I think she'll behave."

She then turned her attention back to Millie. She looked at her friend for a full minute before she nodded, satisfied Millie finally understood the need for manners and patience. "Okay, let's go."

Millie bounded out of the car and marched—literally, with head down and arms pumping at her sides—toward the entrance of the police station. Trish groaned and lowered her head on the steering wheel.

Edna chuckled and opened the car door. "I'm so glad she understood you."

"Yeah, I believe I got my message across. It's my forceful personality."

"Well, let's go see if we can prevent a full-scale war."

But, thankfully, fate stepped in. Larry was standing outside on the porch, casually leaning against the front door with his arms crossed. Millie was gesturing with her arms and doing her fancy footwork again, but it appeared that Larry wasn't going to be as easily fooled as the young officer had been. He nodded every so often, his head tilted down as he listened to Millie, but he didn't budge from the door.

A thought struck Trish as she and Edna drew closer to the pair at the front door. Was it coincidence that Larry just happened to be standing at the door at precisely the same time they drove up, or had Henry installed surveillance cameras in the shrubbery to warn him whenever Millie happened to come by? Of course, it wouldn't be strange at all for Larry to be on his way out when they arrived, or that he might have just stepped outside for a break, but just to be on the safe side, Trish glanced around surreptitiously and plastered a big smile on her face. "Hello, Larry."

"Hello, ladies," Larry said with a twinkle in his eyes. "Maybe you can help me convince Millie that I'm not lying. Henry really isn't here right now."

"Oh, Millie," Edna admonished with a frown. "Larry is our friend. If he told you that Henry isn't in, then he's not in. We'll just come back later."

"Yes," Trish said quickly, her smile still in place. "That's a good idea. And we'll call first next time."

Millie peered at Trish. "Why are you smiling at the bushes?"

"I'm not!"

"You know," Larry said, cocking his head to the side. "I *do* work here. Even though Henry isn't here, there may be something I can help you with."

Edna looked at Trish, and Trish looked at Millie. Finally, Millie shrugged. She moved in close to Larry and signaled for him to lean down. In a quiet voice, she said, "We've trusted you before, young man. I guess we can trust you again. I'm warning you, though, what I'm about to tell you has to stay between us. We're going to share information that is critical to our case, but only to keep you in the loop. You know, professional courtesy. Understood?"

Trish had to give Larry credit. While she was struggling to keep a straight face, and Edna looked as if she might bite her lip in two, Larry just nodded and said in a serious tone, "Understood. What case are we talking about?"

"Well, we don't exactly have a name for it, yet," Millie confided. "But it has to do with the car thefts and the insurance company my daughter works for."

Trish sensed the change in Larry's attitude. He straightened, and with his hands on his hips and a stern look on his face, he said, "Millie, that's a real case. What information do you have?"

"Of course it's a real case! Did you think I was making one up?"

"You cannot get involved in police matters, Millie. This isn't the first time we've talked about this. If you have real information, you have to tell the authorities, and then you have to stay out of it."

Trish tried to intervene. "It's not real information, Larry. It's—"

"What is wrong with everyone today?" Millie demanded. "Larry is surprised I'm talking about a *real* case, and now you're suggesting I don't have *real* information! Has everyone lost their marbles?"

Not *us*, Trish almost said, but Edna wisely jumped in. "What we're trying to say, although not too well," she said with a pointed look at Millie, "is that we believe the agency that Michelle works for is being intentionally targeted in this rash of car thefts. And Millie may have come up with a reason. What if someone is trying to ruin someone's integrity so that they would appear to be an unfit . . . person? Maybe make them appear to be a thief or something? The bad person could be stealing cars to make the good person look bad."

Nope, it didn't sound any better coming out of someone else's mouth, Trish thought. But they had humored Millie, reported their suspicion, and now it was time to get out of there before they embarrassed themselves any further. But, naturally, Millie's thoughts were running in a different direction.

"If our theory gets out, we'll know who the Gabby Gus is," Millie threatened as she stood tall—well, stood, anyway—with her arms crossed in front of her and her chin jutting out. "And, don't get all territorial, either. Henry has already told us he's not interested in this case, so we're taking it over."

It looked as though Larry was trying hard not to laugh out loud, but he wasn't very successful at hiding his amusement. "I have never been accused of being a Gabby Gus."

"There's always a first time," Millie warned.

Edna gave Larry an apologetic look. "Henry never said he wasn't interested. He said the crimes were out of his jurisdiction."

Millie sighed. "Oh, Edna, don't be so naïve. Out of his jurisdiction or not interested, it's the same thing. Personally, I think he believes the whole situation is beneath him. If he's not out trying to solve a murder, or handing out speeding tickets, then he's not going to waste his time."

Uh-oh, Trish thought, turning a bright smile to the bougainvillea bush behind Millie. If Henry heard that, he's not going to be pleased. "Millie," she said calmly, "you know you don't believe that. You're just frustrated and want some suggestions on how you can help."

Millie looked closely at Trish. "Why are you smiling at the bushes?"

"I'm not!"

"Actually, you were," Edna piped in, a concerned look on her face.

Millie turned back to Larry. "I'm not frustrated. We're going to solve this case. And whether Henry wants to look into the car thefts or not is irrelevant, because I'll bet you a dollar to a doughnut he won't have a choice now that the poor lady's body was found at the insurance office. By the way, any news on that?"

"Again, I can't talk about it, Millie," Larry said patiently. "And you have to be very careful about accusing innocent people. Look, I know this is difficult, because your daughter is close to the situation, but I can't stress enough the importance of you three staying out of it. This is not a game."

Millie crossed her arms again and rocked back and forth on her heels, giving Larry a look that was probably meant to intimidate. By the look on Larry's face, though, the threat fell far short.

"Well, Larry, I can see you've crossed sides," Millie drawled. "We came here to share information, and you're not willing to reciprocate. That's disappointing. Now we're adversaries, and all I can do is give you fair warning. We're going to find out who is trying to ruin my daughter's reputation, and it will only be a matter of time before we figure out who it is. But this time, we won't be so quiet about who the real detectives are in this town!"

Larry suddenly coughed into his hand, but Trish recognized the move for what it was when she noticed his shoulders shaking. Even after Millie's outright belligerent statement, he was careful to avoid hurting her feelings. *Adversary*, indeed.

Trish reached out and grabbed Millie by the arm. "Time to go," she said with a sigh. "There are bound to be other friendships you want to destroy today."

Millie allowed herself to be pulled away, albeit begrudgingly. Trish turned to give Larry an apologetic smile; then, just to be safe, she let her smile encompass the surrounding bushes. It was ridiculous, she knew. There was no way Henry would have bugged the outside perimeter of the building just to warn him when Millie was near. But it was something Trish knew she would have done had she been in his shoes.

"You're still smiling at the bushes," Millie said.

"I'm not!"

"Actually, you were," Edna murmured.

Thankfully, it was only a short drive to the insurance office from the police station. If Trish had to listen to one more minute of Millie's tirade over her perception of police incompetence, she would have searched for the nearest cliff and driven right off it.

Michelle was sitting at her desk in the front reception area, and an overweight, middle-aged man wearing jeans and a faded blue T-shirt sat in the chair beside her. Michelle looked up when the little bell sounded over the door. She gave the three women a tight smile, but the man ignored them. His face was flushed and his eyes were dark slits in his puffy face.

Trish placed a finger to her lips and motioned for Millie and Edna to follow her over to the chairs in the small waiting area. She didn't want to interrupt Michelle while she was working.

The office was tastefully decorated in soft, tan walls with clean, white trim. Beautiful oil paintings of peaceful landscapes adorned the walls, and the windows were covered with faux wooden blinds and earth-tone valances. The décor was completed with an industrial-strength floor tile in a swirl pattern of creams and browns, and several live plants were strategically placed to benefit from the natural light.

There were four comfortable chairs in the waiting area, along with a small table displaying a variety of magazines, and a cabinet in the corner held a fresh pot of coffee and containers of sugar and creamer. Beside the cabinet was a small refrigerator with a glass front full of bottled water.

A chest-high counter separated the front waiting area from the offices. Michelle's space was wide open and situated in the middle of the area on the opposite side of the counter. There were two doors behind her desk that led to another office and a restroom.

Trish sank into one of the chairs and literally felt herself relax. *Now this is an office*, she thought, wondering if Richard needed any more help. She could get used to working in a place like this. But then she thought about all the turmoil going on behind the comfortable environment and decided her cluttered office at home was just fine.

Edna leaned forward in her chair. "That man doesn't look too happy," she whispered.

Millie nodded in agreement. She got up and sauntered over to the coffeepot, keeping one eye on Michelle's client. Trish hid her grin. Heaven help him if he upset Millie's daughter.

"Well?" the man asked abruptly. His voice was loud, deep, and raspy, and he started drumming his fingertips impatiently on the corner of Michelle's desk.

After a moment, Michelle turned from her computer screen and shook her head. "I'm sorry, Mr. Drury," she said in a patient tone. "That's all the information I can give you at the moment. Your claim has been filed, and one of our representatives will be contacting you soon."

"That's just not good enough!" Mr. Drury practically shouted. "What am I supposed to do in the meantime?"

Edna jumped at the man's outburst, and Millie's eyes popped open wide in anger. Trish prayed that Millie wasn't going to intervene. So far, the man was only exhibiting bad manners, not making threatening comments. Besides, he knew they were there. Surely he wouldn't do anything foolish when he knew potential witnesses sat just a few feet away.

Millie clamped her lips tight, but it was obvious she wasn't going to remain silent much longer. Trish prayed the man would finish up his business and leave. She had faith in her friend; in an all-out brawl, she was sure Millie could take him, but Trish had been through enough drama for one day.

"I'm very sorry for your trouble," Michelle said. "I wish there was something we could do."

"I just bet you do," the man sneered as he rose and glared down at Michelle. "I know how you insurance people work. You charge outrageous premiums, then when someone has a claim, you stall until you make enough money off of the interest so you're not actually out anything."

"I'm sorry you feel that way." Michelle's voice was firm. "You will be hearing from the adjuster soon."

"Is that what you told Elaine Blakely? Did she come down here to file a claim and you gave her the same brush off? Did she end up *dead* because her insurance company wouldn't honor the policy, and she threatened to expose you?"

Edna gasped out loud at the same moment Millie jumped out of her chair and stomped over toward her daughter, her expression one of fierce anger and motherly protection.

Michelle's face turned white. She stood and faced Mr. Drury. "That's a despicable thing to say," she said, her voice shaking with emotion. "I think you had better leave now."

"You heard the lady," Millie said as she stopped right beside Michelle and faced Mr. Drury, her hands clenched in fists and planted on her hips. Her Bruce Willis imitation didn't seem to faze Mr. Drury, who straightened and looked down at her, his lips curled back in a snarl. For a moment, no one said anything. Then, with an insolent smile, Mr. Drury turned and sauntered out of the office. He never even acknowledged Trish and Edna, who were sitting in the corner chairs.

As soon as the door closed behind him, they rushed over to Millie and Michelle. "What a horrible man." Edna shuddered.

Michelle sank into her chair. "You can say that again."

Millie waved her hand dismissively. "Don't worry about him. He's nothing but a bully. I hope you keep a gun here, though. You never know when an irate client could walk in and go wacko."

"Mother! Of course I don't have a gun!"

"Well, now I know what to get you for Christmas."

Trish bit her lip. *Just what every girl wants.* "What was he so upset about?"

Michelle sighed. "What else? His car was stolen, and he wants the insurance money now."

"Oh, dear," Edna said. "When are those thieves going to get caught?"

"Not soon enough for me," Michelle muttered angrily. "But this isn't the first time Mr. Drury has filed a claim. He has had two other cars stolen in recent years. In the past, his policy has paid off pretty quickly. Now, with all the suspicion of fraud, the home office is taking much longer to settle claims. It's making our job here almost impossible, because the clients come to us for information. We're the ones they get mad at."

"Don't worry, sweetheart, we're on the case," Millie said,

patting her daughter's shoulder comfortingly. "It's just a matter of time." She glanced over at the empty office adjoining the reception area. "Where's Richard, by the way?"

"Unfortunately, he stepped out right before Mr. Drury came in. But I don't think I would have changed places with him. Mrs. Blakely's son arrived in town this morning to deal with his mother's affairs. You're not going to believe this, but her car has evidently been stolen."

"You've got to be kidding me!" Trish exclaimed.

Michelle sighed. "I wish I were. Richard went over there personally. Nobody seems to know exactly when it happened. The son is pretty distraught, to say the least. First, to lose his mother and then to have her car stolen. It's just a little too much."

A chill ran up Trish's spine. Something tugged at her mind, but it wasn't clear enough to decipher. A thought, a memory . . . *something*. She had a feeling that something of importance had been said, or something had happened that didn't make sense, but nothing came together in a cohesive manner to shatter through the fog of her thoughts. She finally shoved the feeling away. *If it was important, it will come back to me*, she told herself as she turned her attention back to the conversation.

"I should say so," Edna said, visibly angry. "When they finally catch whoever is doing this, I hope they hang them!"

"My thoughts exactly," Millie grinned. "I'm proud of you, Edna. You're finally getting some backbone." She intentionally ignored the look Edna sent her. Rubbing her hands together, Millie looked around the office. "Okay, here's what we're going to do. We need a list of your clients who have had their cars stolen."

"Uh . . . I don't know if that's legal, Mom."

"Of course, it is. We don't need any personal or financial information, just their names and addresses. It's nothing more than a mailing list. Insurance companies sell their mailing lists all the time."

Trish frowned. "And we need this list because—?"

"Because we need to find a pattern, something that connects

all these cases. This isn't coincidence," Millie stated emphatically. "There's a common link, and we're going to find it."

"Don't you think the police or the insurance investigators have already thought of that, dear?" Edna asked. "I mean, it's a good idea," she added quickly when Millie frowned, "but I'm sure someone is already working on that angle."

"Well, if they are, they sure aren't going to share any information with us, Edna. We're on our own, I'm afraid."

Trish rolled her eyes. This game of playing detectives had gone on long enough. The situation was tragic, and more than a little suspicious, but there really wasn't anything they could do. Millie was getting cocky about their supposed role in the investigation, and despite her well intentions, she could end up getting them in real trouble with the police.

Trish needed to get Millie away from the office. Hopefully, Trish would be able to talk some sense into her friend before Millie bought a magnifying glass and a pipe. "I'm sure Michelle needs to get back to work, Millie. Let's give her a break and get out of her way." Michelle could thank her later.

Or not, she amended when Michelle pursed her lips and looked at her computer screen. "I'm making an executive decision," she said. "I'm going to print out the information you requested, Mom. You can do with it what you will. I just want you all to know that I appreciate what you're doing. You may not be able to find any connection, but just knowing you care enough to try means more to me than I can say." She punched some keys on the keyboard and the sound of a printer could be heard in Richard's office. "I'll be right back," she said as she jumped from her chair.

"Do you have any idea what we're going to look for?" Edna asked Millie.

Millie shook her head. "We'll know it when we see it."

A few minutes later, Michelle came back carrying a folder. "Here you go."

Edna took the folder while Millie hugged Michelle. "Everything is going to be just fine, sweetheart. Hang in there."

Michelle gave a small smile. "I don't have a choice."

They were walking out the door when Millie said, "Look

on the bright side, girls. At least we don't have to sit here and deal with people like that horrible Mr. Drury."

And then it hit Trish. She knew what that elusive thought had been earlier.

If Mrs. Blakely's son just now discovered that her car had been stolen, then how had Mr. Drury known about it?

Chapter Six

Millie sat down at the kitchen table, opened the folder Michelle had given them, and then gave a low whistle. "I didn't realize there were so many victims in this car-stealing business. We've got our work cut out for us, girls."

Edna carried three freshly poured cups of coffee to the table. "We should admit to ourselves that we don't have any idea what we're doing," she said and sighed. "Those names are useless to us."

Trish emerged from the pantry carrying a new bag of chocolate chip cookies. "You're probably right," she said as she sat down and tore the bag open. "But I still say there is something strange about George Drury knowing Elaine Blakely's car was stolen. It doesn't make sense. Mrs. Blakely's body was found a couple of days ago, and even Michelle and Richard didn't know why she was at the office. If it hadn't been for her son reporting it this morning, then nobody would know about it, still. So how did Mr. Drury find out?"

Millie grinned and reached for a cookie. "You're finally getting into detective mode, aren't you?"

Trish cocked an eyebrow. "Say again?"

"Don't be upset. It's a good thing. You'll be more help, now. Besides, I think it's contagious. Any minute now, Edna is going to say something detective-like."

Edna stuck her nose in the air. "That's elementary, my dear Watson." She giggled when Trish and Millie both groaned.

"You two need to work some more on your detective-ese," Millie joked. "In the meantime, you're wrong about George Drury being involved. I'm telling you, it's Tony. He's got motive, and he had opportunity. It's pretty much an open-and-shut case. We just have to figure out how to nail him."

"You heard what Larry said, Millie. Be careful about accusing innocent people," Edna said seriously. "You're suspicious about Tony because it fits your scenario. True detectives work the facts until a suspect is revealed. They don't dream up a suspect and then try to make the facts fit their suspicion."

Millie was unfazed. "You'll see I'm right. But I do agree with one thing you said. We need to work the facts, so let's start with the lists." She pushed the sugar bowl and cookies to the side and spread out the paperwork. "Okay, let's organize."

It wasn't that easy. In two months, twenty-four cars had been stolen from different areas of the city, but there didn't seem to be any pattern emerging. Tired and frustrated, Trish pushed away from the table. "This is insane. We don't even know what we're looking for."

Edna sighed. "I know. And the print is so small I'm getting a headache."

"Boy, does this sound familiar," Millie said with a pout as she stood and started gathering the papers. "I had to pull you two along last time we worked a case, kicking and screaming the whole time. It's a good thing I'm not a quitter, because your defeatist attitude is really bringing me down. Just because the answer didn't jump up and slap us in the face is no reason to give up." She shoved the papers into the folder and grabbed her purse. "When you two are ready to apologize, you know where to find me!" she yelled, then stormed out of the kitchen.

"Oh, dear—"

Trish held up a hand. Sure enough, Millie marched back in, her face a masterpiece of storm clouds. "Well, you won't know where to find me, because I didn't tell you. I'm going back over to the insurance office. We need more detailed information. Now you'll know where to find me!"

The front door slammed, and Trish sighed. "She's a piece of work, isn't she?"

"That she is," Edna said and sighed, getting up to put her cup in the sink. "I need to go check on the home front and get dinner started. Joe's going to wonder what I've been doing all day."

Trish grinned as she walked her friend to the door. "What are you going to tell him?"

"Why, the truth, of course."

"The *truth*-truth, or the *kinda*-truth?"

Edna bit her lip. "The kinda-truth."

Trish laughed and opened the door, just in time to see Millie get into her car. Millie drove a powder-blue, older-model Buick, one that was big enough to save her in case she was ever in an accident, which in Trish's mind was only a matter of time.

Millie sat on three seat cushions to help her see over the hood of her car, and that was why Trish and Edna never, ever rode anywhere with her. Another reason was her actual driving ability. Millie could break the speed limit just backing out of her driveway. Like now. Trish winced at the sound of squealing tires as Millie slammed on the brakes at the end of the drive-way, turned her car forward, and then traveled down the street at the speed of sound.

Trish sent up a silent prayer that Millie would arrive safely where she was going, and then back home again, in one piece.

An hour later, Trish was working in her office when she heard the unmistakable sound of Millie returning. She hit the print button on her computer and then stretched. Out of habit, she wanted to look across the street and make sure Millie—and her car—were okay. She grabbed her coffee cup and ambled down the hallway.

She was just about to open the front door when the door-bell rang. She jumped, causing coffee to slosh all over her and the floor. Biting back an expletive, she took a deep breath and opened the door. Millie stood there, hands on hips, looking angry enough to bite a nail in two.

Trish glared at her. "We're not going to apologize, so get over it. You were acting like a jackass, and *you* need to apologize to *us*!"

"When frogs fly," Millie said with a wave of her hand as she pushed past Trish and stomped to the kitchen. "You're not going to believe what just happened!"

"Please, come in and tell me about it," Trish said drily and shut the door.

Millie poured herself a cup of coffee. "Let's sit down. I'm so mad my hands are shaking."

"What happened?" Trish asked, grabbing a wad of paper towels to blot the coffee from her shirt.

Millie sat at the table and leaned forward. Trish took a second look at her. Millie's eyes were as big as flying saucers, and steam seemed ready to erupt from her ears. *She really is mad*, Trish thought, her interest piqued.

"I know who smashed my garbage can and ran into my mailbox!"

It took Trish a minute to realize what Millie was talking about. "Oh! How did you find that out?" An image of Millie cruising the local high school parking lot looking for a car with the indent of a little red postal flag was unimaginable. But, hey, if it worked.

"You know I went to see Michelle, right?" When Trish nodded, Millie continued. "Well, I got a new list with the types of cars stolen and the year and model. I told Michelle not to worry, that we'd get this solved in no time, when I turned around and ran right into Barbara."

"Barbara?" Trish was puzzled. She didn't know anyone named Barbara. Then she remembered. "You mean Richard's old girlfriend?"

Millie nodded. "The one and only. And, let me tell you, the look she gave me was not friendly. I don't know why she doesn't like me."

"Gee, I don't know. Could it have something to do with you being rude to her at the restaurant?"

"No, that's not it," she said, shaking her head. "I think she's jealous that I'm friends with Richard. Regardless, her look was so cold I almost needed a jacket. I didn't hang around long after she got there. Evidently, Barbara was there to make a payment, so I told Michelle I'd see her later, and I left. That's when I saw it."

The thought of Barbara being jealous of Millie was too . . . *cute*. It took Trish a moment to pull her thoughts back to what Millie was saying. "What did you see?"

"Barbara's car!"

Trish cocked an eyebrow. "Sorry, I'm confused. Why is that important?"

"Because it's evidence!"

"Would you please finish a complete thought?" Trish snapped. "These three- and four-syllable sentences are driving me crazy. What are you talking about?"

Millie sighed dramatically and began talking in a slow cadence. "I left the insurance office and walked to the parking lot. There were only three cars there: mine, Michelle's, and Barbara's. And before you ask, I knew it was her car because I checked the list," she said smugly, but at least she was talking normally now. Her eyes were alight with fire. "It just so happens that Barbara's car has a dent on the driver's-side front bumper."

"You believe that because Barbara's car has a dent, she hit your mailbox?"

Millie nodded, her smile getting a little bigger.

"Why, of course. That makes perfect sense," Trish said wryly. "But just to be sure, why don't you check other cars for dents? I mean, I'm sure the junkyard is full of dented cars that could possibly have rammed your mailbox."

"Because I don't need to check any other cars."

"I know I'm going to regret asking," Trish muttered, "but why not?"

Millie reached into her pocket. "Because I doubt if any other cars have something like this stuck in their grille."

Trish peered closely at the object in Millie's hand. It looked suspiciously like the handle of a garbage can.

"If you won't go with me, I'll drive myself!"

"No!" Trish and Edna both shouted with horrified looks. Millie wanted to drive over to Barbara's house and get a picture of her car before Barbara had a chance to get it repaired, something Trish and Edna were steadfast against.

"You can't drive during the day, much less at night. You are not going anywhere," Trish stated firmly.

Millie stomped her foot like an angry child. "You can't stop me!"

"I can sit on you, you old bat!"

"So now you're threatening to kill me?"

Trish's eyes narrowed. "Millie—"

"Millie, dear," Edna said quickly. "It makes no sense to go look at Barbara's car tonight. What if the address on that list is wrong? It could be a mailing address instead of a physical one. Besides, you don't even know if she's home. Let's sit down and be rational about this."

"And all of those questions can be answered with one quick drive over there. I don't want to sit down, and I don't want to be rational! Look, girls," Millie implored, "I can't explain why I feel this is so important, but I do. I really need to go check this out. I'll even swing for ice cream cones on the way back." When that didn't seem to change her friends' minds, she continued. "You don't understand. It wasn't your property destroyed. I feel so . . . *violated*. I'm just an old woman living alone with nobody to fight my battles for me."

Trish rolled her eyes. Millie's voice was getting weaker as she talked, and the pitiful look on her face would melt an iceberg. That is, if it was believable. Millie was the *youngest* older woman Trish had ever met, and Millie certainly didn't need anybody fighting her battles for her. In fact, it was the exact opposite. Millie needed someone to *keep* her from fighting.

"I just feel that if I can prove to myself that it was Barbara, then I'll know I still have some small shred of independence left. And I'll be able to sleep again at night, knowing it wasn't just some random act of violence."

Oh, oh, Trish thought, noticing that Edna appeared ready to cry. Trish needed to say something fast before Edna gave in to Millie's tactics, but it was too late.

"If it's that important to you, dear," Edna said, as she leaned over and gave Millie a hug, "then, of course, we'll go with you. But don't you ever feel like you're alone. You'll always have us right by your side."

"Thank you, Edna. That means the world to me." Over Edna's shoulder, Millie winked at Trish. Her voice seemed much stronger now.

Trish gave a deep sigh. "Okay, Millie, you won this round. I'll go get my keys. But first, I'm looking up the address for the closest nursing home. We'll drop you off there on the way back."

"Trish!" Edna exclaimed.

Millie patted Edna's shoulder. "Don't worry about it," she said. "She's just teasing. I need to run home and get something, but I'll be right back. Trish, get the car started, and Edna, you need to call Joe."

"When are you going to learn?" Trish asked Edna as soon as Millie had scooted out the front door. "You fall for Millie's tricks all the time."

"I know," Edna agreed with a shake of her head. "One of these days she's going to be shocked when she can't pull one over on me."

"She's not the only one who will be shocked. By the way, what are you going to tell Joe?"

Edna walked over to the phone. "That we're going to go get ice cream."

Trish tapped lightly on the horn to let Millie know they were out front. "She said she just had to run home to grab something. I wonder what's taking her so long."

Night had fallen over the quiet neighborhood, and a brisk breeze had sprung up, ushering in another cold front. Lights were coming on in the houses, and the comforting smell of firewood smoke wafted through the air. Trish shivered, wishing she had brought her coat. She could be sitting in front of her own fireplace, watching television and sipping hot cocoa, instead of venturing out in the cold to find a mischievous car that might or might not be parked in its owner's driveway, and that might or might not have been involved in the damage at Millie's. *Geez* . . . she really needed to make more friends and rethink her whole social life.

"Here she comes now," Edna said as Millie's front door opened. Then she looked more closely. "What is that she's carrying?"

Trish shrugged. "I don't know, but it looks like she's bringing everything but the kitchen sink."

Millie scrambled into the backseat amid a lot of grunting and groaning, and then something landed on the floorboard with a loud thud. Trish and Edna both turned in their seats and stared at her in openmouthed amazement.

Millie pulled a pair of dark sunglasses from her purse, slipped them on her nose, and leaned back in the seat. "What are we waiting for?" she asked, completely unaware of the spectacle she made. She was wearing a straw gardening hat with purple daisies stitched on the brim, a black sweatsuit with black tennis shoes, and from her neck hung a pair of binoculars that looked as if they originated from the Civil War era.

"What's with the sunglasses?" Trish asked. "And what was that noise?"

"I don't want Barbara to recognize me if she happens to be outside when we drive by. And I brought my baseball bat for protection. We don't know what kind of neighborhood Barbara lives in. And, just in case we need a distraction, I brought my megaphone."

"Oh, of course." Trish gave Edna a look that said "Millie needs to be committed" before turning around and backing out of Millie's driveway.

Barbara Ferguson lived in an upscale neighborhood not far from Grand River. Millie's baseball bat probably wouldn't be necessary. The subdivision was fairly new, with a few houses still under construction. Two-story and large one-story structures built with brick, rock, and stucco made up the majority of the homes on the street Barbara lived on, and the fresh landscaping of young trees and bushes in the tiny front yards was evidence this area of the subdivision had been completed only recently.

The street was quiet and had a streetlight at each end of the block. Lights were on in most of the houses, but almost all of the driveways were empty. The fact that these people might actually use their garages for the purpose intended instead of just as a storage area was something the ladies hadn't considered.

All three of them peered out the car windows to find the

house number as Trish drove slowly down the street. Halfway down the block, Edna said, "Here it is. This one on the right, with the tan stucco exterior. Is that Barbara's car, Millie?" A soft light from the garage reflected off a silver Mercedes sedan parked in the driveway. From what they could see, the car appeared to be in perfect condition.

Millie had her nose pressed up to the glass. "Hmm . . . I think so. I'll have to get out to see the front of it, though. Pull up a little bit, Trish, and I'll go check it out."

Trish bit her lip as she edged closer to the curb right past Barbara's house. Millie's plan to investigate Barbara's car had seemed harebrained when they had discussed it. Now that they were actually sitting in front of Barbara's house, the plan seemed downright insane. "I don't think this is such a good idea, Millie. What if someone sees you?"

"That's why I wore a disguise! Besides, I'll only be a second."

Millie pulled her camera out of her purse and opened the car door. Bending low, she started tiptoeing across Barbara's yard toward the driveway, and that's when Trish noticed she was also carrying the bat. "I don't have a good feeling about this."

Edna sunk low in the seat. "Me, neither."

They watched Millie make her way to the driveway and then slowly circle the car. When she was standing at the hood, she bent down to look at it closely and then raised her fist in a success gesture. She lowered the bat to the ground and snapped a couple of pictures. Trish glanced quickly at the neighboring houses, hoping the flash had not aroused any suspicions, but everything seemed perfectly fine.

Edna let out a deep breath as Millie headed back toward them. "I'm glad that's over and we can get out of here," she whispered.

Trish was about to agree when she saw Millie stop beside Barbara's mailbox. Her eyes widened as she saw Millie struggling to raise the bat over her head. "Oh, no!" she exclaimed, just as Millie took a swing at the mailbox. *Clang!* The loud ringing sound reverberated through the still night as Millie hit the ground, the force of her swing knocking her on her rear.

Momentarily stunned, Millie shook her head, and then she scrambled to her feet, grabbed the bat, and rushed to their car.

"What are you waiting for?" she gasped. "Let's get out of here!" Millie struggled to drag the bat in the car before slamming the door. She was breathing hard and . . . *laughing!*

Trish noticed a couple of porch lights come on and decided now was not the time to lecture Millie on her behavior. She pressed her foot to the floor and she clamped her lips tight. *Great. Just for the fun of it, why don't we attract more attention to ourselves?*

Trish rounded the corner, wheels screeching, and then forced her foot to the brake, slowing the car down to the speed limit. Her hands were shaking so badly she couldn't loosen her grip on the steering wheel. It was a good thing, because had she been able to, she would have reached into the back seat and strangled Millie.

"What were you thinking?" she demanded, turning to glare at Millie. "Do you realize you just damaged government property?"

"Watch where you are going, dear," Edna said calmly. "We sure don't want to get in a wreck and have the police arrive."

Trish turned back around, but she cast a quick look at Edna. Her friend wasn't quite as calm as her voice portrayed. Her face was pale, her eyes were opened wide, and her hands were clasped tightly in her lap. *She wants to clobber Millie, too,* Trish thought, comforted by the knowledge that she wasn't the only one considering murder. The Three Musketeers were getting ready to lose a member.

Millie scooted forward and placed her hands on the front seats. She was still chuckling. "Wow! That was fun!"

Edna turned slowly. "*Fun?* Millie, do you realize you probably just committed a felony?"

"Hogwash! You two need to stop overreacting. Anyway, if it is a felony, I bet Barbara's is worse. She destroyed my garbage can *and* my mailbox."

Trish was dismayed at Millie's flippant attitude. "This is serious, Millie."

"I'm not joking, either. I can claim I was emotionally attached to my mailbox and went temporarily insane," she said matter-of-factly. "There's nothing to worry about, girls."

"Okay, wiseacre," Trish said sardonically. "And how will you explain temporary insanity when you took the time to grab your bat and drive all the way over here? It sounds like premeditation to me, and probably to any jury too."

Millie leaned back in her seat. "Well, I hadn't really thought about it from that viewpoint. Maybe we better go home now."

And she didn't sound like she was laughing anymore.

Chapter Seven

Trish awoke early the next morning with a dull headache, a stiff neck, and a strange feeling that today might not be a real good day. She swallowed two aspirin with her coffee and walked over to the kitchen window. With a deep sigh, she looked over at Millie's house. She still couldn't believe what the crazy old lady had done last night. In Millie's mind, she and Barbara were now even, but Trish didn't think the police would see it that way. Or Barbara, for that matter, because Trish had no doubt that Barbara would know exactly who had attacked her mailbox.

But the question remained: why would Barbara intentionally run her car into Millie's garbage can and mailbox in the first place? Barbara came across as snooty and a little spoiled, but to do something that childish didn't make sense.

And Millie's belief that Barbara was jealous because Millie was friends with Richard made less sense. Adults did not go around vindicating their little green monsters by destroying their enemy's garbage cans. Of course, it could be that Barbara was unstable. If that were the case, they would be smart to stay out of her way. Trish made a mental note to find out more about Barbara Ferguson from Michelle. If Barbara really was gunning for Millie, the more information they had, the better.

Trish took a sip of coffee and started to turn away when she suddenly froze. A car was pulling into her driveway and, with a sinking feeling in the pit of her stomach, she knew who was behind the wheel.

She ran for the phone. "Millie!" she exclaimed as soon as her friend answered. "Get over here now! Larry just pulled up.

And call Edna!" Trish slammed the phone down and ran back to the window. Larry was starting to get out of his car.

Why is he coming to my house? Millie's the criminal, not me. But then reality set in. She was just as guilty as Millie. She had driven the getaway car. It was possible that they could keep Edna out of jail, though. Trish could say they had forced Edna to come along. Her thoughts were careening around nervously, and she instantly regretted notifying Millie and Edna. Neither of them would know the story she was about to tell Larry. Quickly, she picked up the phone again, but at that same instant the doorbell rang.

Trish took a deep breath and slowly replaced the receiver. She had to calm down. If she answered the door looking as guilty as she felt, the best lawyer in town wouldn't be able to help her.

She rubbed her hands down her side, lifted her shoulders, and walked to the door. The phrase "dead man walking" crept up in her subconscious, but she resisted the urge to run out the back door and hide.

Taking a deep, calming breath, she plastered a big smile on her face and opened the door.

"Larry, what a nice surprise! Please, come in." Oh boy, she was going to have to do better than this. Her voice sounded wooden, and she knew that her smile, frozen in place, was going to arouse suspicion. "Would you like some coffee?"

Larry raised an eyebrow. "Uh . . . sure. Thank you."

Trish started to close the door behind him when she saw Millie's head pop out her front door across the street. Trish tried to signal her to stay away with a wave, but Larry turned just then and gave her a funny look.

"Darn flies," she said, and quickly shut the door. "Can't keep them out of the house."

Larry cocked his head, a confused look on his face. "Trish, is everything all right?"

She laughed a bit too loudly. "Of course," she said, propelling him into the kitchen. "Everything is fine."

Trish knew he wasn't convinced. He sat down at the table while she poured him a cup of coffee, and while her back was to him, she lowered the wattage in her smile a few degrees. "So, how are you?"

Larry accepted his coffee with a thank-you. "I was hoping I might find Millie and Edna here too."

Trish gulped and sat down before her legs gave out. "Uh . . . well, I think they're—"

At that moment the front door crashed open and then slammed shut. Millie barreled into the kitchen and then came to a screeching halt. Her hair was covered in pink sponge rollers, and she hadn't bothered to change out of her purple robe and yellow slippers. The open neck of her robe exposed a ruffled pajama top in bright pink. She looked exactly like what Trish imagined a wild woman who had escaped a hospital for the severely insane would look like. If Larry had been any less of a man, he would have jumped out of his chair and run for his life.

Millie quickly composed her features and headed nonchalantly for the coffeepot. "Hello, Larry," she said. "I didn't realize you were here."

Trish cringed and forced herself not to crawl under the table. There was no way Millie would have missed seeing Larry's car in the driveway, and he was obviously thinking the same thing if his twinkling eyes were anything to go by.

"I just got here a few minutes ago," he said. "How are you this morning?"

"Oh, fine," Millie said as she sat down across from him. "Just fine. I wanted to come over to thank Trish for a wonderful time last night. We had dinner here and then watched a movie. All night. Yes, we were here all night. We watched *Top Gun*. I just love Tom Cruise in that movie. In fact, we watched it twice." Millie faked a yawn and covered her mouth with her hand. "Excuse me. I'm still tired from being up so late. We were here all night."

Larry grinned. "So you said." He looked at Trish. "All night, huh?"

Unfortunately, Trish knew she had that deer-in-the-headlight look. She wasn't good at lying, especially to policemen. "Uh—"

"*Yoo-hoo!*" a voice rang out. "I'm sorry, but the door was

unlocked, so I just came on in." Edna looked at Larry then and pasted a startled expression on her face. "Larry! What a nice surprise."

Larry burst out laughing and held his hands up. "Enough, I surrender! Either you all want something from me, or you all want to *keep* something from me. Which is it?"

Millie stirred creamer into her coffee. "I don't know what you mean," she said primly. "I was merely explaining that we all watched television last night here at Trish's house. *Top Gun.* A great movie. We watched it twice."

"I need some coffee," Edna said, her voice high-pitched. "Does anyone want a refill?"

"Okay, now that you all three know what you were doing last night," he said with a teasing grin, "I guess I can tell you why I stopped by."

Trish held her breath, Millie briskly stirred more creamer into her cup and Edna spilled coffee onto the counter. The time had come to face reality, and unless Tom Cruise was going to buzz by in his fighter jet, they weren't going to be able to avoid it.

"We've started an investigation into the car thefts."

Millie jumped up so quickly one of her curlers fell out and landed on the floor. "That's impossible!" she said indignantly. "I told you we were here—*what did you say?*"

Larry's lips twisted wryly. "I know you were concerned, and I just wanted to put your mind at ease."

Trish released her breath, and Edna carried her coffee to the table. Millie sat back down, a slow smile crossing her face.

"That is really good news, Larry," Edna said. "What happened to change your mind?"

"Well—"

"Wait a minute," Millie said. "You didn't change your mind because we were concerned. It's because of Elaine Blakely's murder, isn't it? You think the events are related, so you *have* to get involved now."

"Millie, you know I'm not going into specifics. Nice try, though," Larry smiled.

Millie jumped up again, and another curler hit the floor as

she flung her arms around Larry's shoulders. "I knew it! I knew you were on our side," she said with a wide grin. "Now the first thing we need to do is come up with a plan."

"I'm on the side of the truth," Larry said gently. "And there won't be a plan. This isn't something I can discuss or share information with you. Now that we're officially looking into the thefts now, you all need to stay out of it and let us do our job."

Trish was still reeling from relief that Larry had not come over to confront them about their fall into the criminal world last night, so it took her a moment to realize what Larry *wasn't* saying. And then it hit her. With a feeling of dread, she knew that Michelle and Richard were a part of the investigation.

The very idea was ridiculous, but Trish knew from past experience that the police would consider cold, hard facts and reasonable suspicion, not intuition or even common sense, and certainly not the passionate protests of a mother.

On the other hand, Trish surmised, maybe an investigation would be helpful. She was positive the officials wouldn't be able to link Michelle or Richard to any wrongdoing, so they would have to start looking outside the immediate operators to find the real culprits. This could turn out to be a positive turn of events.

Millie looked at him for a moment. "I see," she said, nodding slowly. "You think my daughter and her boss could be involved, don't you? Well, I hope you realize that we won't be able to share any information we get with you, either. That is, not until we're ready to hand over the bad guys, because while you're busy going after innocent people, we'll be doing the real detective work."

"Millie," Larry said gently, "we don't go after innocent people. When an investigation starts, everyone who could even remotely be connected is looked at. Someone might know something that they don't even realize is important. That information could help develop leads. You know this from your previous work."

Trish glanced at Larry. Bless him, she thought to herself. In an effort to smooth ruffled feathers, not only did he understate the fact that Michelle would have to be looked at, he also gave Millie kudos for her understanding of the way the mind of a detective works. Everyone at the table, excluding Millie, of course, knew what a crock that was, but it was very nice of him to say it, nevertheless.

Millie exhaled loudly and stood, a stubborn expression on her face. "You do what you have to, Larry," she said, placing her hands on her hips and giving him a serious look. "I'm warning you, though. When you question my daughter about what she may or may not know, if you use bright lights, starvation, or snowboarding techniques, you'll have me to answer to."

Larry's eyebrows drew together. "Snowboarding?" Then his face cleared. "Oh! You mean *waterboarding*." His eyes danced and he appeared to be struggling with his composure. "I promise you, Millie, we don't use any of those techniques on anybody."

"Well, we have work to do, Larry, so we have to be going. I can't say we'll be talking to you soon, because, until elephants do cartwheels, you're on a need-to know communication level. Come on, girls, let's go." With that remark, Millie tossed her head and marched out of the kitchen, two more curlers left in her wake.

Trish, Edna, and Larry all looked at each other. In a few seconds, Millie walked back in and sat down. "This is our place, Larry. You'll have to be the one to leave."

Larry nodded and stood. "Of course." Leaning down, he dropped a quick kiss on top of Millie's head. "I'll be in touch," he said to the ladies. "Thank you for the coffee."

"You're welcome," Trish said, standing to walk him to the door.

Edna lifted her hand in a wave. "Good-bye, Larry. Thanks for coming by."

Trish walked out on the front porch with Larry and quietly closed the door behind her. "Please don't take Millie too seriously, Larry. She's very upset right now."

"I know," he said and nodded. "The best we can hope for is that the case is solved soon. In the meantime, I have a job to do. This is a serious matter." He started to leave, but then he turned back suddenly. "By the way, what were you ladies *really* doing last night?"

Trish's stomach flipped over. "Uh . . ."

Larry chuckled and gave her a wink before turning to leave.

Later that afternoon, Trish sat down with a tall glass of iced tea. Two more rooms to go and all her housework would be caught up. She wasn't the world's greatest housekeeper by any stretch, but normally she felt a sense of accomplishment when the science projects in the refrigerator had been cleaned out and the fuzzy balls of *something* had been removed from under the furniture. That wasn't the case this time, though.

Her thoughts centered on Millie, and they had for most of the afternoon. Millie had left shortly after Larry had departed, saying only that she had a couple of things she needed to take care of. Her friend normally wasn't the reserved, secretive type, but Trish could have sworn she had actually heard the wheels turning in Millie's brain right before she had rinsed out her coffee cup and left.

So now Trish found herself distracted, waiting for whatever it was that Millie had been concocting, because there was no doubt Millie was up to something. And knowing Millie as well as she did, that *something* could be anything.

Edna had sensed the scheming going on in Millie's mind, also. She had left shortly after Larry and Millie had, stating that she had better take care of a few things, too, so that when Trish called her—and Edna had no doubt that she would—with information on Millie's latest escapade, she would be free to help Trish put out the fire.

Trish grinned and got up to place her glass in the sink. As she and Edna had learned the hard way, it was wise never to underestimate Millie. Grabbing the broom, she started toward the guest bathroom, anxious to finish her chores before, as Edna had said, there was a fire to put out.

Thirty minutes later, she was sitting on the side of the tub, red-faced and out of breath. This was why Trish refused to join an exercise club. With all the twisting, turning, stretching, and bending it took to deep-clean a bathroom, all the weekly requirements for exercise in a healthy lifestyle were met. Groaning, she pushed herself up, gathered all the cleaning supplies, and made her way toward the kitchen. This called for an energy boost, something along the lines of chocolate chip cookies and coffee.

She had just sat down with her snack when the doorbell rang. She let out a frustrated sigh. "I am going to rip that doorbell off the wall, and if it's a salesman, I'm going to rip something else off, too."

Trish opened the door and her eyebrows rose. "What in the world—?"

Two huge, slender cardboard boxes were on the porch, leaning against the side of her wall, and two men in gray uniforms were pulling another one from the open bed of a large delivery truck. One of the men stopped and waved to her. "Good afternoon, ma'am. I rang your bell to let you know we were here."

Trish heard her phone ring, but she ignored it. She rushed down the steps. "Wait a minute! I'm afraid you have the wrong address. I didn't order anything."

The men stopped and looked at each other. They lowered the box they were carrying and while one of them balanced it on the ground, the other one pulled a folded sheet of paper from his shirt pocket. He looked at the paper, then at Trish's address. "It says that this order is supposed to be delivered here," he said.

"I don't care what the order says," Trish said firmly. "I didn't order anything."

Just then Millie stepped out onto her front porch. "Trish," she yelled at the top of her voice from across the street. "Stop arguing with them and let them do their job." Millie was wearing her favorite faded-blue overalls and her head was wrapped in a towel. "If you'd answer your phone, you wouldn't embarrass yourself like this. I'll be over in a minute." And with that, Millie marched back into her house and slammed the door.

Trish fumed. She hadn't been embarrassed until Millie had used her foghorn voice to let the whole neighborhood know there was something going on that was probably worth watching. She spun around and indicated with a jerk of her head that the men should continue.

"Where do you want these?" the man asked kindly.

"I don't even know what *these* are."

"They're chalkboards. Three of them," he said, clearly struggling to keep the box balanced.

"Chalkboards," Trish repeated flatly. "Of course. Just put them in the hallway."

When the men had all three boxes leaning on the wall in the front hallway, she signed the delivery order. "Thank you, ma'am. Have a great afternoon."

"I'm sure I will," Trish said. "Killing old ladies is a hobby of mine."

Trish closed her front door and headed for the phone. "Edna," she said when her friend answered. "You better get over here. And bring your firefighter's equipment."

Chapter Eight

Trish and Edna were sitting in Trish's living room when Millie bounded in the front door. She was still wearing her overalls and the big towel on her head.

"You're going to catch a cold if you run outside with your hair wet," Edna chided.

"What? Oh, yeah, I forgot," Millie replied as she reached up and pulled the towel off, tossing it onto the floor. "I didn't wash my hair. I was raking leaves in my backyard. Whenever I get under that big oak tree in the corner, the blackbirds use my head for target practice. It's almost impossible to wash bird dookie out of your hair."

Trish grimaced. "Bird dookie?"

"You heard me." Millie looked over at the boxes still standing where the deliverymen had left them.

"I think it would be a good idea if you told us what this is about," Trish said.

"Yes, dear, why did you have three chalkboards delivered to Trish's house?" Edna asked.

Millie walked over to one of the boxes and tried to move it. "I thought it would be obvious." She grunted as she tried to nudge it forward, then to pull it toward her. "That list Michelle printed out for us is too confusing." She turned around and placed her back against the box and pushed, but the box refused to move.

"We're going to set these boards up and write the information on them so we can find a pattern to these car thefts." Millie laid down on her back on the floor and balanced her feet against the edge of the box. "That's what they do on TV, and they always get the bad guy."

Millie pushed with her legs, but instead of moving the box, she only succeeded in scooting her body across the floor. Turning her head, she looked over at Edna and Trish. "I could use some help here!" she exclaimed.

"Oh, for goodness' sake," Trish muttered as she got up and helped Millie off the floor. "I thought you had stopped watching all those detective shows. They're not real life, Millie; they're entertainment. Have you ever seen a chalkboard in Henry's office?"

"You just made my point," Millie said, straightening out the legs on her overalls.

Edna grinned. "I don't think we're going to be able to move these boxes."

"Call Joe," Millie said. "He'll help us."

That wiped the grin from Edna's face. "Uh, Joe doesn't really know anything about Michelle and Richard's connection to the car thefts, yet."

Millie looked at her. "How could he not know?"

"Of course he knows about the *incidents*. But the news didn't report anything about the insurance company's connection."

"What about Mrs. Blakely's body being found in front of their office?" Trish asked.

"Well, the news just reported the block number, not the specific location."

Trish cocked her head. "Why didn't you tell him the whole story?"

"Because Joe will have a fit if he finds out we're even entertaining the idea of looking into the situation. You know what he said after we got involved in Susan Wiley's murder."

"Yeah," Millie nodded. "Something about witnessing our own murders."

"Well, not exactly, but the meaning was close to the same thing."

"I don't see what the problem is," Millie said, shrugging her shoulders. "We shouldn't be afraid to tell Joe we're going to put our heads together to see if there is a common thread running among the cars that have been stolen. There's also another way to look at it. Joe will think it's mighty strange that we never mentioned anything about the company Michelle works for being the target of an investigation. Common sense will tell him that I'm concerned as her mother."

Nobody spoke for a moment. Trish bit her lip and looked at Edna. "Flimsy, but it's the truth. At least it's the truth so far."

Edna gave a deep sigh. "Okay, I guess it makes sense. But I'm warning you both, not one word about our trip over to Barbara's house. I'm serious about not lying to Joe, but I'm not quite ready to explain to him that his wife may have committed a felony. That could push his 'understanding button' a little too far."

Millie chuckled. "Fat chance of that. The man loves you so much it's disgusting. I'll never understand why, though, the way you're always lying to him."

"Millie!" Edna gasped. "That's not fair! I never lied to my husband until I got involved in your crazy schemes to investigate crimes. And I only lied to protect your butt!"

Trish hid her grin. If she remembered correctly, a few months ago Edna had been as passionate about finding out who had killed their friend as she and Millie had, even going so far as to drive the getaway car when Trish and Millie had broken into their main suspect's trailer. Joe still didn't know the full story on that particular escapade, and, if they could keep Millie from bragging about it, he never would.

Joe came over a few minutes after Edna called. Trish made a fresh pot of coffee and set out a plate of cookies, and they all sat in the living room. Before Trish could even ask him how he was doing, Millie blurted out her near-death experience regarding the crash into her trash can, and she told it with even more drama this time.

"Don't worry about it, Millie. I'll fix your mailbox this afternoon," Joe said. "I don't know if you remember, but the same thing happened to Mr. Greenburg a few years ago. It's a shame, but there's not much you can do when kids decide to destroy property just for fun."

Trish and Edna held their breath, afraid that Millie would

tell Joe that bored teenagers were not responsible for her property damage. They exhaled when Millie continued. "Hmph," she said with a sniff. "I don't remember that, but he probably deserved it. I, however, did not."

Mr. Greenburg lived next door to Millie. Widowed many years ago, he used to spend quite a bit of time working in his beautiful cactus garden, which just happened to be on the side of his house that was next to Millie's. She swore she'd caught him looking in her bedroom window and had reported him as a Peeping Tom to the police. Of course, the fact that Mr. Greenburg was eighty-five years old and as shy as a rabbit made it hard to believe, but Millie was adamant, and when the police refused to do anything about it, she placed her shotgun in her window sill.

The garden had dried up and withered before Trish moved into the neighborhood, but she suspected Mr. Greenburg had stopped working on it due more to his belief he was living next door to a crazy woman than out of regret that Millie now kept her curtains closed.

"I seriously doubt that Mr. Greenburg asked for his mailbox to be destroyed, but regardless, I'll repair yours. It will be as good as new."

"Thank you, Joe," Millie beamed. "You're pretty handy to have around."

Edna fidgeted in her seat. Millie had just given the perfect segue into the reason they had called Joe. She was going to have to tell him about their interest in the car thefts.

Trish kept her face expressionless. Joe Radcliff was a distinguished man with an intelligent, dry sense of humor. He was also a man who obviously adored his wife, so it always tickled Trish to watch the interaction between them when Edna was involved in something that she knew her husband might not approve of.

Millie spoke first. "Since you're in a fixin'-things mood, Joe, would you mind terribly putting a few chalkboards together for Trish? She ordered them and forgot to ask if they came preassembled. They didn't."

If looks could kill, Millie would have died halfway through

her statement. Trish couldn't believe the ease in which Millie could twist the facts of an incident and leave someone—usually Trish—looking like a complete fool.

"I see," Joe said, his blue eyes twinkling. "Bribing me with coffee, are you? Well, ladies, I'm happy to help." He stood and moved toward the boxes. "It'll cost you dinner at the very least, though."

"Deal!" Millie chuckled. "See, Trish? I told you Joe wouldn't mind helping." Then, with Joe's back turned, she gave Trish a wink.

Trish clasped her hands tightly together. It would be impossible to actually shake Millie until her teeth rattled. Too many witnesses. But the intent must have been obvious on her face, because Edna jumped up and, with a frown at Millie, turned to her husband.

"Do you need any help, dear?"

"I think I'm going to need a Phillips screwdriver."

"I know where Trish keeps one," Millie said, scrambling out of her chair. "I'll be right back."

Trish didn't even try to deceive herself that Millie's mad dash from the room was out of fear for her life, because she had seen the laughter threatening to erupt on her friend's face. Trish was going to have to work harder on her intimidation tactics.

While Joe worked on the chalkboards, the ladies kept up a steady stream of nervous chatter, all of them afraid that if they gave Joe the chance, he would ask what the chalkboards were for. They talked about the weather, politics, and the recent Dallas Cowboys' football season while Edna kept getting up to refill Joe's coffee cup. But from the frequent laughter coming from behind the chalkboards, it was pretty obvious their ploy wasn't working.

It seemed like only a matter of minutes before Joe had all the chalkboards assembled. Trish bit her lip in dismay. Her formal living room, the one room in which she had given in to an unusual urge and decorated with ultrafeminine colors and fabrics when she had kicked her husband out, had been taken over by three monstrous cyborgs with blank, empty faces.

"Where do you want to put them?" Joe asked, pushing the empty cardboard boxes out the front door. "They don't really match the décor in your living room." He grinned.

"I noticed," Trish muttered.

"Don't worry about it, dear," Edna said to Joe. "They have rollers on the legs, and Millie and I can help Trish situate them. You go on home and start the grill for the steaks, and I'll be there in a minute."

Joe shook his head. "In a minute. First, after listening to you three discuss the poor pass the Speaker of the House threw to Kobe Bryant during the World Series while that snowstorm raged inside the new covered stadium, my curiosity has sky-rocketed. So, just what are these chalkboards going to be used for?" Joe looked at all three of them, his laughter barely held in check.

"Uh . . ." Trish stalled, her eyes darting quickly to Edna, who looked as if she had just been splattered with bird dookie. Trish was not going to lie to Joe, but she would sure appreciate it if Edna would intervene right about now so she would have an idea on how much they were going to tell him.

"Recipes," Millie stated boldly.

Edna's mouth dropped open, and Trish groaned. Had Millie not understood Edna's demand that they not lie to her husband? Then she mentally slapped her forehead. Of course Millie had understood. But as usual, she had just decided to do things her own way.

Joe cocked an eyebrow. "Recipes?"

Edna forced a laugh and gave Millie a killer look. "Millie is teasing you, sweetheart. Actually, we're going to do something pretty interesting. You've heard about the recent spike in stolen cars, haven't you?" She waited until Joe nodded. Poor man, he definitely looked confused.

"Well," Edna continued, "Millie's daughter, Michelle, works for the insurance company that insured a large number of those cars. We thought we'd just mess around and see if we can find some kind of pattern the crooks used."

Joe looked at the ladies, then at the chalkboards, then back at the ladies. Finally, he walked over to a chair and sat down.

Edna kept her smile in place, but her hands were going to be blistered if she kept twisting them together.

"I didn't realize Michelle's company was in any way connected to the thefts," Joe said. "Has she asked for your help?"

"Some things a daughter doesn't need to ask for. A mother just knows," Millie said as she stood and walked to the front door. "Well, Joe, we sure appreciate your help. Thanks for coming by."

Joe ignored her. "How are you going to use the chalkboards?"

"We thought we'd make a list of all the cars stolen, then break it down into the types of cars, the addresses, the dates, and any other similarities we can think of," Trish said.

"I told Trish it was probably a waste of time, but you know how stubborn she can be," Millie said dismissively. "Well, Joe, we know you have other things to do. Thanks again for all your help," she added, gesturing toward the door.

Joe continued to ignore her. He appeared to be mulling something over in his mind. "Actually," he finally said, "that's not such a bad idea."

"It isn't?" Edna asked, startled at Joe's response.

Millie walked back to her chair and flopped down. She crossed her arms over her chest and muttered under her breath, "It was my idea."

"Well, it certainly couldn't hurt," Joe said. "And it sounds like something you three would enjoy doing. I'm sure the investigators are already doing something similar, but it would be interesting to see how your analysis matches up with theirs."

"You really think so, dear?" Edna asked, obviously relieved.

Joe shrugged. "I don't see any harm in it," he said as he stood. "In fact, if you'd like some help, just let me know. I suppose you got a list from Michelle?"

"Yes," Trish said. "Millie asked her for it. Michelle's really upset about all of this."

"I can see why she would be," he said. "Now, do you need help moving the chalkboards?"

"No, the legs are on rollers. We can move them ourselves," Trish said.

"Okay, then, I'll meet you at home, dear," he said to Edna.

Then he turned and looked at Millie, who was still pouting. "And, Millie, you are more than welcome for the help." With a grin he let himself out the front door.

Trish looked at Millie and Edna. "Are you as surprised as I am?"

"I sure am," Edna said. "What I'm more surprised about though, is that we were able to tell the truth without having to go into a lot of detail. I feel much better about this."

"It's just a matter of time before you start worrying about something else, Edna."

"Just ignore her," Trish said. "She's just upset that she didn't get the credit for the plan."

"I am not!" Millie exclaimed. "What I'm upset about is that you two were just sitting there all gaga because Joe liked the idea. Did you forget that he doesn't know that Michelle and Richard are under investigation or that Mrs. Blakely's body was found at the insurance office? What's he going to say when he finds out we didn't tell him everything?"

"But I am going to tell him all that, Millie," Edna said. "I'm sure he'll be just as interested in our plan as he is now."

"Yeah, right." Millie sighed loudly as she stood and placed her hands on her hips. "Well, the main thing is that the chalkboards are ready to use. Where do we want to put them?"

"I have a suggestion," Trish said.

Chapter Nine

Thursday morning was cold, overcast, and damp, a perfect match for the gloom in Trish's house. All the ladies had accomplished in the last couple of hours was to decide how to best organize the information from the list Michelle had given them onto the chalkboards.

They had experimented, moving the chalkboards from room to room last evening, but the living room had turned out to be the best place for them, after all. Pushing the furniture against the far wall, they then aligned the chalkboards in front of the furniture, side by side so they could look at them consecutively. Trish's lovely living room had been converted into a frenetic schoolroom, and she was not happy about it at all.

"I think we need one more chalkboard," Millie said and grunted. She was standing on her toes on the top rung of a small stepstool and still had trouble reaching the upper section of her board.

"No," Trish said without pausing. She was logging the types of cars stolen on her board while Edna recorded the dates of the thefts and Millie jotted down the addresses and areas where the cars had been stolen.

Edna stopped writing and looked at Millie. "What do we need another board for?"

Millie shrugged. "It might be helpful to know the victims' ages. The more information we have, the better."

Trish dropped her chalk in the holder and dusted off her hands. "Nope, it's not going to happen. We're not putting one more chalkboard in this house. Just look at my living room!

Everything is already covered in chalk dust," she said. "Soon we're not going to be able to breathe!"

Millie stepped down and wiped her hands on the seat of her jeans. "Yeah, I probably need to get some face masks."

"And don't you worry, dear," Edna said to Trish. "I'll help you clean up."

"I'm still trying to figure out why we couldn't have done this at your house, Millie," Trish said. "It was your bright idea."

"I was busy. I wouldn't have heard the delivery truck. Besides, I knew you were home working in your office, so it only made sense to have the boards delivered to your house."

Trish shook her head. What made sense to Millie hardly ever made sense to anybody else.

Millie crossed her arms and sauntered in front of the chalkboards, pausing at each one to look over the information, not unlike a general inspecting his troops. "Okay, what do we have so far?" she drawled. "Anybody notice a pattern taking shape?"

"The only pattern I see is that we have all entered approximately two lines," Trish said with a twist to her lips. "It's time for a break."

Edna grinned. "I agree. It's important that we pace ourselves."

Millie looked over her shoulder and saw that they were serious. "At this rate we should finish around Christmas," she muttered, following them into the kitchen.

They were on their second pot of coffee and in a heated debate about the declining tradition of not wearing white before Memorial Day when Millie stood up and stretched. "Come on, ladies," she said. "Back to work."

Grinning, Edna pushed away from the table. "Persistent little thing, isn't she?"

Trish sighed. "Very."

The drizzle had finally stopped and the clouds had disappeared earlier in the afternoon, but the temperature was still chilly. The heater kicked in, causing Trish to blink. Pulling the blanket from her guest bed up to her neck, she yawned and rubbed her eyes. Her rear was numb and her back ached, but she wasn't ready to give up yet.

The ladies had worked for hours, transferring all the information on the lists to their respective boards. Too tired to do anything more, they relaxed over cups of coffee before Edna and Millie had gone home. But even though Trish had tried to do some work for her bookkeeping clients, she kept experiencing a strange, niggling feeling that she was missing something important. So she had pulled a chair from the kitchen and placed it in the foyer, and for the last hour she had been staring at the chalkboards. So far, she hadn't been able to figure out what was troubling her.

Trish felt strongly that chasing after Tony Matson was a waste of time, but Millie was adamant that he should remain at the top of their list of suspects. Of course, Tony was the *only* one on their list, so it was inevitable that Millie would use any hint of suspicious activity to implicate him. And Trish was also concerned that Millie wasn't quite as insistent that Tony wouldn't go so far as to murder someone to frame Michelle as she had been just a few days ago.

She stood up and stretched. Organizing the information on the boards the way they had was very helpful, she had to admit, but there still didn't appear to be any rhyme or reason to how the stolen cars were selected. Trish moved closer and crossed her arms as she forced herself to look slowly at each board again.

Her gaze fell on George Drury's name. She had a funny feeling about that man, and it had nothing to do with his rude and abrupt behavior in Michelle's office the other day. *Hmm . . . 2009 Dodge Intrepid, white, stolen on March 1, just about three weeks ago.* She pored over the boards again. Drury's car was one of three Intrepids stolen in the last two months. The other two were different colors and stolen from different areas of town. No clues there.

Frustrated, Trish reached up and massaged the back of her neck. Her gaze fell on Mrs. Blakely's name. *2010 Camry, red, stolen on or around March 21*, just two days ago. The date couldn't be determined because, as Michelle had told them, it wasn't reported stolen until after her death, when the son had discovered it was missing. According to the information on the boards, several other Camrys had also been stolen, but they were different colors and nowhere near Mrs. Blakely's address.

Suddenly, Trish noticed a remarkable coincidence. Why hadn't she seen it before? Both George Drury and Mrs. Blakely lived on the same street. Quickly, she scanned the boards. There had been a couple of incidents in which two cars had been stolen from the same street. It had happened both times over a month ago, and the crimes were approximately three weeks apart. Was that some sort of clue? Excited, she looked over the boards again. She noted the types of cars in specific time frames, she looked at colors of cars in certain areas, and she even compared dates and colors. But the result left her more confused than ever.

She let out a deep breath. She was exhausted and definitely wasn't making any more progress tonight. When had her intention to just keep Millie busy so her friend would feel productive change into this aggressive search for clues? Trish didn't have the answer, but she had to acknowledge that she was enjoying the challenge. She'd never admit that to Millie, though.

Yawning, she checked the lock on the front door and turned out the light. She was about to turn away when, from the corner of her eye, she caught the muted beam of headlights. At first, she didn't think anything about it, but after a couple of seconds, it became obvious the car wasn't moving. Cautiously, she made her way to the window and pulled the curtain back just far enough that she could peek out. The car was stopped in the middle of the street, but it was positioned in front of Millie's house. It looked—*no, it couldn't be*—it looked like Barbara Ferguson's car!

Trish gasped, dropped the curtain, and threw the blanket from the chair across her shoulders. In her haste to get outside, she fumbled with the lock on the front door, and by the time she'd made it out onto the front porch, the car was halfway down the street. It was too dark to positively identify it, but Trish would have sworn it had been Barbara's car.

But that begged the question: what was Barbara doing in this neighborhood, and why had she paused at Millie's house? Trish shivered and pulled the blanket tighter. Maybe the woman really was unbalanced, as Michelle had joked. What if there was some truth to that? Or, it could be that Barbara had come back over to exact revenge against Millie for damaging her mailbox. She evidently hadn't called the police, even though Trish was certain that Barbara knew exactly who was behind the mischief. What if she was planning on retaliating?

Trish looked across the street to Millie's house, where the only light came from the front-porch fixture. Full-grown shrubs alongside the porch and across the front of the elegant stone structure were cast in shadows, and the two massive oak trees, sentinels standing proudly in the middle of a rock-bordered flower bed, blocked the view of the moon with their thick branches and remaining leaves. Millie's house was tucked in for the night, peaceful and quiet, unaware that it had just been scrutinized.

Trish couldn't say for certain that it had been Barbara, so she decided she would keep what she saw to herself. She didn't know if Millie was in any danger or not, but if Trish was able to determine that it was in fact Barbara trying to intimidate Millie, she would notify Henry and Larry immediately. The two men probably considered Millie a huge thorn in their sides, but there was no way they would let anything happen to her.

Trish gave one last look down the street in the direction the car had gone. She prayed it had just been someone lost, looking at house numbers to get their bearings, but she felt in her heart that wasn't the answer. With a troubled sigh, she went inside and locked her door.

As was becoming the norm, Millie came over early the next morning. She looked fresh and rested, wearing a bright turquoise sweatsuit and balancing a tray with a two-layer chocolate cake in one hand and a plate of fudge brownies in the other. Trish felt her waistline expand by two inches just looking at them.

"You look like hell," Millie said breezily as she brushed past Trish. "You're going to have to start getting some sleep if you're going to be worth a flip in helping us solve this case."

Trish wondered how Miss Perky would look with chocolate icing smeared across her face. But she knew that what Millie had said was true. She had spent a restless night, waking up at the tiniest sound and creeping to her front window to make sure Barbara hadn't returned to terrorize her friend.

"These are for energy," Millie said, placing the goodies on the kitchen table. "We've got a lot to accomplish today. I called Edna. She'll be over in a minute, and we can get down to work."

Trish poured herself and Millie cups of coffee. "What did you do, bake all night?"

"Nope, did it this morning. I put the cake in the oven, and I jogged around the block. Then I put the brownies in the oven and jogged around the block again."

Trish grinned as she carried the cups to the table. Millie didn't jog. She walked briskly, scoping out the neighborhood for juicy tidbits of gossip. But then, suddenly, Millie's words registered, and she almost tripped. Millie had a habit of going for a walk whenever the mood hit her. Occasionally, if it was at a decent hour, Edna would join her, but more often than not Millie walked alone.

She had been doing this for as long as Trish had known her, so it would sound pretty strange for Trish to demand that she not walk by herself any longer. Millie's safety was top priority, however, and until Trish was sure Barbara was not a threat, she couldn't let Millie go gallivanting off alone.

Swallowing, Trish knew she was going to bitterly regret what she was about to say. "Uh, I've been meaning to tell you that I want to start walking with you."

"Really?"

Trish forced a smile. "Yes. Whenever you decide to go for a walk, I want you to call me. I mean it, okay?"

Millie raised her eyebrows and leaned back to look at Trish's rear end. "It's about time."

Edna arrived in time to share the caffeine and chocolate breakfast but where the "energy" seemed to work for Millie, it almost made Trish and Edna comatose. Chocolate cake for breakfast wasn't such a good idea.

Copying Trish's idea from the night before, they each carried a chair into the foyer to analyze the information on the chalkboards while they sipped coffee. After a few minutes,

Millie leaned back in her chair and crossed her arms. "Let's go over them one more time," she said in a tone similar to that of a frustrated teacher with unruly students.

"We've been throwing ideas around for thirty minutes," Trish said. "We need to back away from it for a while and then look at it with fresh eyes."

"We could call Joe," Edna suggested. "He said he would help."

Millie agreed. "Not a bad idea."

Trish stood with a moan, rubbing her stomach. "First, I want to talk to you both. I'm very interested in finding out more about George Drury."

Edna looked confused. "George Drury? Who is he?"

"He's the man from the insurance office," Millie said. "Trish, I'm telling you you're barking up the wrong tree. Tony Matson is our man, and the clues we need are written somewhere on those chalkboards."

"Look, I'm not saying that Drury is or isn't involved in the car thefts, and I'm not saying your ex-son-in-law is or isn't involved, but I don't think it's wise to focus all our efforts on one individual," Trish said. "Personally, I don't believe Tony Matson is a part of any of this, but I'm willing to check out your theory for your sake. I expect you to do the same for me when I have a feeling about someone. The Three Musketeers is an equal opportunity group, not a dictatorship."

Millie snorted. "Oh, for heaven's sake—"

"Trish has a point, dear," Edna said. "I'm sure professional investigators don't put all their eggs in one basket until they've checked out the whole flock."

Millie looked at Edna. "Did you just make that up?"

Edna stuck her nose in the air. "You know what I meant."

"We check out George Drury *and* Tony Matson, and anyone else we get suspicious about, or we drop this right now," Trish said firmly.

Millie threw her hands in the air. "Okay! You win. And just to show you I'm a fair, reasonable person, we're going to investigate old George first. Then, after we're done wasting our time, we'll look at Tony."

"Gee, that sounds fair and reasonable," Trish said wryly.

"What are we going to do?" Edna asked, her voice sounding a little nervous. "How are we going to find out if Mr. Drury's involved in this or not?"

"We'll come up with a plan tomorrow, right after Trish and I finish our walk."

Trish forced a smile. "Great."

The next morning, Edna joined Trish and Millie for an early-morning walk, and they discussed ways in which to find out more about George Drury. But they hadn't really decided on one course of action until soon after their walk, when they had piled in Trish's car and driven by his house. *Bingo!* The house next door to Drury's was vacant and had a FOR SALE sign in the yard. A plan had started to take shape.

"Why me?" Edna demanded.

"Because you're the only one who can pull it off," Millie said, pushing her back down onto the stool. "Now sit still."

They were crammed into Edna's bathroom, getting her ready for her part in the plan. Joe had left for his weekly golf game with his sons, Lewis and Stan, so the women had the house to themselves. Millie called it fate, but Edna refused to comment. Joe's offer to help had only extended to the mental aspect of figuring out the pattern the crooks were using. He wouldn't be pleased that they were going to actively investigate a possible suspect.

"Honey, you don't have a thing to worry about. Millie and I will be right next door," Trish said in a soothing tone. But it was hard to keep the uneasiness from her voice. The plan wasn't without its faults, but it was the best they could come up with under the circumstances.

"You two being next door is not going to help me if I fumble my words," Edna said.

"Edna, Mr. Drury didn't come across as the smartest raisin in the box," Millie said as she pulled Edna's hair into a French twist. "We're going to make you look professional and snooty. All you have to do is ask intelligent questions and act aloof, and he'll never guess you're not representing the insurance company. Remember, your goal is to find out if he's aware of the other stolen cars insured by Security Insurance and what he knows about Mrs. Blakely."

"Gee, is that all?" Edna asked.

Millie lifted the can of hair spray and soaked Edna's hair. "Okay, we're almost done."

"Millie!" Edna exclaimed through a coughing fit. "It's not even windy outside! My hair isn't going to budge . . . for days!"

"We have to be certain. It's hard to look snooty with your hair falling over your eyes."

Trish waved the fumes away. Her mind was still stuck on the phrase "the smartest raisin in the box." George Drury may not be the smartest raisin, but he could very well be the meanest. She slipped a light brown suit off its hanger and handed it to Edna. "This looks very professional," she said helpfully. "You'll look like you know exactly what you're talking about."

Edna pursed her lips. "Don't think I don't realize you two are just trying to butter me up. The way I *look* isn't going to matter."

"Edna, if you're uncomfortable about this, let's not do it," Trish said. "We'll think of something else."

Millie's head snapped up. "What do you mean, 'We'll think of something else'? That's all we did this morning! We've decided on a course of action, and we're going to follow it. Edna has to do this part. She's the only one Drury never got a good look at. Besides, if we get too many plans in the works, we'll get confused. We could end up approaching Drury dressed like firemen and telling him we're there to sell Avon!" she said dramatically.

Millie paused and tilted her head. "Hey, wait a minute. That worked pretty well last time. Maybe we should consider it. I've still got the Avon bag in the closet."

"I doubt old George is going to be interested in face cream or eye shadow," Trish said.

Millie sighed. "Yeah, you're right. There hasn't been a product developed that will help that ugly mug, and he knows it."

Edna started giggling, then laughing outright. "Okay, okay, let's get this over with. Hand me those low-heeled pumps, Trish. I may need to make a run for it."

Trish looked at her for a minute. "Are you sure?"

"Of course, she's sure," Millie answered. "This is going to be a piece of cake. Besides, we need to hurry and cross Drury off our list so we can go after the *real* bad guy."

"Let me guess," Trish said dryly. "Tony Matson?"

"Wow, you're correct on the very first guess," Millie said egregiously. "That has to be a record for you."

Chapter Ten

George Drury's house was located in the middle of the block, and as Edna drove down the street, she was relieved to notice that none of the neighbors appeared to be outside, even though it was a beautiful, clear afternoon. This was a normal, working-class neighborhood, and the neighbors were working.

She parked her car alongside the curb in front of George's house and furtively looked in her rearview mirror. Trish and Millie had pulled into the driveway of the vacant house next door and were just getting out of the car. They both wore red T-shirts and jeans, with red baseball caps on their heads. They were hoping that nobody would notice them, but if anyone did, Trish and Millie were prepared to pretend to be operators of a lawn service. While Edna watched, they pulled out a broom, a rake, and a box of trash bags from Trish's trunk. Then Trish reached up and pulled lightly at the bill of her cap, the signal that she and Millie were all set.

Edna forced herself to loosen her grip on the steering wheel. Her friends were counting on her. She wouldn't let them down, but still, she wished wholeheartedly that she was anywhere but parked in front of George Drury's house getting ready to face him. She took a deep breath, reached for the "professional-looking" notepad she had brought with her, and climbed out of the car. The sooner she got this over with, the sooner they could all get back to Trish's house and have some coffee, and maybe some leftover cake, to settle their nerves.

George Drury lived in an attractive red-brick house with white trim, but it was completely void of personality. The front yard appeared sterile; the lawn was cut and the shrubbery was trimmed, and likely handled by a yard service. The driveway was empty, of course. The wide front porch was bare and shades were drawn across the windows. Mr. Drury probably never came outside in the daylight. Instantly Edna felt ashamed. Just because the man didn't have flowering plants and bushes in his yard or little statues greeting her on the porch didn't mean he was evil. She gathered what courage she had left and knocked on the front door. She couldn't see Trish or Millie, but she knew they would be keeping their eyes on her. That thought didn't quite bring as much comfort as she would have liked, but it was better than being here all alone. Somewhat.

Edna tried to focus on her assignment. Trish had wanted to ask Michelle what sort of questions an insurance investigator would ask, but Millie was firm in her desire not to let her daughter know what they were doing. It could put Michelle in an awkward position, Millie had reasoned, especially since her reputation and her job could very well be on the line. Suspicion that Michelle had attempted to transfer evidence or find a scapegoat would surely seal her fate.

Still, Edna felt pretty sure they had come up with plausible, intelligent questions on their own. She just hoped she could pull it off, because Millie's statement that "nothing can go wrong; it's a foolproof plan" just begged for fate to step in and prove her wrong.

Edna straightened her shoulders and pasted a *snooty* look on her face. This time she rang the doorbell, reminding herself she was doing this for Michelle. That seemed to help—some.

But after several seconds she started thinking this had been a waste of time. George Drury obviously wasn't home. She looked over her shoulder to see if Trish or Millie were close enough to notice, and suddenly she heard the sound of a lock turning.

Her eyes opened wide and her head snapped around just as George Drury opened the door. She remembered to clamp her mouth shut and stick her nose in the air, but it was too late. So much for snooty. She looked—and felt—alarmed, and there was nothing she could do about it.

Drury was bigger than she remembered and, if it was possible, he looked even more unpleasant than he had that day in the insurance office. He wore jeans and a white T-shirt under a loose, dark-blue flannel shirt. He hadn't bothered to comb his hair, and his five-o'clock shadow looked like it had passed midnight.

George Drury's eyes narrowed, and Edna panicked. Did he recognize her? Oh, Lord, they were all in big trouble if he connected her to Michelle and Security Insurance. She breathed a sigh of relief, though, when he spoke and his words held no hint of recognition.

"Look, lady, I don't know what you're selling, but I don't want any," he said in a gruff voice, and then he started to close the door.

"Wait!" Edna said in a rush.

George cocked an eyebrow and waited. Edna swallowed and tried to gather her scattered wits. She had to pull herself together; there wasn't going to be another opportunity like this to question him.

"I'm not selling anything," she said, and then her mind went blank. She couldn't remember one single question she and the girls had worked so hard on earlier. "Um . . . I'm here about your car."

That got his attention. He opened the door wider and leaned against the doorjamb, crossing his arms over his chest. "What about my car?" George Drury towered over Edna, looking down at her as though she were nothing more than an irritating pest. "Are you a cop?"

A cop? Why would he assume that she was from the police department? Well, regardless, his comment bolstered her courage some. Maybe she appeared more professional than she felt.

Stalling for time, Edna made a presentation out of opening her notebook while her mind scrambled for a way to handle a believable interview. "I am not a police officer," she said evenly. "Are you Mr. George Drury?"

Drury tilted his head. "Who wants to know?"

"My name is Clara Watson. I'm conducting an insurance interview regarding your stolen car."

"Is that so?"

Mille shrugged gracefully. "I apologize if this is an inconvenience, but it will take only a few minutes of your time."

"So you're with the insurance company?"

"Well, in a way. I actually investigate claims and the way they are handled." Edna smiled and prayed he wouldn't ask what company she worked for, because she couldn't remember the name they had invented. "Now, if you don't mind answering a few questions?"

All of a sudden Drury seemed eager to cooperate. This had been Trish's idea, to play on Drury's anger at his perceived ill treatment by Security Insurance, and it looked like it was working.

Drury pushed away from the door frame and planted his hands on his hips. "What I want to know is, why I haven't gotten my money yet?"

Edna nodded sympathetically. "I'm hearing those same comments from quite a few individuals, Mr. Drury. Let's get some basic information out of the way. Tell me the year and make of the car, the date it was stolen, and where it was located at the time of the theft."

Edna already knew the answers to the questions, but she made a show of writing the information down as Drury impatiently related the facts. "I don't know the exact time," he said. "It happened overnight. It could have been anytime between eight P.M. and seven A.M. It was taken right out of my driveway."

"I understand," she said. Then, to keep up the pretense, she asked him about his claim-filing experience. She listened quietly while he ranted about Security Insurance and Michelle. She jotted down notes every so often and kept a pleasant expression on her face despite the fact that he was really making her angry with his derogatory remarks about her best friend's daughter. If Drury happened to look closely at Edna's notebook, he would see *Jerk! Big Jerk! Bigger Jerk!* scribbled on the page.

She closed the notebook and looked at him. "I'm sure everything will be taken care of soon. Your comments have been very helpful." *Gag!*

"So how much longer is it going to take for them to settle my claim?" he wanted to know.

"I can't say for sure. That's really not my department," she said apologetically. "I know that quite a few insurance companies are under a lot of pressure right now, with this wave of stolen cars hitting the city." Edna waited. If Drury said anything about Security Insurance taking the majority of the claims, then it would be evidence he knew more than he should.

"That's not my problem," he said harshly.

"No, no, it's not. It's just unfortunate." Edna was a little disappointed he hadn't said more. She was running out of ideas on ways to keep the discussion going, and she still had to find out what he knew about Elaine Blakely. She needn't have worried, though.

"I don't know if you're aware that my neighbor down the street had her car stolen, too."

She hid her excitement. "Was this recently? What's your neighbor's name?"

Drury nodded. "Blakely. Elaine Blakely."

"Hmm . . . doesn't sound familiar. Her case must be assigned to someone else."

Drury barked out a laugh. "I doubt it. She was murdered."

The cold, brutal way he blurted out the horrible incident sent chills down Edna's spine.

"I didn't know her well," he continued, "but I happened to be walking by her house the morning she discovered her car had been stolen. She had come outside to get the morning paper, and she was so upset she couldn't think straight."

"I can imagine," Edna said. "Something like that is quite a shock, as you well know."

"Yeah. I told her my car had been stolen a couple of weeks earlier and that she better notify her insurance company right away, because it could take forever for them to take care of her. Turns out she was covered by Security Insurance, just like me." Drury grinned and shook his head. "I didn't think the crazy old lady would take me so literally. I guess she called a cab and went straight over to the insurance office. And they weren't even open yet! She must have been waiting outside the office when some thugs attacked her."

Edna was so furious she didn't trust herself to speak. How dare he talk about that poor woman as if she were a nutcase! Edna slowly took several deep breaths and used every ounce of willpower she had to keep her expression flat. "Well, I thank you for your time, Mr. Drury. Have a good day." She smiled tightly and turned to leave.

"Wait a minute!" he said, taking a couple of steps out on his porch. "When do I get my money?"

Edna never broke her stride. "They'll notify you," she said over her shoulder.

Out of the corner of her eye, she saw Millie and Trish next door, and it appeared as if they were talking to somebody. Edna didn't dare turn her head to look. She didn't want to draw Drury's attention to the "workers" right next door. She'd meet them back at Trish's house, as had been pre-arranged, but they'd better hurry. She needed coffee, and she needed it bad.

"The way you peeled out of there, I thought he had threatened you or something," Trish said as she placed a cup of coffee in front of Edna.

"You couldn't have been too worried. It took you almost an hour to get here," Edna said with a pout. "It's a good thing I wasn't on fire."

"If we had seen smoke, we would have come running." Millie grinned. Edna didn't return the smile.

"Edna, we are sorry, honey. We were trying to get away from that neighbor who wanted to know how much we charged for weekly yard service. Well, at least *I* was. Millie was trying to negotiate an exorbitant rate."

"Yeah, and I would have clinched the deal if Trish had been doing a better job. I think the neighbor was afraid Trish would just lean on the broom while I did all the work."

"We don't do yard service, you old bat!"

"That's not the point," Millie replied. "I would have told him we couldn't do his yard *after* I won the negotiating."

Trish sat down heavily and looked to the heavens. "Give me

strength," she muttered. "Can you forget about the yard work for a minute and let Edna finish her story?"

Millie shrugged. "Sure."

Trish turned to Edna. "You really don't believe Drury is involved in the car thefts at all?"

Edna sipped her coffee. "No. He's a horrible human being, but I doubt he has enough ambition to be an active criminal. All he wants is his money. If he had said that one more time, I would have gotten ill."

"Well, I think you showed a lot of restraint by not punching him when he showed such little respect for Mrs. Blakely. I think I would have punched him," Millie said.

"I just wanted to get away from him."

"I would have sworn he was involved somehow. Especially when he knew about Mrs. Blakely's car before even the police did," Trish said.

"He explained that. He had talked to her the morning it happened. He said she called a cab and went straight to the insurance office. He thinks she was killed there while waiting for them to open the office."

Trish sighed. "Back to square one."

"Nope, that's where you're wrong," Millie said, getting up to refill her cup. "Now we go after Tony. If we had checked him out first, instead of wasting our time on George Drury, we could be sitting here celebrating another victory under our belts."

"Okay, smart aleck," Trish said, leaning back in her chair. "Do you have any idea on how we're going to go about it?"

"I'm telling you both, I am not going to pose as another insurance investigator," Edna warned with a hint of steel in her voice. "I think I lost ten years of my life, I was so frightened."

"Listen to Miss Scaredy Cat, would you?" Millie said to Trish. "And after she did such a fantastic job. Besides, who wants to live forever?"

"No!" Edna repeated.

Millie shrugged her shoulders. "It doesn't matter. I wasn't going to ask you to do that, anyway. I'm going to use the head-on approach."

Trish raised an eyebrow. "What do you mean?"

Mitzi Kelly

"I'm going to confront him head on."

Edna chewed on her bottom lip. "Do you think that's wise?"

"No, I think it's a terrible idea, and that's why I'm going to do it, you nincompoop! Of course I think it's a good idea."

Edna sniffed and turned her head.

"Look, I know Tony," Millie said. "He'd see through any kind of ruse. I'm going to hit him with the facts and then see what he does. If he knows we're on to him, he'll make a mistake."

Trish looked at Millie. Strangely, she could see the sense in Millie's plan. Up front, straightforward, catch him off guard. She liked it. No games or tricks. "This might be one of the best ideas you've had, Millie."

"I know," she said smugly as she rose from the table. "Let's eat some cake. I'm starving. Then, tomorrow after our walk, we'll invent some reason to go see Tony."

Edna's eyes opened wide. "*Invent?* But you just said—"

"I know what I said. I'm going to hit him with the facts. First, I need to know what those facts are going to be, though. Do you guys want ice cream with your cake?"

It was late, and Trish could barely keep her eyes open, but she had done enough work to guarantee she could finish tomorrow. Marking the place on the bank reconciliation she was working on, she closed her financial program and then checked her e-mail to make sure she had responded to any important messages from her clients.

A message suddenly popped up from *mmorrow007* with the subject line: *hwkl*.

Perplexed, she opened the message, wondering if Millie was already falling into the habit of using only consonants to form words, something that drove Trish nuts. But the message made even less sense than the heading: *Ainwibw ua iyrausw nt qubsiq11111.*

Trish shook her head and shut down her computer. It was bad enough that Millie used the phone and the front door indiscriminately, contacting her friends at all times of the day—and night—with whatever thought popped into her head. Now that she also had e-mail capability, there would be no escaping the social-contact nightmare.

Trish turned off the light in her office and carried her coffee cup to the kitchen. She was rinsing it out when a frightening thought occurred to her. As unpredictable as Millie was, it was still strange for her to have sent an entire message in code. Unless it wasn't code. *What if Millie had experienced a stroke?*

The cup clattered in the sink as Trish rushed to grab a sweater and then ran out the door. Time was critical for stroke victims and it had already been—what, five minutes?—since the message had been sent.

No, no, no, please, no! Trish kept repeating the phrase silently as she hurried across the street. Out of breath, she pounded on Millie's door. "Millie! Millie, can you hear me?" she shouted.

Trish stepped back, her eyes darting quickly across the front of Millie's house. There were no lights on, and she couldn't tell if any of the windows were open. She pounded on the door again, her eyes filling as her heart pounded in her chest.

She was about to run around to the back of the house when the inside-entrance light flipped on and she heard the lock click open on the front door. An almost dizzying wave of relief spread through her when Millie poked her head out. At least she was still walking on her own. That had to be a good sign.

"Well, thanks a lot!" Millie said angrily.

Taken aback, Trish's eyes opened wide. The last thing she had expected was *anger*. But she didn't really have any experience with this sort of thing. Maybe it was normal for emotions to go haywire.

"Hold your arms up and smile," Trish said suddenly as she recalled something she had read about an individual's ability to obey simple commands in determining whether a stroke had actually occurred.

"What are you—?"

"Just do it!" Trish demanded.

In slow motion and with extreme exaggeration, Millie clenched her teeth and opened her mouth wide. She then raised her arms in front of her, struggling with the weight of her shotgun.

Trish looked at her. "What are you doing with the shotgun?" she asked quietly, her voice bland as she took a deep breath and wiped at her eyes.

Millie lowered her arms with a gusty breath. "Protecting myself!"

"Against what?" Trish's tone hadn't changed. Her heart still wasn't beating at a normal rate yet, since irritation was now replacing fear.

"There was someone at my window! Didn't you get my e-mail message?"

"What I got was a bunch of gobbledygook," Trish said. "It wasn't even in English."

"Oh. Well, it was dark. I didn't want to turn on any lights so I must have hit the wrong keys. What I wrote was, '*Help! Someone is outside my window!*' If you didn't understand it, how did you know to come over?"

Trish looked around uneasily. "I thought maybe you had suffered a stroke," she said. "How do you know somebody was outside your window? And why didn't you just use the phone and call me?"

"Because I heard someone moving around, and I couldn't use the phone because whoever it was would have heard me talking! By the way, you need to do something about this obsession you have with me dying. Anyway, I wanted you to look outside to see if you could see anybody. Instead, you come rushing over here like your house was on fire. I'm sure you scared them away."

"Excuse me for wanting to make sure you weren't helplessly lying on the floor," Trish said shortly. "I didn't see anybody lurking around, though. Are you sure it wasn't your imagination?"

"I don't get my gun out for nothing."

Actually, she did, but Trish wasn't going to argue the point. "Which window?" she asked with a deep sigh.

Maybe Millie really had heard something, but it could have been an animal or a branch brushing against something in the breeze. Of course, the fact that there wasn't a breeze tonight made that unlikely. Still, if somebody had been close to Millie's house, surely Trish would have seen them when she came running over. But would she have? Her focus had been solely on getting to Millie; she hadn't really paid much attention to her surroundings at all.

Millie pointed with her shotgun. "That one over there," she said. "The dining room window."

"Go put that thing away," Trish demanded, "and get a flashlight."

Millie propped the gun against the wall—not exactly what Trish had meant by putting it away—and hurried to the kitchen. She returned with a flashlight, handed it to Trish, and then flipped on the outside lights.

"There's nobody there *now*," Millie said, following Trish over to the window.

"I agree, but if somebody was looking in your window, there might be footprints."

"Oh, good idea!"

Trish bent down and shone the light on the ground around the bougainvillea bushes under the dining room window. Millie was peering over her shoulder. "Do you see anything?"

Trish was silent for a moment. "I don't think so. Unfortunately, the ground is too dry and hard to know for certain. I'm more inclined to believe it was a dog looking for a quiet place to sleep." With Millie following close behind, she cast the light over a wider area on the ground and up through the bushes, moving toward the side of the house until the entire front area had been checked.

Trish looked at Millie and shrugged. "Nothing here," she said as they walked back to the porch. She handed Millie the flashlight and, with a pointed look at the shotgun, said, "Go put that up. You're going to end up hurting a Girl Scout or something if you don't stop grabbing it every time someone comes to your door. Now, lock up, and I'll see you in the morning."

Millie nodded. "Thanks for coming over, anyway. I was so sure I heard someone messing around out there. Oh well, it was probably a dog, like you said." Grabbing the shotgun, she turned and lifted her hand. "Good night."

Trish waited until she heard the lock on Millie's door before she hurried back home, a shiver racing up her spine that had nothing to do with the chilly night. What she had told Millie was the truth, the ground *was* too dry and hard to tell anything for sure, but it did appear as if the area had recently been disturbed, nonetheless. A smattering of dry leaves were piled evenly on the ground from the foundation of the house to the base of the bushes—except for the area right under the dining room window. Also, several branches on the adjoining bushes under that same window were bent and broken about waist high. At face value, that was probably irrelevant, except for the fact that none of the other bushes, or the leaves gathered around the foundation, appeared to have been disturbed at all.

Still, it could have been a dog . . .

Chapter Eleven

Trish might as well give up on trying to get any sleep. She didn't know if it was from the emotional stress of believing Millie had suffered a stroke, or the real fear that somebody had been outside her friend's window, or the disgusting experience with George Drury, but it was four thirty in the morning, and she had been tossing for the last hour. Of course, the threat of seeing Millie again in her purple spandex pants and white high-top tennis shoes for their morning walk could also be the reason.

Frustrated, she threw the covers off and trudged to the kitchen. Coffee might be a mistake, but she didn't have any whiskey.

Five minutes later, she was seated in the foyer, looking at the chalkboards. Maybe now that George Drury had pretty much been ruled out as a suspect, she could review the information with fresh eyes. There was something here; she just knew it. Some clue, some pattern . . . *something.*

There was, of course, always the possibility that all the stolen cars had been randomly selected, but it was just too much of a coincidence that Security Insurance insured the bulk of them. Unlike most people Trish knew, she did believe in coincidences, just not one this big.

And there was another reason she had been drawn to the information on the chalkboards. In the back of her mind, she hoped that maybe she and her friends could help solve Elaine Blakely's murder. The thought of Mrs. Blakely being dismissed so easily by someone like Drury as nothing more than just a senile old lady tore at Trish's heart.

It had been so sad driving by the poor woman's house yesterday after dealing with George Drury. It had sat silent and alone toward the end of the block, seemingly in mourning for its owner. Trish had a horrible habit of assigning human emotion to inanimate objects, but she couldn't help it. The beautiful pink rose bushes in front had even appeared to be grieving, knowing they were deserted and wouldn't be receiving the loving care they were accustomed to.

Trish hadn't mentioned her feelings to Millie when they passed the house. One crazy old lady in their group was enough. Still, it would be wonderful to bring some sort of justice to Mrs. Blakely's memory.

But half an hour later, Trish reconciled herself to the fact that her fresh eyes weren't any better than her old eyes. Rubbing her neck, she stood up and made her way to the kitchen. She needed to make a grocery list, start some laundry, and tackle a financial statement for one of her clients. By the time she finished, it should be time for her walk with Millie. Yippee.

Trish was doodling on her notepad beside the items "lettuce and toilet paper," which she had written down, when an idea struck her. She paused, then slowly finished the design of her doodle. Her eyes opened wide. Quickly, she ran to her office and grabbed a city map. Then she gathered paper, pen, and coffee and hurried into the living room. What if the pattern they were looking for wasn't in the name of the victim, or the date of the thefts, or the type of car? What if it was *actually* a pattern—a design?

Trish hunkered down in front of the chalkboards, and for the next hour, she methodically drew patterns on her notepad, then checked the boards, then repeated the process over and over. Her coffee had grown cold, forgotten on the floor beside her amid a pile of crumbled paper. After what seemed like an eternity, she slowly pushed herself off the floor and gaped at the chalkboards.

"That's it," she whispered.

She placed a trembling hand to her mouth and stumbled backward to the chair, where she plopped down and stared. "Holy-moly!" she shouted.

She couldn't wait to tell Millie and Edna. She ran to her window and looked across the street. It was still dark outside, but it looked like there was light shining through Millie's kitchen window. Trish picked up her notepad, the map, and the list Michelle had supplied them with and practically ran across the street. She sort of hoped Millie was still asleep. It was time for her friend to feel what it was like to get woken up from a deep sleep.

Trish resisted the urge to lay her finger heavily on Millie's doorbell and pound incessantly on her door. It would serve the old bat right, she thought childishly, but there was that shotgun to consider. Instead, she knocked lightly three times, and the door opened almost immediately.

Trish didn't wait for an invitation. She rushed inside, anxious to explain her discovery. "You're not going to believe . . . *What are you doing?*"

"Getting ready to fix breakfast. Want some?" Millie was holding a blue-and-white bottle in one hand and a bathroom plunger in the other.

Trish looked pointedly at the plunger. "Uh . . . no, thanks."

Millie shrugged. "Suit yourself. Is it time for our walk already?" she asked over her shoulder as she headed for the kitchen.

"No," Trish replied, following at a safe distance. "It's still dark outside."

"Good, because I was going to tell you that you really shouldn't wear your robe and slippers to go walking. I did that once, and my feet hurt for days."

Trish looked down at herself. She had been in such a hurry to come over that she hadn't given her outfit a second thought. *Great. My worst nightmare is coming true. I am turning into a taller Millie!*

Trish sat down at Millie's table. "What I have to tell you is much more important than a walk or what I'm wearing. You're not going to . . . Wait a minute. I can't stand it any longer," she said with a small shudder as Millie laid the plunger on the counter and started to pour coffee. "Have you lost your mind? What in the world are you doing with a plunger in the kitchen?"

Millie looked confused for a moment, then her face cleared. "Oh, you mean my fertilizer mixer?"

Trish gagged.

"I don't call it a plunger in polite company," Millie grinned. "I buy that liquid fertilizer you have to mix with water. Since I have so many plants, I use a big gallon bucket and that mixer tool is the best thing I've found to really get the stuff mixed. You start that suction thing going on the bottom of the bucket, and you've got the best-mixed plant fertilizer you can get."

Ah, yes, the blue bottle. It all made perfect sense, Trish thought wryly. "How do you know for sure that you don't get your . . . *tools* mixed up?"

Millie grabbed the plunger and held it up for Trish to see. Written in red magic marker on the wooden handle were the words *mixer tool.* "Besides, I never take my mixer tool into the bathroom. That would be crazy."

Trish raised an eyebrow and just looked at her friend.

Unfazed, Millie put her mixer tool back on the counter and finished pouring the coffee. "What did you want to tell me?"

Trish accepted her cup of coffee with a smile. "First, call Edna. I want to tell you both at the same time."

"Why didn't you call her before you came over?"

"Because she won't get frightened receiving a call from you at this ungodly hour. She might panic if it's from me."

Millie nodded. "You've got a point."

Twenty minutes later, Edna walked in looking as perfect as always. "Good morning," she said cheerfully.

"It certainly is," Trish said, ready to bust with her news. "Pour yourself some coffee and come sit down."

"And hurry," Millie grumbled. "Trish wants us to wait until after she talks to us before we fix breakfast."

"I think you'll live," Trish said drily as she placed the papers she had brought with her in stacks. "Now, pull your chairs closer. What I'm about to show you is going to blow your minds."

Edna grinned as she scooted her chair over. "This sounds exciting."

Trish took a clean piece of paper and drew a tic-tac-toe design large enough to cover the whole page. Then, in each square, she sketched a triangle inside of a rectangular box.

Millie placed her elbow on the table and rested her chin in her hand. "Great. I haven't played 'connect the dots' in ages," she said and sighed.

"I'm going to connect my palm to your cheek if you don't hush," Trish muttered without looking up. She repeated the pattern in the final square. "Now, Edna," she said, handing her friend the list Michelle had printed, "give me the address and the date of the first stolen car."

Edna skimmed down the list and called out the information. Trish carefully wrote the address and then the date on the top left corner of the rectangle. "Okay," she said. "Now give me the details on the second theft."

Edna repeated the process while Trish recorded the information on the design in the first square. She had started on the upper left corner of the rectangle, then gone down, across, up, and back to the first point. Next, she switched to the triangle, starting at the top, then to the bottom left tip, and then across to the right tip. Trish smiled. She could hear the excitement building in Edna's voice. She cast a glance at Millie, who was still slumped over the table looking completely bored. Spoilsport.

Edna called out another address with the date, and Trish completed the pattern by marking the information at the top of the triangle again. Leaning back in her chair, she looked at her friends with a wide smile. "Well?" she asked eagerly. "Aren't you going to congratulate me?"

Edna smiled, but she looked slightly confused. "It's a nice design, Trish."

Millie snorted. "This is what we held off breakfast for?" she exclaimed, her voice incredulous. "Give me some paper. I can draw more elaborate designs and write the same information down with better penmanship."

Trish frowned and looked down at the paper. Why didn't her friends understand? But after a few seconds it dawned on her. "Oops!" she giggled. "I got ahead of myself." She reached for the city map and opened it on the table. She located the address where the first car was stolen from and wrote the number one beside it. She did the same thing for the rest of the addresses, numbering them consecutively from the information on her paper. When she had finished, she traced a line on the map from number one to number nine.

Edna gasped. "Oh, my goodness, Trish, you did it! You found the pattern!"

Trish flushed. "Well, I *think* so. This is how I believe the crooks are choosing which cars to steal," she said, reaching for a clean piece of paper. "First, they draw this design." She drew another tic-tac-toe design on the page with a rectangle and triangle in each square. "Then they place it over a section of the city map. They start at the upper-left-hand corner of the rectangle and trace the pattern of the rectangle and then the triangle on the map. Once they've done that, I think they match it up with an address from an insured vehicle to the corners and points that's as close as possible."

Millie kneeled in her chair and leaned across the table. She looked at the map, then at Trish's paper. A smile spread across her face and she let out a loud *whoop*. "Way to go!" she said, giving Trish a slap on the back. "You're turning out to be worth your weight in gold. Well, almost. So now we can find out whose car will be targeted next?"

"Hopefully," Trish said. She was so happy to have been able to help with the puzzle that she was even willing to ignore Millie's teasing. "They must be doing this for entertainment, sort of like a game, because it's a silly pattern. But, so far at least, it's matching up to the victims' addresses and time frames of the thefts."

"So how do we figure out who is going to be hit next?" Millie asked, her eyes bright with excitement.

"We have a little more work to do. We need to get a new list from Michelle with *all* of their clients. Then we need to mark off the areas that have already been hit. After that, we should be able to pinpoint the next target."

"I can't imagine how you figured this out," Edna said. "This is truly amazing."

"It was a fluke," Trish admitted. "But I'm pretty sure this

design was created to use as a type of grid. We'll probably need to tinker some with the dates to estimate when the next car will be stolen. Then we'll go see Henry and show him what we've got."

Millie's smile disappeared. "We'll do *what*?"

Trish looked at her. "Of course we're going to show Henry. What did you think we were going to do?"

Millie climbed off her chair. "We have to prove our theory first, Trish," she said as she walked over to the refrigerator and started pulling out eggs, bacon, and jelly. "We can't take a chance that Henry will dismiss the evidence."

"I think this is going to be hard to dismiss," Edna said, getting up to help Millie prepare breakfast. "I'm sure Henry will take it seriously."

Millie pulled the bread out and placed four slices in the toaster. "Just like he did when we told him Sam Wiley didn't murder his wife, right? Yes, it's obvious he trusts our judgment."

Fascinated, Trish watched Edna move around Millie's kitchen, completely unalarmed by the plunger on the counter top. Either she already knew what it was used for, or with all the latest—and greatest—kitchen gadgets scattered around, she hadn't really noticed it.

"That was a different situation, Millie," Trish said, gathering up the map and papers. "We're trying to prevent another crime. I'm sure Henry will be grateful."

"I can't believe you two are so eager to turn everything we know over to Henry," Millie said, her voice full of exasperation. "We had the idea for the chalkboard analysis, we discovered the pattern, and we're going to do even more work to try and figure out who the next victim is. And after everything *we* have done, we're going to let Henry take the collar?"

Trish rolled her eyes. "Don't start that 'collar' stuff again. This isn't a competition."

"Of course it is! Henry insulted our intelligence, and we've got to show him he had better start taking us seriously."

"Girls," Edna said quietly. "We can't forget there's a good chance a murder is connected to these car thefts."

"Even more reason for us to keep this to ourselves, even if

it's just for a little while," Millie said earnestly. "Let's test our theory to make sure we're right. Then, let's find out what we can regarding Tony's involvement," she implored. "Henry doesn't like theories; he likes proof. And the more real evidence we can give him, the faster he can solve Elaine Blakely's murder."

Millie kept pleading her case all during breakfast. Trish knew that Millie had a legitimate point but wasn't sure that investigating this on their own was the smart thing to do. Finally, she turned to Edna. "What do you think?"

"I honestly don't know," Edna said, shaking her head. "Millie, I know how important this is to you because of Michelle, but what if we do something wrong, and it makes it harder for the police to solve the case? Are you sure you want to take that chance?"

Millie looked at Edna with a sad, pleading expression. "Yes, I do," she said softly.

Edna was silent for a minute. "Well, I guess we can try," she said.

Trish held back a laugh. Millie knew just how to work on Edna's emotions.

Millie clapped her hands together and scooted her chair back. "Terrific! Now, Trish and I need to change clothes, and then we'll all go for a walk. We need to keep our energy up, you know. It's important that we stay in shape. We can start working on our theory as soon as we get back."

"Uh . . . Edna, you go with Millie," Trish said quickly. "I'm going to run over to the insurance office and get Michelle to print out an entire new list of all of their clients. We've been scribbling and scratching names off the pages we have, and it's too hard to read." It would also give her a chance to get some information about Barbara Ferguson.

"Are you sure you don't want to go with us?" Millie asked, looking pointedly at Trish's rear again.

"Yes!" Sticking her nose in the air, Trish grabbed her paperwork and headed home. If she were a witch, she would snap her fingers and curse Millie with a big backside . . . and a muzzle.

Chapter Twelve

Michelle hung up the phone when Trish pushed through the door of the insurance office. "Good morning, Trish. How are you?"

"I'm fine, dear. How are you?" But Trish really didn't need to ask. The dark circles under Michelle's eyes and the tired expression on her face were answer enough. "Am I interrupting you?"

"No, of course not. I was just talking to a client who called to ask about her claim. It seems like that's about all I do lately," she said, getting up from her chair. "I can't do much except try to keep everybody patient since the home office has taken over handling the claims. I was just getting ready to fix a cup of coffee. Care to join me?"

"I'd love some. I'm not even close to my quota of ten pots a day yet."

Michelle grinned. "I don't know how you guys do it. I'd never be able to sleep."

"When you're our age, sleep is highly overrated." Trish sat down beside Michelle's desk and accepted the coffee with a smile. "Are you here alone?"

Michelle nodded. "Richard will be here in a little while. He wanted to stop by the police station to see if there are any developments."

"I doubt if they'll tell him anything, but I understand his frustration."

"Yeah, to say the least. At this point, he's more concerned about Mrs. Blakely's murder than the thefts. He's worried about me opening up the office by myself. He always makes sure he's here before I arrive in the mornings."

"That's a good idea. You can't be too careful. At least until the police get to the bottom of this."

"And let's hope that's soon." Michelle sighed as she sat down at her desk. "How is Mom doing?"

"She's fine. I saw her this morning, and when I left the house a little while ago she and Edna were going for a walk."

Michelle chuckled. "Checking out the neighbors again, huh?"

"Exactly."

"I'm taking the kids over there for a couple of hours tonight. I have to put the finishing touches on Carol's surprise birthday party this weekend, and I don't want them at home."

"That's right, the big sixteen!"

Michelle smiled. "Yes, and I'm not going to let this other stuff ruin it."

"Your mother has been talking about it for a month. Has she told you what gift she bought?"

"Oh, yes, and I'm not sure I'm ever going to forgive her. *An electric guitar!* What was she thinking?"

"She said she wants to see Carol as the lead guitarist in a rock and roll band," Trish laughed. "In case you haven't noticed, Michelle, your mother is slightly crazy."

"Don't I know it. Carol is going to love it, though. I just hope I survive the practice sessions," she said with a shudder.

"She said that one day Carol was pretending she was playing a guitar while she was listening to some music, so she decided to get her a real one. Crazy or not, she's got a big heart."

"Mom's always believed that following your dreams is the most important thing you can do." Michelle took a sip of her coffee. "I really hate that she's worried about me. That's the worst part of this whole thing."

Trish placed a hand over Michelle's. "That's what mothers do. But she also knows everything is going to be fine. She just hates that you have to go through this."

Michelle smiled and squeezed Trish's hand. "She is the eternal optimist, isn't she? Well, I hope she's right. I just want this over with and for life to get back to normal."

"It will, dear; it will. You just hang in there." It broke Trish's heart to see Michelle so upset. She had never been fortunate enough to have children of her own, but over the years she had come to think of Michelle as family. Trish wanted so badly to jump up and shout that they may have found a major clue in the selection of the cars stolen, but that would be cruel. What if there was a glitch in their discovery, a huge coincidence that had nothing to do with the stolen cars at all? No, she couldn't take a chance on getting Michelle's hopes up. When she was sure, absolutely positive that their findings held water, then they would break the news to Michelle. And she couldn't wait to get started.

"I need to ask you a favor," she said. "We've been working hard on breaking down the information on the list you gave us, but your mother spilled coffee all over it. It's so hard to read now, and I was hoping you could print out another list with the names and addresses of all your clients."

Michelle shrugged. "Sure. Have you found anything interesting, yet?"

If you only knew. "It's hard to say. Listen, I have something else that's on my mind," she said, anxious to change the subject. "Were you serious when you mentioned that Barbara Ferguson may be a stalker?" She had to be careful. She didn't want to add to Michelle's worries, but if Barbara was indeed a threat, Millie and Michelle were both going to need to be aware of it. First, Trish needed to find out if Michelle had been serious.

Surprised, Michelle raised her eyebrows. "*Barbara?* What makes you ask about her?"

"Uh, well . . . I think I may have seen her at the grocery store yesterday."

Michelle frowned. "Well, the grocery story would be a first for her, but it doesn't surprise me. Even though there are stores and restaurants closer to her home in San Antonio, she always seems to frequent the ones here in Grand River. And I know why. She wants to be anywhere Richard is."

"Ah," Trish nodded knowingly. "She's not thrilled about being the *ex*-girlfriend, is she?"

"Hardly," Michelle snorted. "If Barbara had her way, I'd be

Mitzi Kelly

booted out of here so fast Superman would have a hard time catching me."

"You mean . . . I mean, I don't want to pry, but are you and Richard—?"

"No!" Michelle exclaimed, a slight blush reddening her cheeks. "Of course not. Richard and I are just friends. We're professional colleagues. We just work together."

Me thinks the lady doth protest too much, Trish thought in amusement, but she kept her expression flat. It seemed to her that Michelle could do a lot worse than Richard Kelp.

"Barbara probably thinks we're more than friends, though," Michelle continued. "She does her best to insult me every time she sees me. She worked here for a while, and now she thinks she owns this place *and* Richard."

"Barbara worked here at the office?" Now, that could be an awkward situation.

Michelle nodded. "Yes. She filled in back in September when I took the kids to Florida. It was right before her relationship with Richard ended. She had experience working in an insurance office, and at the time it seemed like the perfect solution. Richard bought me a huge bouquet of roses when I got back." Michelle chuckled. "He said Barbara drove him crazy the entire time. It wasn't long after that they broke up. She's been trying to wheedle her way back into his life ever since."

Trish clucked sympathetically, but her mind was racing. Now was the time for the important question. "That must be fun," she said wryly. "Do you think Barbara is, um . . . dangerous?"

Michelle grinned. "Only to herself. I'm sure her self-esteem is suffering terribly. She'll get tired of this after a while and move on. I just hope it's sooner rather than later. It's really getting on my nerves. Every time you turn around, she's there."

"What does Richard think about it?"

"That's the only fun thing about this. He gets so embarrassed it's ridiculous," she said, her eyes twinkling. "He doesn't know how to tell her to leave him alone. He said the breakup was horrible."

Maybe he'd better find a way to let Barbara know there was no hope of continuing their relationship, Trish thought. Stalking was a serious business, and if Barbara hadn't crossed the line into psychotic disillusionment, then she was living in a fantasy world, at best. Still, Trish had no better feel for whether Barbara was dangerous, or not.

Michelle hit a few keys on her computer and then got up to go get the list of clients she had just printed. Restless, Trish stood and ambled around the office. She was anxious to get back home and work on the pattern she believed would help catch the car thieves. If it worked, would it also lead the police to Mrs. Blakely's murderer? She sincerely hoped so. Then life, as Michelle put it, could really return to normal.

"This darn printer," Michelle called out from the back office. "It keeps jamming. I'll be with you in a minute."

"That's fine, dear. No rush." Trish stopped in front of Michelle's desk to look at the framed pictures of her children. My, they were growing fast. There was also a professional photo of Millie sitting prim and proper in a Queen Anne chair, obviously taken quite a few years ago because now, as far as Trish knew, Millie wouldn't dare be caught in a *dress*.

A big red *X* caught her eye on the desk calendar. Looking closer, she saw *Tony* scribbled on today's date, and the *X* covered his name. Hmm . . . she wondered what that was all about. Poor Michelle, she had enough on her plate without having to deal with her ex-husband, too. If Millie was right in her assessment of Tony Matson's character, he sounded like a real piece of work.

When she heard the printer start back up, she moved to her chair and sat down. Seeing the information on Michelle's calendar was completely innocent, but Trish still felt as if she had intruded.

A few minutes later, Michelle handed her the new list. "Hope you find something useful," she said.

"Me, too." Trish smiled as she stood and gathered her purse. "Call me if you need anything, sweetie. Even if it's just to talk."

Michelle gave her a hug. "I will. I promise."

Trish stared in amused disbelief when she pulled into her driveway. Millie and Edna were sitting in the front yard, legs spread out in front of them as they stretched, attempting to touch their toes. The spectacle was made more entertaining by Millie's bright orange sweatsuit and an orange sweatband across her forehead. The red tennis shoes were what stole the show, though. She was surprised the neighbors weren't out in droves to watch the display.

As usual, Edna was dressed appropriately, in a soft lavender sweatsuit with white walking shoes. She looked *normal*, so to be seen in public with her bizarre friend took guts, especially while they were exercising. Trish's admiration for Edna knew no bounds.

"It's about time you got here," Millie grunted as she struggled to her feet. "We had to keep moving so our muscles wouldn't tighten up."

Edna brushed the seat of her pants off. "I tried to tell her that if our muscles tighten up after just walking, we're in pretty bad shape."

Millie shrugged. "You should have seen Trish after our first walk. She was practically limping."

It was true, but Trish didn't like being reminded of it. "Why didn't you just use your key to go inside the house?"

Millie pulled at the sides of her pants. "Where would we carry a key?"

Trish grinned. "You've got a point," she said, opening the door. "You could have gone to your own house, though."

"If we had known you were going to take so long, we would have. Did you get the list?" Millie asked, heading straight for the kitchen to start a pot of coffee.

"Yes. I've been trying to think of how best to lay out all the information so we can work on it. And before you suggest anything, Millie, I am not putting another chalkboard in this house."

"How is Michelle doing?"

Trish didn't want to worry Millie any more than was necessary, so she hedged just a bit. "She's doing fine. She's anxious to get this all over with, of course, but she looked and sounded pretty good."

"I can't wait until this is over, too," Millie said and sighed.

"I know, honey," Trish said. "Just keep the faith. I have a feeling we're on the right track."

"Of course we are," Millie said, her spirit back in full force. "And just think how happy Michelle is going to be when Tony is behind bars."

Edna put the sugar and creamer on the table. "Stop convicting someone until there is actual evidence," she said sternly. "And speaking of getting evidence, why don't we erase the board that has the types of cars listed? That information doesn't seem useful."

"You're right," Trish said. "We can use that board to write down the addresses that correspond to our pattern."

It was a tedious, time-consuming process, but finally, after three hours, the pattern was falling into place. Millie had made a quick phone call to Michelle to verify the address of the last stolen car. After locating that address on the city map, they had used it as a starting point and drawn several test patterns, with Edna identifying any of the surrounding streets with the same streets on the list Michelle had provided.

"That's the last one," Millie said, her voice full of wonder. "We know who's going to have their car stolen next."

Trish was almost giddy with excitement. Still, this was just an experiment. Nothing definitive had been proven yet. But it sure looked promising, though. "If our calculations prove correct, it's going to happen tonight."

"I wish we had one of those police radios," Edna said, her smile animated. "We'd know when a call came in reporting the theft."

Millie looked at her. "Edna, I can't believe I'm going to say this, but that's a great idea."

Edna rolled her eyes, but her smile was still in place. "You're such a charmer."

Trish laughed. "Forget it, girls. We'll just have to wait until we can check with Michelle. It almost makes me want to go sit outside that house, though, and see if something happens."

"Another great idea!" Millie exclaimed. "Let's do it—oh, darn it, I can't," she said, her disappointment evident. "My grandkids are coming over tonight."

Ah, that explains the X *on Michelle's calendar.* "For goodness' sake, I was just kidding," Trish said. "We're not going to
sit and watch a house to see if a car gets stolen. We'll find out
soon enough. You just enjoy your grandchildren tonight, and
try not to let any of your insane qualities rub off on them."

Trish was up early the next morning. It seemed insensitive to
be hoping that a car had been stolen last night, but she couldn't
help but pray that's exactly what happened. She jumped only
slightly when the doorbell rang. She had been expecting it, and
she was prepared. A fresh pot of coffee was ready, store-bought
cinnamon rolls were on the table, and she was dressed.

"Good morning, Millie," she said as she opened the door.

"How did you know it was me?" Millie asked as she came
in and headed straight for the kitchen. Trish had to admit she
almost looked forward to discovering what her friend would
choose to wear on any given day. Today she had chosen a soft
purple cardigan over a white turtleneck sweater, lime-green
leggings, and her white high-top tennis shoes.

"I guess I'm getting used to these early-morning visits.
Um . . . are you cold?"

"It's still a little nippy in the mornings. I don't like to be cold
while I'm walking. Not good for the muscles."

Trish groaned. "I didn't think you'd want to walk this morning. We need to work on our *case.*"

Millie grinned. "We can do that while we walk. Besides,
Michelle will be at the office in a couple of hours. I'll give her
a call and see if she knows anything. If I had my car stolen,
I would notify my insurance company immediately after I
called the police, wouldn't you?"

"I guess you're right," she sighed. "I think I'll go crazy waiting for news, though. We can work on another grid on the map,
or we can dust my living room. You choose."

"We can do both right after our walk. I called Edna, and
she'll be over in a minute, so finish your coffee and go get
dressed."

"I am dressed!"

Millie looked down her nose. "Oh."

Trish gritted her teeth and went to get her tennis shoes. What was wrong with her jeans and flannel shirt? They were going to *walk*, for heaven's sake, not go shopping. Well, she decided, this was going to be her last walk with Millie. She wasn't even sure what she was worried about anyway. Millie could take on Barbara Ferguson anytime and win hands down.

Half an hour later, Trish discovered that Millie and Edna enjoyed speed walking. This had to be Edna's fault, because Millie hadn't tried to torture her this way on their previous walk. Struggling to keep up, she tried to hide the fact she was out of breath while she plotted her revenge on Edna. How embarrassing to have her two older friends cruise effortlessly around the neighborhood while she staggered behind them on rubbery legs, desperately gasping for air. The good news, though, was that they were back on their own block, and soon Trish could make some excuse to go to her bedroom and die in peace.

Suddenly Millie stopped. *Wham!* Millie stumbled when Trish ran into her but was able to stay upright. Trish, however, was sprawled on the ground.

"Oh, dear," Edna exclaimed as she hurried to help. "Are you all right, Trish?"

"She's fine," Millie snapped, rubbing her shoulder. "I'm the one who was knocked into tomorrow!"

Trish glared up at her from her prone position, only half-heartedly accepting Edna's assistance. It felt so good to lie still for a moment. "Why did you stop so suddenly?"

"Because there's a moving van in front of Sam's old house."

Trish craned her neck to see. Sure enough, a big orange-and-white van was parked in their old friend's driveway. The three women froze, transfixed at the scene with mixed emotions, relief that the vacant house would now have an occupant and sadness that a part of their history was ending.

Susan Wiley, their neighbor of many, many years and a good friend, had been murdered in that house. Her husband, Sam, had tried to keep the house and pick up the pieces of his life, but the tragedy had been too much for him. Dealing with his wife's murder and going through the horrible ordeal of being accused of the crime had forced him to leave. They heard from him every now and then, a postcard sent from Arizona letting them know he and his housekeeper, Claire, were doing fine. And he never failed to end his correspondence with a heartfelt thank-you for their help in clearing his name.

"Joe told me the other day that he had heard the house had sold," Edna whispered.

Millie didn't say a word, but her lips were pinched together tightly. Trish's heart broke for her. Millie had known Susan longer than any of them, and Trish knew that Millie's pain from the loss of her friend was still raw.

Trish struggled to her feet. "It will be good to have people living in the house again," she said gently, placing an arm across Millie's shoulders.

Millie nodded. "I know. That house was meant to be lived in. Sam and Susan filled it with so much love and energy," she said. "So, let's go meet the jerks who bought it." And while Edna's mouth dropped open and Trish's eyebrows rose to her hairline, Millie put her speed-walking skills to use and headed for the house.

The *jerks* turned out to be only one jerk. Patrick Bailey, or Pat, as he said he preferred to be called, was tall and lanky, ruggedly handsome with expressive brown eyes. His voice was deep and smooth, and Trish got the impression he wasn't one to waste words. She estimated his age to be around fifty-five by the slight graying at his temples and the character lines around his eyes and mouth. He appeared to be a down-to-earth sort of guy, open and friendly, and Trish was able to surmise this because he didn't bonk Millie on the head when she stormed up and asked him who he was.

"So, do you have family, Pat?"

"Well," he drawled, "none that will be living here. My parents passed away years ago, and my son is in the navy, traveling the world. And for some reason, my ex-wife didn't want to move here with me."

Edna blushed. "I'm terribly sorry. I didn't mean to pry."

Pat laughed, his eyes crinkling in amusement. "You weren't prying. My divorce was several years ago, but we remained friends. In fact, you'll probably meet my ex one of these days when my son visits," he said, crossing his arms over his chest. "The truth is that I took an early retirement and decided to move somewhere that had a little slower pace of life."

"Oh?" Edna replied. "Where are you from?"

"Not far," he grinned. "Houston. I'll never leave Texas, but Houston was just a little too hectic for me."

"What did you do for a living?" Millie asked bluntly.

Pat didn't miss a beat. "I was an engineer for an oil and gas company."

Millie seemed to be sizing him up. Finally, she smiled and said, "Isn't that a coincidence? Trish is, too."

Trish looked at Millie as if she had lost her mind. "I'm not an engineer!"

"No, but you're divorced."

Trish's face felt as if it were on fire. She gave an apologetic smile to Pat and grabbed Millie by the arm. "It was very nice meeting you, Pat. We're going to get out of your hair now. Oh, and please don't call the cops if you hear gunshots and loud screaming."

"Welcome to the neighborhood!" Edna said over her shoulder as she hurried to catch up with her friends.

Pat's laughter followed them down the street.

Chapter Thirteen

Trish was too embarrassed to say anything about Millie's blatant attempt at matchmaking on the way home, but she did believe she had mastered the art of speed walking. As soon as they all settled in her kitchen, though, she turned to her now ex-friend. "Millie, I can't believe—"

"Hold that thought," Millie said and headed straight for the telephone.

Trish turned to Edna and shook her head in exasperation. "I really am going to kill her, you know."

Edna grinned. "I can't say I'd blame you, but why don't we have some coffee instead?"

While Edna pulled out the coffee cups, they could hear Millie mumbling, "I see, hmm . . . are you sure? Okay, I'll talk to you later, sweetheart."

Millie hung up the phone and sighed loudly. "Well, girls," she said, sinking into one of the chairs, "it looks like our pattern was wrong."

"Oh, no," Trish said as disappointment engulfed her. She had been so sure their theory had merit. Darn it!

Edna carried the cups to the table. "So a car wasn't stolen last night?"

"Oh, a car was stolen, all right," Millie said, adding creamer to her coffee. "Just not from the street we thought it would be on. Poor Michelle, she sounded pretty upset."

"She'd be even more upset if she knew we'd had a theory and it failed," Trish said dispiritedly.

"What's wrong with you two?" Edna asked. "We're not giving

up that easily. So we didn't succeed on the first try. Big whoop! We'll try again."

Trish looked at Edna. *Big whoop?* "Why are you so fired up? You weren't that crazy about us getting involved in the first place."

Edna straightened in her chair. "I just think we should keep trying to figure out how these stolen cars are being selected, that's all."

Millie peered at Edna through narrowed eyes. "Something's gotten into you. What is it?"

Edna took a deep breath and leaned back in her chair. "When we were standing in Susan's—I mean, Pat Bailey's—front yard, I remembered all we went through to help right an injustice. Well, this is no different, except that there are more victims. There are the car owners, and Michelle and Richard, and poor Mrs. Blakely." She paused and looked at them. "I just want to help."

"You're right, Edna. I knew there was a good reason I kept you around," Millie said with a wink. "Trish, where's that map of yours? We're going to try the same pattern once more, and if we're wrong again, we'll think of something else. But the one thing we won't do is quit!"

Trish half expected the theme song from *Rocky* to start up. Still, Edna's determination and Millie's enthusiasm were contagious. She got up and retrieved the map from the living room, and they spread it out on the kitchen table.

"Let's find the street the car was stolen from last night and use it as a starting point for our grid," Millie said.

Trish located the specified coordinates, and Millie searched for the street name. "Here it is," she said. "Tophill Drive. Hand me our grid pattern."

Edna handed her their homemade grid, and Trish leaned closer to see. The name of the street sounded vaguely familiar. Suddenly her breath caught in her throat. "Wait!" she said, her eyes opening wide. "Look at this, girls. Look where Tophill Drive is located!"

Millie and Edna both looked closer, their faces mere inches

from the map. Edna gasped, placing a hand over her mouth as she sat back down. "I don't believe it."

"What?" Millie asked. "What don't you believe?"

Trish waited a moment for Millie to see what she and Edna had discovered. She couldn't believe it, either. Their theory had worked, after all! But obviously, Millie was having trouble seeing what they had. "Millie, Tophill Drive is one street over from Northridge," Trish said impatiently.

"Oh," Millie said absently as she kept perusing the map. Suddenly her head snapped up. "Oh!"

Trish grinned. "Exactly! I think it's safe to say that being only one street away from our estimate constitutes success!"

Edna clasped her hands together, her eyes sparkling with excitement. "Should we call Michelle and tell her?"

"No," Millie said, after giving it some thought. "Let's tell Henry what we've found out, first."

Edna's cup dropped to the table. "What did you just say?" she asked, grabbing a napkin to wipe up the mess.

Astounded, Trish reached over and placed her hand on Millie's forehead. "She doesn't have a fever," she told Edna.

Millie swatted Trish's hand away. "Oh, stop it! This is going to be hard enough on Michelle. It's obvious now that Tony is guilty. I think it will be better if she hears it from Henry instead of us."

Trish groaned. "You're not still accusing Tony Matson, are you?"

Millie crossed her arms over her chest and leaned back in her chair. "Well, he did cancel a movie date with the kids last night, didn't he?"

Trish started to reply but then clamped her lips shut. Actually, that *was* a very interesting fact.

Henry wasn't in the best of moods when they faced him that afternoon. Millie, as her usual adorable little self, had barreled into his office once again and had proceeded to unroll the map over the papers he had been looking at. In the process, she had knocked his cup of coffee into his lap and scattered his pencil holder—which held pencils, pens, loose change, paper clips, and a letter opener—all over the floor.

Edna had quickly rushed to pick up the mess, apologizing profusely for Millie's behavior while steam billowed out of Henry's ears. Unfazed, Millie ignored his temper as she explained their grid pattern, their successful prediction of the area in which a car would be stolen from, and Tony's suspicious cancellation of his date with his kids.

"First of all," Henry said, his voice deceptively calm. "I don't have time to go over this with you. I have a meeting in ten minutes. You can leave me the information, and I'll call you if I have any questions. But you are not, and I repeat, not a part of this investigation. And if I hear you accusing anybody again without any evidence whatsoever, I'll inform that person about the slander laws and encourage them to pursue a lawsuit!"

"We're not leaving anything with you, Henry," Millie said stubbornly. "Not after you threatened us like that. We're trying to help you do your job, and this is the thanks we get?"

"You know what I'm going to do?" Henry snarled. "You're always accusing me of sitting here doing nothing while crime runs rampant in our little city. Well, I think I'll take some of that free time I have and open an investigation into each of your mental statuses. I'll rig the results if I have to, so I can claim you are a threat to society and lock you up for the rest of your lives."

Henry's voice had risen to a shout by the time he finished his tirade. Trish was sure every single person in the department, which thankfully wasn't many, had heard him.

Edna's mouth fell open as she looked up and stared at Henry. Trish just sat silently, afraid to move in case he pulled out his gun. Millie, however, just gave him a bored look. "Are you through throwing your little hissy fit?"

Henry's face turned even redder. "Out," he said, pointing toward the door. "Out!"

Millie glared at him as she began to fold up the map. "Okay, buster, this is the last time we offer you any assistance. You just made a huge mistake. When we give interviews after solving this crime for you, we're going to make a point of letting the whole world know that our chief of police, Henry Espinoza, would rather sit and work crossword puzzles than help the citizens of his community!"

Trish got up and headed for the door. Hopefully, she could make her escape before Henry called for handcuffs. Edna followed, her back stiff, obviously still upset about having her mental status questioned. It was hard for Trish to feel insulted, though, since she questioned it herself so often.

With one last ferocious look at Henry, Millie walked out and, just for good measure, she slammed the door. When she reached the young officer she had previously tangled with, who was with sitting at the front desk, she leaned close and whispered, "You might want to go check on the chief. We frightened him so bad he wet his pants."

Ignoring the startled look on his face, she rushed to catch up with Trish and Edna. "I think that went well, don't you?"

"I think Henry's right," Edna whispered when Trish opened the door. "We really have lost our minds."

"Why are you whispering?" Millie called from the kitchen. "I can't hear you."

Trish rolled her eyes. "That's why she's whispering, you old goose!"

Trish and Edna entered the kitchen, where Millie was busy stuffing a backpack with packages of cheese crackers, cookies, nuts, and bottled water. A tall thermos, presumably holding coffee, sat on the table next to the backpack. "Are you chickening out again, Edna?" Millie asked while she added several napkins, a flashlight, and her binoculars to the mix.

"I'm not chickening out," Edna replied, "but I think I need to have my head examined."

"Henry offered to do that for you free of charge and you got upset," Millie said with an impish grin. "What changed your mind?"

"Joe," Edna said and sighed as she sank down into a chair.

Millie looked up. "Uh-oh."

"I'm afraid he's not very happy right now."

"Oh, honey," Trish said, placing a cup of coffee in front of Edna. "Is this causing problems for you?"

"Sort of," Edna admitted. "It's not too serious, but I hate to go against Joe's wishes. He's worried about us going out tonight. He's not thrilled we've moved beyond passive analyzing into active probing."

"What did you tell him?" Millie asked.

"The truth. He wanted us to wait until tomorrow when he could come with us, but I explained that according to our analysis, a car would be stolen tonight, not tomorrow," she said. "He understands why we feel we have to do this, and he's even proud that we may have cracked the pattern, but he's extremely unhappy we're going to attempt to actually witness the theft."

Millie sat down and patted Edna's hand. "I'm very proud of you for telling Joe the truth. What did he say about Henry treating us like dingbats?"

Edna swallowed. "I may have forgotten to mention that to him."

"That's not really important, anyway," Trish said quickly, before Millie could start teasing Edna. "Is Joe coming home tonight from his trip to Dallas?"

"No, he'll be home tomorrow. He has one more conference tonight, and then he'll leave from there in the morning. He made me promise to take my cell phone with me and call him immediately if anything happens. I hate to see him so worried."

"Well, we'll just make sure he realizes he's worrying needlessly. We aren't going to do anything stupid," she said with a sideways look at Millie.

"What? I didn't say anything."

"That was just a warning," Trish said sternly. "We can't do anything that will get Edna in trouble. Understood?"

Millie shrugged. "Of course," she said innocently as she pushed away from the table. "I think we're ready to go. Let's go catch some bad guys!"

Trish grabbed the backpack. "How much did you put in here, Millie?" she asked, struggling with the weight. "Do you think we're going to starve in the next couple of hours?"

"Don't complain," Millie said as she reached for the thermos. "I didn't see anyone else offering to bring snacks."

"I would have," Edna said.

"Oh, heaven forbid," Millie said wryly. "You brought *salad* to our last stakeout."

They were going to be watching two different houses tonight. Using their grid, they had pinpointed the likely target, but another one of Security Insurance's clients lived two blocks away. Knowing their grid pattern could be proportionally incorrect, they were careful this time to check nearby streets for other potential victims. Their plan was to go back and forth between the two houses, spending a half hour at each in the hope of witnessing a crime in progress.

A car thief would most likely want the cover of darkness, and since the victims' reports did indeed suggest that the thefts occurred between the time the owners went to bed at night and before they woke up in the morning, the ladies had arranged to start their surveillance at ten P.M.

Trish yawned, trying to follow the directions Millie called out to her. The darkness of the night was complete, making it difficult for them to locate the street they wanted. If they had been using their heads, they would have made a practice run to the address instead of trying to see signs blurred by halogen street lights and obscured by thick, heavy tree branches. The moon had even decided not to cooperate in their "quest for truth and justice," as Millie called their activity, by hiding its helpful rays behind a thick layer of cloud cover.

Traffic was light, but it still took about twenty minutes to get to Lynwood Street. Located in an older section of San Antonio, the homes on that street were unique both in design and structure, their stately presence well established. The friends located the two-story rock home with the red SUV in the driveway midway down the block.

Edna leaned forward from the backseat. "It's still there," she said quietly.

"So far," Millie muttered, sounding disappointed.

Trish cruised by the house, making note of areas in which

to park when they returned. Then she drove to the end of the block and turned left. The neighborhood was dark and quiet, with residents tucked into their homes for the night. Every once in a while they would see a porch light on, or muted light from inside a house behind heavy drapes, but there was no activity outside at all, nothing that could alert the inhabitants to a crime in process.

It was too late to question whether this had been a good idea. It had sounded good at the time, easy and safe, but Trish was beginning to have second thoughts. An eerie feeling was starting to take hold, and she glanced at her companions to see if they felt it too. Edna sat stiffly in the middle of the backseat, her eyes darting from side to side as if she were expecting someone to jump in the car. Yes, Edna was definitely feeling the tension.

Millie, however, not so much. An air of excitement emanated from her as she leaned forward with her hands on the dashboard, her eyes open wide as she peered through the inky darkness. Trish shut her mouth and kept her thoughts to herself. She was not in the mood for any teasing from Millie about being a scaredy cat. Besides, she wasn't *scared*; she was just . . . antsy.

Trish went two blocks up and turned onto Hickory Grove.

"Turn here," Millie blurted.

Trish looked at her. "I just did," she said drily. Okay, maybe Millie wasn't quite as unaffected as she appeared.

Millie consulted her notes and called out the address. "We're looking for a black Dodge pickup."

And there it was. Almost to the end of the block, it was parked at the curb in front of a house that appeared to be deserted. The grass was overgrown, and a newspaper lay in the middle of the empty driveway. Trish pulled over to the curb two houses away under a heavy canopy of branches. There weren't any lights on at the house with the truck, but that didn't necessarily mean anything; there wasn't any light showing from the houses on either side of it, either.

"If I were a car thief," Edna said quietly, "this is the one I'd steal. Nobody would ever know."

Trish nodded. "I agree. Should we watch this one first?"

"I guess it really doesn't matter," Millie said, "but I think we should stick to the plan. Any variation could cause us to make a mistake. What if they separate us, and we're questioned? One of us might be so nervous we'd accidently say we were at the wrong house first. Then *we'd* become suspects."

Edna shook her head. "Millie, that makes absolutely no sense whatsoever. And don't think I don't know whom you were referring to when you said one of us would become nervous."

Millie leaned back in the seat. "If the shoe fits—"

"I heard that!"

"It's a little early to be getting on each other's nerves, don't you think?" Trish admonished.

"I'm not getting on her nerves. Edna loves me."

"Oh, for goodness' sake," Edna muttered, but there was a smile in her voice.

Trish pulled away from the curb. "Okay, to make sure we don't mess up during our *interrogation*, let's follow the plan and go watch the other one first." Circling back to Lynwood Street, she parked several houses away from the SUV. She cracked open the windows and cut off the engine, immediately plunging them into total darkness.

"Now we wait," she said, hunkering down in the seat until she could just see over the steering wheel.

After a few minutes of complete silence, Edna's voice rang out a little uneasily. "I wish we had brought something to do while we waited."

"I can't think of anything we could do that wouldn't require light," Trish said with a yawn.

The night creatures must have accepted their presence, because the women were soon being serenaded by the lively sound of crickets and locusts in full swing. Then another sound joined the mix. A zipper was being pulled, followed by a loud rustling noise, drowning out the concert from outside the car.

"What's that?" Edna murmured.

"I'm hungry. I'm getting us something to eat." Millie's head must have been buried in the backpack, because her voice sounded as if it came from a long way away. "Here, Trish," she said, "I don't know what I'm giving you, though. I can't see a thing."

"How can you be hungry?" Trish asked. "We just stopped for hamburgers less than an hour ago."

"I always eat when I get bored."

"I don't know how you can be bored," Edna fretted. "I'm starting to think we should go on home and figure out another way to see who's stealing the cars."

Trish could sense Millie's irritation even though she couldn't see her. "You two sound like a couple of whiny babies," she hissed. " 'I don't know how you can be hungry' . . . 'I don't know how you can be bored.' Well, I don't know how you two can be so gutless!"

"That's not fair, Millie, and you know it," Trish said.

Millie sighed. "You're right. I'm sorry, girls. I'm just praying for all I'm worth that we can solve this tonight so Michelle can relax, and waiting for something to happen is driving me nuts. You have both been so supportive, and I really do appreciate it."

Trish wished they had some light so she could see if Edna's eyebrows were as far up her forehead as her own were. Coming from Millie, that apology was almost eloquent.

"That's okay, dear," Edna said gently. "We understand." And to prove it, she graciously accepted what Millie said might be a package of peanuts.

Trish rolled her eyes, but the gesture was lost in the dark. "Okay, give me some crackers," she said in resignation. After all, her motto had always been, *when in doubt, eat!*

Soon the sound of their munching joined the symphony outside. The hardest thing about this night surveillance, Trish thought with another yawn, was staying awake. Too many nights with too little sleep were catching up with her.

Rubbing her eyes, she sat up straight in her seat. "Let's go check on the truck now."

It was still there, parked in the same spot. If Edna had been nervous before, she must be jumping out of her skin now. This street seemed darker, quieter, more deserted, and the truck stood out like an invitation, a lone vehicle on the street in front of a gloomy, empty house.

"This truck is going to be stolen tonight," Millie said, excitement building in her voice. "I can feel it in my bones."

Trish felt the hairs stand up on the back of her neck. "I think you're right," she said in a low voice. Trish had never been a car thief, in this life or in the past, but wouldn't a criminal look for the easiest target with the least possibility of getting caught? And this target seemed perfect.

"I'll get the camera ready," Millie said in a rush as she bent down and rifled through the backpack.

"I wonder if the camera is going to be able to give us anything useful," Edna said. "There's so little light."

Trish had wondered the same thing. Their plan had seemed simple when they discussed it earlier this evening. Sit and wait for the thief, or thieves, snap a picture of the theft in process, and then hightail it to the San Antonio police substation a couple of miles away. Crime solved! And with very little danger to themselves. Yes, it had sounded so easy, but Trish should have known better. With their track record, if something *sounded* easy and simple, then surely there were going to be major roadblocks.

"I've got an idea," Millie said. "When the car is stolen, we'll follow it until there's a street that's better lit, or something that will give us enough light to take a picture of the car and the creep inside. That will be just as good as getting a picture of it being broken into."

Edna hesitated. "I don't know—"

"Do you have a better idea?" Millie snapped.

"I'm not sure it's a good idea, either, but I don't think we've got much choice," Trish said to Edna. "We can't waste this opportunity."

Edna leaned back in her seat and remained silent. She was not happy about this turn of events and probably wondering what Joe was going to say if, and when, he found out.

One problem at a time, Trish thought, turning her attention back to the truck. Along with the excitement building at actively getting involved in catching a criminal, there was also an air of trepidation. Trish didn't want to voice her thoughts out loud, but she couldn't erase the fact from her mind that a woman had been murdered, and even though it had yet been proven that her murder was tied to the car thefts, something had led even the police to suspect it did.

A few minutes later they heard the familiar rustling of paper. "What do you guys want to eat this time?"

Chapter Fourteen

Edna was yawning incessantly, and Trish's vision was starting to blur. Millie was the only one who seemed alert and focused.

It was well after midnight now. They had worked their way through all the snacks in Millie's backpack, drunk all the coffee in the thermos, and even dashed over to an all-night café so they could use the ladies' room. Joe had called about an hour ago, and Edna had assured him that they were fine and would be going home before too much longer.

"You know," Millie said, breaking the silence, "our new neighbor seems like a very nice young man."

Trish grinned. Midfifties isn't usually considered "young," but she agreed with Millie; Pat Bailey did seem very nice. She also knew where Millie was going with her comment.

"Don't even think about it," she said.

"What ever are you talking about?" Millie asked with mock innocence.

"I liked him," Edna added. "I think he's going to make a good neighbor, and Joe would love it if he plays golf."

Trish didn't respond. She knew if she showed the slightest interest in their new neighbor, Millie would arrange a date, or worse . . . a wedding.

"I think we need to go check on the SUV again," she said drily as she started up the car.

By now she was so used to driving around the street, parking in front of the gray-sided house, and turning off her lights that it took her a full minute to realize something was wrong. In total shock, she peered through the windshield.

Edna was in the middle of another yawn, and Millie had her head buried in the backpack checking to see if maybe she had missed a package of crackers, when Trish groaned loudly.

Edna clamped her mouth closed and Millie jumped, bumping her head on the dashboard. "Ouch!" she said, rubbing her head. "What's wrong?"

Trish just nodded toward the empty driveway before she remembered they couldn't see her movement in the darkness. "The SUV," she said angrily. "It's gone."

Edna let out a surprised gasp. "Oh, no!"

Millie snapped her head around. "I don't believe it!" she exclaimed. "The idiot stole the wrong car!"

Trish leaned her forehead on the steering wheel. "I doubt if *the idiot* is looking at it that way, Millie."

"Maybe it hasn't really been stolen," Edna said hopefully. "It could be the owner of the car had to run an errand or something. Let's don't think the worst until we know for sure."

"Dear Ms. Pollyanna," Millie said wryly, "we won't be able to find out if it was reported stolen until tomorrow. In the meantime, I'm going to *think the worst* and assume the car was stolen, because there isn't a single light on in the house. If the owner had to run an errand, I'm pretty sure he or she would have at least turned the porch light on."

"You're probably right," she said and sighed. "I just didn't want it to be true."

Trish started her car and pulled away. "I wish it wasn't true, either. We were so close! It couldn't have happened more than thirty minutes ago."

They lapsed into a disappointed silence, but they still kept a sharp eye out for the red SUV during the ride home. The odds of seeing it on the highway were slim, but it was difficult to accept failure when they had been within minutes of discovering who was behind the thefts.

"There is a bright side to this," Edna said when they turned onto their street.

Millie snorted. "Here we go again—"

"I'm serious! We now know, without a shadow of a doubt,

that we've discovered the pattern the thief is using to select which cars to steal."

Trish pulled in front of Edna's house and turned to look at her. "You're right," she said and smiled. "And how often are there going to be two addresses so close together that it's hard to decide which one will be hit?"

"You've both got a point," Millie conceded, "but there's something even more important we've uncovered."

Trish frowned. "What's that?"

"Whoever is stealing cars insured by Security Insurance is using the same list we are."

The three women looked at each other. The ramifications of that were huge. It could mean that the list of the insurance company's clients had been sold or distributed for any number of reasons, and it would be possible to find out who had re-quested such a list . . . or it could mean it was an inside job, just as the home office suspected.

"Look," Trish said quickly. "We're tired, and we need to get some rest. We'll go over all of this in the morning. Edna, we'll stay here until you're safe inside your house. Turn your porch light off and on as soon as you lock your door. And don't for-get to call Joe."

Edna nodded. "Good night, girls," she said. "I'll see you in the morning."

As soon as Edna signaled that she was inside with the door locked, Trish turned the car around and drove the short distance to Millie's house. "Well, this has been an eventful night, hasn't it?" she asked, trying to gauge Millie's mood.

"Boy, you can say that again. And as soon as we get confir-mation in the morning about the stolen SUV, we need to get all the information we can about the next target. We should prob-ably make a dry run to see what lighting is there and where would be a good place to park. And I definitely need to bring more food. You two sure eat a lot when you're nervous."

Trish grinned. Millie was fine. "Lock your doors and do the thing with the porch light. I'll see you in the morning."

"Yep," Millie said, scrambling out of the car. "By the way,

I'm going to be looking out my front window until you turn your porch light off and on too. And, you know, we may need to walk earlier than we have been. Our days are sure getting busy."

Trish's grin faded.

Millie flipped her porch light off and on, and Trish pulled into her own driveway. She was bone tired. She climbed out of the car and walked to the front door. If they did indeed get confirmation about the SUV being stolen, she was going to talk to Edna and Millie about turning all of their information over to the San Antonio police.

She knew Edna would be fine with that, but Millie wouldn't be happy. Realistically, though, what were three old women—well, two, she amended—really going to do if they confronted the car thieves? Take a picture and run to the nearest police station? No, after the events from this evening, it was obvious that wasn't going to be effective. It wouldn't provide enough evidence for a conviction, and it would only alert the thief, or thieves, that their strategy had been detected.

Trish closed her door and locked it. She had just used her porch light to let Millie know she was safely inside when she thought she heard a car engine start up. Puzzled, she went to her window and looked outside but she didn't see a thing. She couldn't hear anything now, either. Hmm . . . probably just her imagination acting up. Lord knows she had experienced enough drama for one night.

Larry Thompson was Trish's knight in shining armor. She had been racking her brain for a reason not to walk with Millie and Edna this morning, but Millie had easily shot down all her excuses. Resigned, she had just started for her bedroom to change her shoes when the doorbell rang.

"Good morning," Larry said with a warm smile.

Trish's welcome probably seemed a bit too enthusiastic, but he couldn't possibly know he had just saved her from a fate worse than death. "Come in," she said eagerly.

Larry stopped suddenly in the hallway and raised a questioning eyebrow. "Redecorating?"

Trish followed his gaze. The chalkboards. "No," she said, forcing a laugh. "That's just a project we're working on. Come on into the kitchen. Millie and Edna are here."

"Good morning, ladies," Larry said when Trish escorted him into the kitchen, a huge smile on her face, knowing the morning walk had been delayed . . . or better yet, cancelled.

Edna greeted him cheerfully and got up to pour him a cup of coffee, but Millie peered at him suspiciously. "What are you doing here?"

Larry grinned, not in the least insulted. "I decided to swing by on my way to the office. I saw the lights on and took a chance you would all be together."

"Hmm . . . well, what do you want?"

"Millie! Stop being rude," Edna said as she handed Larry a cup.

"Well, I want to know if he's here as a friend or a foe," Millie said.

"A friend," Larry said. "Definitely a friend."

Millie looked at him. "I'll be the judge of that. What's up?"

Larry chuckled and leaned forward, placing his elbows on knees. He looked very attractive this morning, wearing khaki slacks and a black button-down shirt. He really was a good friend, and Trish appreciated his kindness and patience. She just prayed Millie wouldn't ruin the friendship with her blunt, competitive nature where his profession was concerned.

So far, Larry had never allowed Millie's comments regarding his lack of ability to faze him. In fact, he seemed to enjoy the repartee between them, but there could always come a time when Millie crossed the line. Trish just hoped Edna's genuine sweetness would always override Millie's brusqueness.

"Henry told me you all came to see him the other day," he said, his eyes shining as he looked at them.

Millie stood abruptly and gave Larry a withering look. "Don't mention that man's name in my house!"

Trish raised her eyebrows. "Uh, Millie . . . it's *my* house."

Edna took a sip of her coffee and remained silent, probably remembering Henry's comments about their sanity. Edna wouldn't defend Millie's rudeness, but she wasn't going to jump to Henry's defense, either.

"He said that I should stop by to talk to you when I had the chance," Larry said. "He also mentioned something about having to run home to change his pants, but I never quite understood what that had to do with anything." Larry grinned, knowing exactly what had happened with the spilled coffee in the chief's lap.

Millie busied herself at the coffeepot. "His outfit didn't match," she said. "So what else did Henry say?"

"Not much. He said you may have discovered a pattern or something and that I should check it out."

"So Henry was listening, after all," Edna said, slightly perturbed.

"Oh, Edna." Millie chuckled, waving a hand dismissively. "Henry's got that whole macho thing going on. At least we know now that he respects our professional opinions. We might be able to work together, after all."

Larry coughed. "Yes, well, how about you show me what you've discovered?"

And they did. First they showed him the chalkboards and how they had been used to organize the information. Then Trish got the map and the grid while Edna cleared off the center of the kitchen table. Millie got the list that Michelle had printed for them and, practically talking over themselves, they quickly outlined their theory and everything they had done so far to prove it, including the events of last night.

Larry was obviously impressed, though he wasn't happy that they'd put themselves at risk. But before he could lecture them once again on the dangers of investigating on their own, Millie piped in.

"So, do you know if the SUV was reported stolen yet?"

Larry nodded ruefully. "I'm afraid so. At least I'm assuming it was the one you were watching. I heard something on the scanner this morning."

"Well, when are you going to question Tony Matson?"

Larry sighed and placed his elbows on the table. "Okay, Millie. Tell me about Tony Matson."

She didn't hesitate. "He's a first-class scumbag."

Larry nodded. "I gathered that much. But why do you think he could be responsible for the stolen cars?"

"Because he's jealous, vengeful, and arrogant. He'd do anything to smear Michelle's name and get custody of the kids. When he told Michelle he wanted a divorce, he said he would take care of the kids since she didn't have a job and it would be so hard for her." The more Millie talked, the redder her cheeks became. "Well, Michelle floored him when she fought for, and won, custody. Tony did everything he could to make it difficult for Michelle. He has paid child support regularly, but not one dime more. Her car broke down not long after the divorce, and even though that was her only transportation to get the kids where they needed to be, he refused to help. He did offer to take the kids and raise them, though. Pretty considerate of him, wasn't it?"

Larry sat back and crossed his arms over his chest. "But, Millie, his kids are teenagers. Why would he go to all the trouble of having Michelle implicated in a crime when he's only got a few years left to pay child support?"

"I think he's still angry that a judge chose Michelle over him, and that he can't intimidate Michelle. One thing I know about Tony Matson is that he hates to lose. According to Michelle, he almost lost his job once because another Realtor in the firm he works for sold a prestigious piece of property that Tony had scheduled to show later that same week. He was verbally insulting and went on and on about it for days, both at the office and at home. He only calmed down when he was chastised for his behavior, but that was only for appearances. Michelle said he never really forgot that he lost the sale and he placed the blame entirely on the other Realtor."

"Wow, that's a little over the top," Trish said.

"That's what I've been telling all of you!" Millie exclaimed. "*Tony* is over the top. He'll do anything to get his way. And the only thing preventing him from getting his kids is Michelle."

Larry fell silent while Millie watched him closely. Finally, he seemed to reach a decision.

"Okay, Millie, let me give this some thought. In the meantime, I want you to promise me you won't go accusing Tony Matson of anything, in public or private. Understood?"

Millie grinned. "Understood!"

"Good. Now, back to your grid. I have to tell you, I am very proud of all of you. This took quite a bit of work."

Trish and Edna smiled at each other. It was satisfying to have someone in authority acknowledge their work.

"Just remember that when it comes time to present the collars," Millie said.

Trish grimaced. "They don't actually give away *collars*, Millie."

"Oh. Well, just don't forget how much we're contributing to the investigation, Larry. We may need to use you as a reference for our future clients."

Larry nodded soberly. "You got it."

"So what happens now?" Edna asked.

"First of all, I'd like for you to go over your pattern with me one more time. I want to make sure I fully understand it. Then I'll go back to the station and discuss it with Henry."

"That's it?" Millie asked incredulously. "You'll *discuss* it?"

"Millie," Edna said patiently, "they have to talk it over before they can decide on a course of action."

Millie gave a deep sigh. She was about to give Larry free advice on the advantages of action versus discussion when Trish interrupted. "There is something you can do in the meantime."

Everyone stopped and looked at her. "What's that?" Larry asked.

"Be here at ten tonight."

Everyone still just looked at her. Finally, she said, "I'm serious!"

Millie was the first to understand. She started shaking her head. "I don't think that's such a good idea."

"It's a perfect idea! Think about it for a minute," Trish said. "If we catch the bad guys in the act, Larry can arrest them on the spot. Our plan to get a picture of the crime in progress might only warn the criminals that their operation has been discovered. They could go underground for years, or even move on to another city." Trish looked at Millie and added softly, "We don't know that Tony is involved in this. If he's not—which, personally, I don't believe he is—then Michelle and Richard will still be under suspicion and the opportunity to clear their names would be lost."

"Uh, what exactly are you planning?" Larry asked.

Trish glanced at him. If he wanted to join them in trying to catch the criminals red-handed, would he even be able to? He was surely working on his own investigation, trying to prove probable cause where Michelle and Richard were concerned, and if he hadn't made the connection yet, it wouldn't be long before he came to the same conclusion that she and the girls had—the criminals were using the same client information from Security Insurance. It didn't look good.

"I think it's a wonderful idea," Edna said. "And Joe won't worry at all if Larry is with us."

Trish nodded. "Good point."

Larry tried again. "If you're talking about what I think you're talking about—"

"According to the pattern we've found, the thefts have been happening on specific days of the week," Trish told him. "We believe they are going to attempt to steal another car tonight."

Understanding crossed Larry's face. "You've already chosen a likely victim, and you want me to go with you tonight to see if they can be caught before they are successful."

"Exactly!"

Larry looked at Trish. "I've got a better idea. You give me the information, and I'll do the snooping around."

Millie barked out a laugh. "Not on your life! If we decide to bring you in on this, it's only to provide the muscle. I want to be there when the scumbag is caught. We've worked too hard on this to just hand it over."

Trish looked at Edna, who seemed torn between playing Keystone Cops or turning their information over to Larry. Finally, Edna bit her lip and sighed. "I agree with Millie."

"We want to be there, Larry," Trish said. "We're not trying to be difficult, and I know you can get the information anyway when you start analyzing the pattern, but finding out who is behind this is really important to us." They hadn't just picked up the newspaper or watched the news one evening and decided to go on a crime-busting spree. This involved Millie's daughter, and it seemed more and more like Security Insurance was being set up. The question was, was the insurance company itself the target, or could it be Richard? Or even Michelle?

And, if it was, could their lives be in danger?

"I understand," Larry said gently. "I really do. But I can't risk your safety by agreeing to join in an unofficial stakeout. I'll follow up on the lead, and I promise I'll let you know if anything happens. Please listen to what I'm saying," he implored. "This is not a cops-and-robbers show on TV. This is real life, and it's dangerous. I appreciate all you've done, and I understand your passion for wanting to see it through to the end, but you're not trained for the myriad things that could go wrong on a stakeout. I am."

"What could go wrong?" Millie asked in a mocking tone. "You get the wrong doughnuts?"

"Millie, that remark was uncalled for," Edna admonished. "Larry's only trying to help."

Millie sighed. "Okay, Larry, we'll discuss it. That's all we can promise you right now."

Chapter Fifteen

There was still quite a bit of time left before darkness fell. Trish followed Millie's directions and pulled up in front of the red-and-white brick house. "It seems Tony does pretty well for himself," she said, admiring the clean lines of the two-story structure in the quiet, refined cul-de-sac. A portable basketball hoop sat on one side of the two-car driveway, ready to be pulled out at a moment's notice. Expertly trimmed bushes in varying shapes and colors graced the front of the house, and the lawn was a rich, lush green. A brand new Lexus sedan sat on the other side of the driveway.

"It sure doesn't look like he needs to steal cars," Edna muttered.

"He doesn't do it for money," Millie hissed. "He does it to try and destroy Michelle. But the game's over. This could very well be his last day as a free man if we catch him tonight, and I can't wait to see his face when he realizes he's been outsmarted. Now, remember, just follow my lead."

Trish and Edna sighed simultaneously as they climbed out of the car. The minute Larry had left this morning, Millie had adamantly insisted that it was critical to get as much "dirt" on Tony as they possibly could so the case would be airtight.

"You haven't even told us what you're going to say," Edna whispered as she followed Millie to the front door. "We should have rehearsed something."

"Not necessary," Millie replied over her shoulder. "Tony's no match for my quick brain. He'll never suspect a thing."

Trish bit her bottom lip. *Famous last words.*

Millie rang the doorbell while Trish and Edna stood behind her, smiles already in place. The door opened and Trish looked up . . . and up. Tony Matson was at least six foot four, with wavy black hair and piercing blue eyes. He was one of the most attractive men Trish had ever set eyes on.

His welcome smile faded when he saw who was standing on his front porch. "Hello, Millie," he said woodenly. "What can I do for you?"

"Hello, Tony," Millie said, her voice warm and friendly. Trish couldn't imagine what it cost her friend to be nice to this man whom she so thoroughly despised.

"You remember Edna, don't you?" she asked, turning slightly toward her friends. "And this is Trish Anderson, another one of my neighbors."

Edna, of course, had met Tony before, but, as she described it, she never really felt like she knew the man. Everything always seemed like *surface* stuff with him.

Trish looked at Tony Matson. As attractive as he was, she knew enough about appearances not to be fooled. Her own husband had been extremely attractive, and he had turned out to be a real slug. Not unlike Tony. According to Millie, Tony had engaged in an affair—actually a couple of them—during his marriage to Michelle, shattering her dreams and breaking her heart. For that, Millie would never forgive him, and she had never bothered to hide that fact.

Tony gave Trish and Edna a nod, but he clearly wasn't interested in starting up a conversation. He turned back to Millie and repeated, "What can I do for you?"

Millie looked surprised. "Am I too early?" she asked, making a big show of looking at her watch.

"For what?"

"Why, to pick up the kids, of course."

Tony frowned and cocked his head. "Carol and Randy aren't here."

Millie's eyes grew round. "Then where are they?"

"I assume they are in school. Why would you think they were here?"

"Well, isn't that strange?" Millie asked, pretending to search her memory. "I'm sure Michelle asked me to pick up the kids from your house today."

Tony crossed his arms over his chest. "I doubt that. I find it hard to believe Michelle wouldn't know where the kids are."

"Yes, it is hard to believe, isn't it?" Millie said, leaning a little closer to him and looking at him intently. "I wonder if she's got a lot on her mind or something."

Tony shrugged. "I wouldn't know, Millie. Michelle and I don't talk about anything but our children."

Trish watched the exchange with interest. Trish and Edna knew that Millie was hoping against hope that Tony was guilty of stealing the cars and, even better, of Mrs. Blakely's murder. That would make the whole charade worth it.

Trish wasn't convinced that Tony was the culprit, though. Of course, he appeared to be a little wary, probably wondering why Millie was being civil to him, but he didn't look like he was hiding the fact that he moonlighted as a car thief or that he was Jack the Ripper reincarnated. He seemed open, if slightly arrogant, but not *guilty*.

"Well, maybe I misunderstood her. This old mind of mine isn't what it used to be." Millie chuckled. "You don't mind if I borrow your phone to call her, do you?" she asked, pushing past Tony as she entered his house.

Trish kept her smile in place, but inside she was laughing at Millie's gutsiness, and at the startled expression on Tony's face.

"Nice place you got here," Millie called out from an unknown location.

Tony let out a deep breath, but at least he hadn't forgotten his manners. "Come on in," he said to Trish and Edna, holding the door open wider. Trish heard the impatient tone in his voice, but she ignored it. Impatience was one thing she could understand regarding Millie, and she wasn't about to hold that against him.

"Thank you, Tony," Edna said in a respectful manner. "I'm sure Millie will straighten this out in no time."

Tony's house was clean and clutter free. It was a standard

floor plan with a dining room, kitchen, and den on the first floor and probably two bedrooms upstairs. Tastefully decorated in earth tones, it was still patently clear this was a single man's home. No trinkets, no knickknacks, no cutesy details.

Millie was standing at the corner of the kitchen counter where the phone was located. She picked it up with a smile over her shoulder. "I'll find out what's going on."

Tony sighed. "Please just try to be quick. I was getting ready to leave for an appointment."

Millie turned her back on him and started dialing. "Of course."

Edna and Trish stood awkwardly in the den while Tony busied himself gathering his wallet, keys, and cell phone off the dining room table. They hadn't been invited to sit down but under the circumstances that was to be expected.

Millie was talking into the phone, laughing heartily at something "Michelle" said. Then Trish thought she heard a slow ripping sound.

Puzzled, she looked around the room. The sound was coming from the kitchen area. Suddenly, her breath caught in her throat. It looked, from the way Millie was balancing the phone between her neck and shoulder, that she was tearing a page off of the notepad beside the phone, babbling the whole time about her mistake.

Uh-oh. Trish did the only thing she could think of. Stealthily opening the clasp on her purse, she dropped it on the tile floor—hard.

Items scattered everywhere as she opened her eyes wide and placed her hand over her mouth. "Oops."

"Oh, dear," Edna said. "Let me help you. I've told you before you're going to have to get rid of that old purse. The handles are much too fragile." As Edna bent down to grab a lipstick that was rolling toward the sofa, she smiled and gave Trish a wink. She had noticed Millie's actions also.

"This happens all the time," Trish explained apologetically to Tony as she and Edna started cramming everything back into her purse. "Edna's right. I really do need a new purse."

Tony didn't reply, but his stance clearly told them he could not care less whether Trish got a new purse. Clearly, he had run out of patience.

Thankfully, at that moment, Millie replaced the phone and turned to Tony. "Well, I feel foolish," she said with an embarrassed laugh. "Michelle asked me to stop and get *pepperoni* pizza for the kids, not to get the kids from Tony. Get it? *Tony . . . pepperoni?*"

The ladies started walking toward the door, thanking Tony for the use of his phone and apologizing for the confusion.

When they reached the door, Millie turned as if a sudden thought had just crossed her mind. "By the way, Tony, I thought I saw you at The Outback last night. I waved, but I guess you didn't see me." The chain was a popular restaurant in the area. It wouldn't be unusual for either Millie or Tony to dine there occasionally, so Millie's statement was pretty innocuous, but Trish was impressed. Millie was trying to find out what had made Tony cancel his movie date with his children last night.

Tony opened the door and stood to the side. "You were mistaken. I was at a business meeting. And, if you don't mind, I really need to get going. I have a full day of meetings today also."

"Oh, well." Millie shrugged. "They say everybody has a twin. I must have seen yours."

Tony walked outside with them and locked his front door. "I suppose so. Good-bye, ladies," he said curtly, heading toward his car without a backward glance.

"Good-bye, creep," Millie muttered under her breath as she followed Trish and Edna.

Edna giggled and jabbed Trish lightly in the ribs. "There she is," she whispered. "For a minute there, I thought an alien had possessed our dear old friend."

They climbed into the car and Millie shuddered. "Let's get out of here. I think I'm going to be sick."

"*Pepperoni?*" Trish laughed.

"It was all I could think of. Pretty clever, wasn't it?"

Edna grinned. "I don't know if I'd call it clever. Let's just hope Tony doesn't ask Michelle about it."

"It won't matter," Millie said confidently. "Nobody listens to a jailbird."

"I really didn't get the feeling Tony was involved in anything illegal," Trish said doubtfully. "He didn't look like he was trying to hide anything."

"Look at this," Millie said, pulling a crumpled piece of paper from her pocket. "You'll feel differently when you see what I found."

"I can't read while I'm driving. What does it say?"

Millie cleared her throat. "2010 blue Acura."

Trish waited, but Millie didn't say anything else. "That's it?" she asked.

"What else do you want?" Millie snapped. "A written confession? Besides, I saw right through that flimsy excuse he had about being at a business meeting last night. What he was doing last night was stealing an SUV!"

"Well—"

"That note *is* a little strange," Edna said. "I don't know that I'd consider it proof positive, but it sure is interesting. I can't think of a reason to jot down such vague information about a car."

"There could be any number of reasons," Trish argued. "But let's say you're right, Millie. Let's say that the note you have is good evidence that could convict Tony of a premeditated crime. Well, that note would be thrown out of any court, because you didn't come across it legally."

"Oh, dear," Edna said. "She's right, Millie. Remember when you stole Susan's earrings from Tom Jones' trailer? Joe had to put them back before anyone found out. And, believe me, Joe will *not* do that for us again. Besides, you ripped the page off the notepad. We couldn't replace it if we wanted to."

Millie rolled her eyes. "Stop being such a worrywart," she said calmly. "I'll say I found the piece of paper in Tony's trash outside. I saw a show one time where the detective went through somebody's trash trying to get evidence, so that must be legal."

"I am not going to lie," Edna stated emphatically.

Millie looked at her. "Then you'd better stay out of the courtroom."

The ladies didn't want to lie to Larry. They also didn't want him to know they had decided to go on the stakeout, after all. So they did what they thought best; they didn't say anything at all to him, including details about their visit to Tony's earlier this afternoon. Besides, they hadn't found any mention on the list of the insurance company's clients regarding a 2010 blue Acura, so why risk upsetting him?

Edna came in carrying a box of assorted doughnuts to add to Millie's already full backpack. "In honor of Larry," she said, tongue in cheek.

Trish laughed. "And here I thought that was just a stereotype."

Millie finished loading the backpack, and they all piled into Trish's car. The address they were heading for was located in north central San Antonio, close to Six Flags Fiesta Texas.

"I'm almost going to regret it when the car thefts stop," Millie said. "I'm getting to learn the city better than I ever did."

"That's something we should start doing," Edna said. "We could take a drive on Saturday afternoons. Just get in the car and head out and see where we end up. Wouldn't that be fun?"

"Almost as much as cleaning the toilet," Millie said sarcastically.

The park was closed this time of night, and traffic was light. Consequently, they found the street without any problems, and sitting in the driveway, almost at the end of the street, was a dark green Dodge Intrepid.

"Bingo!" Millie said, her nose pressed to the side window.

They couldn't have asked for better stakeout weather. The night was clear and comfortable, a slight breeze allowing them to keep the windows cracked. The full moon, magnificent in the black, starlit sky, cast its rays of soft, muted light over the earth, enabling them to see distinct shapes in the shadowy landscape.

So focused were they on the car in the driveway three houses away that they never noticed the dark-blue sedan that pulled to the curb several houses behind them.

"Stay alert, ladies," Millie whispered. "This could go down pretty fast."

But it didn't.

Not only did it not *go down fast;* it didn't go down at all. In three hours, they had devoured all the food, finished the coffee in the thermos, and whispered among themselves, playing mindless word games in an effort to stay awake. But nothing happened.

Trish struggled to keep her eyes open. Too many nights with too little sleep were starting to wear on her. Still, as she started the car, her heart went out to Millie. Millie had been so sure the thief would be caught tonight. Her disappointment was palpable, and Trish wished she could think of something to say to make her friend feel better. She pulled away from the curb and drove past the Dodge with a frustrated sigh.

"I wish this would have ended tonight, dear, but there are so many reasons that could explain why the thief didn't strike," she said gently. "Our grid pattern is not wrong. That much I'm sure about, and we're not going to stop chasing the degenerate until we catch him—or them, whichever the case may be. And another thing I'm sure of is that we are going to be successful."

Millie turned her head and gave Edna a small smile. "Thanks, kiddo."

Edna reached up and squeezed Millie's shoulder. "I meant what I said, so don't get discouraged. We'll get them next time."

Trish groaned. "If we keep up these stakeouts, I'm going to have to get a bigger car. I'm about to bust!"

"Nonsense," Edna said. "We'll just walk more and start exercising."

"I get enough exercise, thank you very much," Trish said firmly.

Millie turned to her. "I hate to break this to you, but the remote control does not qualify as an exercise machine."

Trish was happy that some of Millie's spunk had returned. It would be cruel to bonk an old, depressed lady on the head.

Trish planned to drop Edna and Millie at their homes and make sure they were safely inside as she had the last time they were out so late, but Millie surprised her by asking if she'd mind if they came in for just a moment to unwind.

Trish resigned herself to the fact that she wasn't going to get much sleep again tonight as she unlocked her door and they all traipsed inside. "I'm not making coffee," she said with a yawn. "There's orange juice and water. Take your pick."

"Nothing for me," Millie said. "I want to make a phone call."

That stopped Trish in her tracks. Make a phone call at this time of night? What had happened to the despondent, tired woman who had basically replied to all conversation in mono-syllables during the ride home?

Edna sat down at the table and stared at Millie. "Who in the world do you want to call? It's two o'clock in the morning!"

"I know," she said absently, pulling things from her purse until she found her small telephone book. "I'm calling Tony. I want to know if he's home."

"And you couldn't call from your own house because—?" Trish asked.

Millie started punching in numbers. "Because if he has that caller ID thingie, he'll know it's me. You have an unlisted number." She listened quietly for a few moments, and then she jumped and quickly hung up the phone. "Darn it, he's home," she muttered.

"Which is exactly where I'm going," Edna said, covering a yawn with her hand. "Home."

"Come on, girls," Trish said tiredly. "I'll walk you both home."

"I was so sure Tony was going to steal that car tonight," Millie said as they headed out the door.

"Well, you never know," Edna said. "It could still happen."

Trish pulled her sweater tight and shook her head. By the tone of their conversation, they could be talking about a grocery list instead of a felony. She had heard about investigators who became so jaded because of all the evil they dealt with that they weren't shocked by anything. She hoped that wasn't happening to them.

Then she started giggling as she realized the direction her thoughts were taking. She sounded just like Millie, spouting off like they were real detectives. Shaking her head, she took a deep breath and stifled her laughter. She desperately needed some sleep.

Chapter Sixteen

Trish padded bleary-eyed down the hallway. She really was going to have to move. Once the doorbell waking you up at the crack of dawn every morning became the norm, it was definitely time to move. She opened the door without raising her eyes, turned on her heels, and headed for the kitchen. "I'll start the coffee," she mumbled.

"That can wait," Millie quickly called after her. "You have to come see this."

Trish took a deep breath and forced herself to turn around. "What?"

Millie was standing on the front porch looking back at her house. When Trish reached the door, Millie pointed across the street. "Look at my car," she exclaimed angrily.

Trish walked out on the porch, blinking several times in an effort to clear her vision, and looked over at Millie's car in her driveway. At first, she didn't notice anything amiss, but then her brain registered what she was seeing. The back window of the Buick was shattered, glass scattered over the trunk of the car and the driveway.

"Oh, Millie!" she said and gasped. "What happened?"

"Someone threw a brick through my car window!" she stated furiously. "Come on, I'll show you."

A little self-consciously, Trish hurried across the street after Millie. While her friend, for once, was fully dressed, in comfortable jeans and a No Fear sweatshirt, with her hair neatly styled, Trish was wearing her robe and slippers, and she knew her hair was sticking straight out. The odds were, though, that none of her neighbors would be out this time of morning, the sun just barely starting to peek over the horizon.

There was a good reason why Trish was not a gambler—the odds were always against her. She was halfway across the street when John Greenburg, Millie's next-door neighbor, opened his door and walked outside. He appeared startled to see her running across the street, but being the gentleman that he was, he simply raised a hand in greeting and bent to pick up his newspaper.

Mr. Greenburg was a tall, slender, distinguished gentleman with a full head of thick, almost white hair. Even though he had to be in his eighties, he handled the upkeep of his yard himself and did an excellent job. The idea that he was once a Peeping Tom, as Millie had claimed, was too ridiculous to consider, and Trish refused to let that accusation color her opinion of him. Trish often wondered if the reason Millie always gave him such a hard time was because she had a crush on him. That would just be so cute, but Millie would fly off the handle if Trish ever voiced that opinion out loud.

"Good morning, Mr. Greenburg," she called out. "Millie's car was vandalized sometime early this morning. You didn't happen to hear anything, did you?"

Frowning, Mr. Greenburg walked farther out in his yard to view the old Buick. "I sure didn't," he said, shaking his head. "That's a downright shame."

Millie planted her hands on her hips and narrowed her eyes. "You didn't do this, did you, John?"

Mr. Greenburg waved a dismissive hand at her and turned to go back inside, but Trish had seen the slight smile on his face.

"You're incorrigible," Trish muttered when she reached Millie's side.

"I know."

Trish was right. *It was cute.*

But there wasn't anything cute about the damage to Millie's car. A large hole provided instant air conditioning from the back window. Shards of glass were everywhere, making Trish wish she had on more than her flimsy slippers. Carefully, she balanced on her toes and maneuvered as close to the rear of the car as she could. Inside on the floorboard of the backseat rested a red, clay-colored brick. Anger enveloped her as she glared at the brick, as if the inanimate object had caused this senseless damage all by itself.

"I bet it was Tony," Millie said resentfully. "He must have known it was me calling him last night. He knows I'm onto him, and this is his way of warning me to back off."

"You can't be serious."

"You bet I am. And he picked on the wrong old lady!"

Trish sighed. If it turned out that Tony had nothing to do with this or the car thefts, Millie was going to have to find a way to apologize to him, even though he couldn't know he was her prime suspect in a felony. Still, it was interesting that of all the cars on this street, Millie's was the one that was targeted. And it *did* happen after her phone call to Tony.

She pushed the ridiculous thought from her mind. "Have you called the police?"

"Not yet. I was so mad when I saw my car that I went straight to your house."

"Well, I appreciate that," Trish said drily, "but you better call them now. You need to file a report."

Millie hesitated. "I was sort of wondering if we could drive by Tony's house first."

Taken aback, Trish looked at her. "You're kidding, right? Why would you want to go to Tony's?" Then it dawned on her. "Oh, no," she said vehemently. "Retaliating for the mailbox was one thing, and we were very lucky we didn't get into trouble for that. You're not about to go throw a brick through Tony's car."

Abruptly, another thought jumped into her mind. There was no doubt that Barbara Ferguson had been responsible for the destruction of Millie's mailbox. And, even though Trish couldn't be absolutely certain the woman was still a menace, she couldn't shake the sudden suspicion that made her wonder if Barbara could be responsible for this childish act as well.

She looked at Millie's car again, and she almost grinned as reality began to sink in. This was an act of adolescent cruelty, nothing more. She was overtired, letting her imagination run away with her and jumping to conclusions based on Millie's unfounded accusations.

"Go call the police," she said sternly, effectively wiping away the look on Millie's face that told her that she had been hoping Trish would change her mind.

Millie pouted. "That won't be necessary."

"You have to report this, Millie. This is serious."

"I meant it wasn't necessary to *call* the police. Larry just pulled up."

Trish whirled around and then groaned. *Will the embarrassment never end? What is Larry doing here so early?* Hastily, she combed her fingers through her hair and pulled her robe tighter.

Larry climbed out of his car, a puzzled look on his face. Trish noticed he looked tired, the dark shadow of a beard apparent on his face, and his hair also was slightly tousled.

"Okay, buster," Millie said, narrowing her eyes. "Where's the bug?"

"The . . . *what?*" Larry stopped and looked at Millie as if she had lost her mind.

"There's no way you could know I needed you unless you have a bug planted somewhere or unless you have telepathic powers. And since I don't believe in all that mental stuff, you had to have installed some kind of listening device, probably hoping I'd say something to give you evidence against my daughter!" Millie was furious, her face turning red as she stretched to her full height—not a very intimidating stance. "I know it's here somewhere, and when I find it, I'm going to sue the police department for invasion of privacy."

Larry coughed and looked down at the ground for a moment. When he raised his head there was an unmistakable light shining from his eyes. "This is strictly a coincidence. I had no idea you needed me, but I'm glad I'm here. What's wrong?"

Millie's anger dissolved immediately, but she didn't bother apologizing. "Oh, well, it's a good thing you're here," she said, stepping aside. "Look at this!"

Larry's eyebrows rose and he let out a low whistle as he

moved closer. Carefully, he inspected the car, walking around
to the other side and peering through the hole. He noticed the
brick, and his lips pulled into a tight line. "When did this
happen?"

"I don't know exactly, but it had to have been between two
and six this morning. I was just getting ready to call the police
when you drove up."

"So it wasn't like this when you got home from the stakeout?"

"No, I would have noticed . . ." Millie's voice trailed off.

Larry cocked his head. "Well?"

Trish groaned. "How did you know?"

"Because I followed you last night."

"You *what*?" Millie demanded. "Isn't that an invasion of privacy or something?"

"No, it's not," Larry said sternly. "I followed you to make
sure you three didn't get into any trouble or run into a dangerous situation. I knew when you didn't call me back yesterday
that you were going to follow up on your lead, so I decided to
tag along as an inconspicuous bodyguard."

"Uh . . . thank you, Larry," Trish said meekly.

Millie stuck her nose in the air. "Hmph."

Larry let out a deep breath. "We're not through talking about
this. I'm going to find a way to convince you ladies that you
need to stay out of police business. But for now, let's get back
to your car. Do you have any idea who would do something
like this?"

"You bet I—"

"No," Trish said quickly. "It's probably just one of those
random things."

"But—"

"You know, kids driving around bored, something like that."
Trish came up beside Millie and placed a comforting, strong-
as-steel comforting, hand on her friend's shoulder.

"I see. Well, I'll take care of filing the report on this for you.
I'm going home to take a shower and then I'll be at the station . . .
in case you think of anything you want to tell me."

Trish and Millie stood side by side like two wooden statues
with plastic smiles until Larry left. As soon as he turned the

corner, Millie stepped back and looked at Trish. "Why didn't you want me to tell him Tony did this?"

"Because you're just guessing," Trish said, her voice grim. "He's never going to take you seriously if you don't stop accusing people you don't like. Now, go get your broom, and we'll pick this glass up before someone gets hurt."

Turning on her heel, Millie stomped to the house, muttering something about Trish eating her words once Tony was arrested.

Trish shook her head and bent to carefully pick up some of the larger shards of glass, setting them aside in a pile. She knew this wasn't a random act, as she had told Larry, but she didn't have a real feel for the person who could have done such a thing, either.

These strange incidents were beginning to pile up, and the one common thread between all of them was Millie. But that didn't make any sense. These attacks couldn't be retaliatory for Millie's involvement in looking for the car thieves, because that wasn't common knowledge. And, if it were, she and Edna would be targets, also. And then there was Barbara Ferguson. Surely Barbara couldn't be that insecure, that childish, to go after an eighty-two-year-old woman because she was friends with her ex-boyfriend. That was just plain crazy.

But a real fear was growing that Millie could be in danger. *But from whom?*

At that moment, Millie came out carrying a broom, a dustpan, and a cardboard box. She had a worried look on her face.

Trish felt a sense of foreboding. *Now what?*

"Michelle called," she said solemnly, handing the broom to Trish and dropping the box on the driveway. "The home office has scheduled an internal audit next week. Richard and Michelle will be on paid leave while it's going on."

"Oh, honey," Trish said softly. "I'm so sorry."

Millie only nodded, her lower lip trembling and her eyes downcast as she made circles in the grass with the toe of her tennis shoe.

Trish laid the broom down and reached for Millie's hands. "It's going to be okay," she said. "Michelle and Richard haven't done anything wrong, and the evidence is going to show that. I'm confident they'll be cleared of any suspicion."

Anger, strong and intense, swelled up in Trish so suddenly it almost took her breath away. To see Millie so heartbroken, so dejected, was almost more than Trish could bear. She honestly did believe that a thorough investigation would clear Michelle and Richard, but, realistically, there was always a chance that they could be swept along in the wave of criminal activity connected to the insurance office and have evidence tilted against them. Many court cases documented the fact that innocent people had been convicted of crimes they had never committed.

Well, that wasn't going to happen. Not if she had anything to say about it. The thief had played his game too long, and he had made a critical mistake—he had made Millie cry.

"We're going on another stakeout tonight, and if the thief doesn't strike, we'll do it again the next night and the next," Trish said with steely determination. "We're going to catch the worm before that audit starts. Pack a ton of food, Millie. We may be out all night tonight. I'll call Edna, and we'll meet at eight o'clock at my house."

Trish turned and headed home. She felt so powerful that she wanted to shout, "I am woman! Hear me roar!" as she crossed the street, but she knew the sentiment would fall short, given her current state of dress. Still, it felt good to be unafraid—to be in control and on a mission.

"Uh . . . Trish?" Millie called out.

Trish stopped and spun around. "Yes?"

"Thank you," Millie said sincerely, and then, with a wink, she added, "but aren't you forgetting something?"

"What?"

Millie held up the broom with a grin.

"Oh, yeah, I forgot."

Trish looked at her watch. It was already starting to get dark, and unfortunately, she was standing in line at the grocery store after picking up the items on Millie's list. Millie wanted certain snacks for their surveillance—things she didn't have in her kitchen, naturally—and since she couldn't drive her own car in its present condition, she had asked Trish to make a quick run to the store. *Quick* had turned into an hour, but Trish wasn't going to complain. Her mouth watered just looking at the junk food Millie had requested.

She carried the sack of goodies to her car and placed it in the front passenger seat. Turning, she looked at her watch again. Darn, she had really wanted to be on the way to the stakeout by now.

"I see you've been grocery shopping too."

Trish's head snapped up. Barbara Ferguson was in her car, idling in the lane right behind Trish's car. She was leaning slightly out her car window, one arm perched casually on the steering wheel. Although her words were polite and she wore a smile, the coldness in her eyes sent chills down Trish's back. "Pardon me?"

"You may not remember me," Barbara said. "I met you the other day when you were with Richard and Michelle."

Wary, Trish forced a smile. "Yes, of course. How are you?"

Barbara was only a few feet away from Trish. There was no way Trish could just wave good-bye and casually sidle around to the driver's side of her car. Besides, unless Barbara moved her car, Trish wouldn't be able to leave. What was she doing here, anyway? Not that long ago Trish had used the excuse to Michelle that she had run into Barbara at the grocery store . . . *ah, that's it. Richard must be here.*

Trish took a step forward. "Well, it was good to see you again."

But Barbara didn't take the hint. She made a show of looking out the side window and then in the rearview mirror. She then turned slowly to Trish. The striking blue eyes that had been so cold a moment ago now appeared vacant, as if she wasn't aware of her own question and couldn't care less about the answer.

Inconspicuously, Trish glanced around. An elderly couple was pushing a grocery cart on the far side of the parking lot, and a woman with an infant struggled to load sacks into her trunk three lanes over. Where were all the people who had been in the crowded store just a moment ago? Not that Trish anticipated an all out-brawl with Barbara, but it would have been comforting to have more people around. This woman was nuts, and Trish felt the need to get away from her as quickly as possible.

"Well?" Barbara asked again. "Is the old lady in the store, or is she at home sticking her nose where it doesn't belong again?" She gave a mirthless laugh at her own comment.

A slow anger started burning in Trish's gut. *She* was the only one who could call Millie an old lady, and crazy or not, it was time for Barbara to back off. If Trish had any doubts before, she was now positive that Barbara was behind the unfortunate incidents plaguing Millie.

Trish moved closer until she was next to Barbara's car. "What's your problem, Barbara?" she asked quietly. Barbara's eyes rounded, and Trish noticed spittle at the corner of Barbara's mouth. Trish almost gagged, but now was not the time to give up the upper hand. She had surprised Barbara, and she needed to press her advantage. "You're running around acting like a child. Crashing into Millie's mailbox, sneaking around her house and throwing bricks through her car window. You think you're being sneaky, but everyone knows you're the one behind these episodes. Do you realize Millie has a shotgun?"

The initial fear that Barbara had shown was fading as a calculating smile crossed her face. Trish stood her ground, but what she really wanted to do was run as far away as she could from this woman. Suddenly, Barbara's countenance changed once again. Her eyes softened, and she gave Trish a wide smile. "You're right, I have been acting like a child. Tell your friend I'm sorry, won't you?" And with a wave, Barbara pulled away.

Trish's mouth dropped open as she stared after Barbara. If Trish hadn't witnessed it, she wouldn't have believed it. She couldn't think of a better example of a split-personality disorder. Barbara was either a great actress, or the woman had some very serious issues.

Trish got in her car, locked the doors, and just sat there for several minutes as she took deep, slow breaths. If she got home and Millie and Edna saw her shaking like a leaf, she would have to tell them what had just transpired. And she had no intention of telling Millie just yet. Millie was worried sick about Michelle, and Trish didn't want to announce any more problems. First things first. Figure out this darn car-theft thing and then tackle the problem with Barbara.

"What did Joe say?" Trish asked as she filled the thermos with coffee.

"I, uh, sort of stretched the truth a little bit."

"Tell me it ain't so!" Millie gasped in exaggeration.

Edna frowned. "Oh, hush, Millie. I feel bad enough as it is. Joe caught a really bad cold while he was in Dallas, and he feels miserable. He'll go if we need him, of course, but I hate to ask him."

Trish paused. She had really hoped Joe would go with them tonight. She was feeling jittery and out of sorts after her encounter with Barbara. Of course, Edna and Millie didn't know anything about that. "What did you tell him?"

"I just told him that we hadn't been very successful with our estimated targets so far and we wanted to do some testing before we scratched it and started over. I said we'd be driving back and forth between three different vehicles we wanted to check out tonight and if by chance we saw anything suspicious, we would be calling Larry."

Millie snorted. "Edna, if you're going to lie, at least make it worth your while."

Trish considered the situation. She wanted no part in deceiving Joe Radcliff. He was so good a friend, and he had offered so much help and support in their little ventures, that it wasn't worth alienating him. But Millie was right—Edna hadn't stretched the truth that much. She had downplayed the fact that they were absolutely certain their grid was accurate, but that didn't mean their targeted car would be stolen *tonight.*

Trish threw some napkins into Millie's backpack. "Okay, let's go."

The ladies strategically parked a few houses away from the black Camaro located on a street not far from downtown San

Antonio. As had become their custom, they cut all the lights and hunkered down with the first round of junk food.

Trish had barely swallowed her first bite when headlights appeared in her rearview mirror. "Incoming," she warned, and they all slid down lower in their seats. They weren't excited or nervous; this had happened several times during their stake-outs. It never even slowed their steady progress through the packaged sweet rolls.

It was the kind of night that made ghost stories so popular. The full moon would occasionally be obscured from view by swiftly moving clouds, causing first moonlight and then dark-ness to intermittently dominate. Occasional gusts of winds made tree branches sway in agitation with a whistling, airy sound as shadows danced haphazardly across the landscape.

Trish yawned, waiting for the car to pass before asking Millie to pour her some coffee. She waited . . . and she waited, and then she felt the hairs stand up on the back of her neck. Slowly, she raised her head. Her eyes opened wide and her sweet roll fell from her hand as she saw a brownish car right beside them moving very slowly with its lights off. If she'd wanted to, she could have reached out and touched it.

But she didn't want to. What she wanted to do was to get out of there. Swallowing loudly, she watched the car glide by in slow motion. "Millie, you brought your camera, didn't you?"

Chapter Seventeen

The three women watched in trembling fascination, hardly daring to breathe, as the car pulled over to the curb next to the driveway where the Camaro was parked. After a few moments, two shadowy figures emerged, each carrying something in their hands as they skulked up the driveway. The house was dark, not even a porch light on, making it even harder to see what was going on. But it didn't take bright lights to figure out that the two characters were up to no good.

Trish stared. This is what they had been hoping and praying for. It was complete validation of their grid pattern and confirmation that the thieves were intentionally targeting cars insured by Security Insurance. Once the bad guys were nabbed and questioned, the police would know how they had obtained the client information, and Michelle and Richard would be cleared of any involvement whatsoever.

The sweet taste of success was only minutes away and—*they were going to miss it!*

"Millie!" she whispered suddenly. "Get your camera!"

"Oh . . . oh!" Millie stammered, frantically scrambling to unzip the backpack. "Turn on the light," she said. "I can't see a thing."

"I can't turn on the light, you dingbat!"

A moment later Millie exclaimed triumphantly, "I got it! I just have to find the darn button that turns it on."

"We really better hurry, girls," Edna said, her voice shaking slightly. She was sitting in the middle of the back seat, bent over so that only the top of her head was visible over the headrest.

Trish let out a disbelieving groan. "Haven't you ever used that thing before?"

"I used it at Christmas when Michelle gave it to me. It was really easy then," Millie said. "There's a zoom thing too, if I can just . . . wait, here it is!"

There was a sudden flash of light. All three women gasped and dove for cover. There was a loud thud from the dashboard. "Ouch!" Millie cried.

"Serves you right," Trish hissed. "I can't believe you didn't check out your camera before bringing it tonight!"

"Well, I've got it figured out now. I'll get the picture this time."

"*If* you didn't scare them away."

Millie slowly raised her head. "I don't think I scared them at all."

Trish peeked over the dashboard, almost afraid to look. One of the men knelt behind the car, changing out the license plate, and the other one had the driver's-side door open. Incredibly, in an unbelievably short amount of time, the license-plate guy was running back to his car while the Camaro slowly backed out of the driveway.

"Is it safe to look?" Edna asked from the back seat.

"Yeah," Millie said in a low voice. "I'd say it's pretty safe."

"Oh, my goodness!" Edna exclaimed upon seeing the empty driveway.

Trish was stunned. If she hadn't seen it with her own eyes, she never would have believed how fast and easy it had been to steal the car. She watched, defeated, as the car the thieves had arrived in pulled out behind the Camaro and traveled down the street. At the corner, the two cars turned left, taking with them the hope Trish had at ending this crime spree tonight.

"What are you waiting for?" Millie snapped.

Trish sighed, started her car, and pulled away from the curb. "You're right. No point hanging around here any longer."

"Not if you want to catch them, there isn't!"

Trish slammed on the brakes, causing the car to rock. "What?"

"You heard me. Now hurry up, or we'll lose them. They're probably taking the car to one of those chop shops, and if we find that, we'll have even better evidence."

"Millie," Edna piped in, her voice filled with uncertainty. "I don't know if that's a good idea. I imagine those places are extremely dangerous."

Trish was about to agree with Edna when she clamped her mouth shut. That *woman roaring* thing was playing in her mind again, and she found herself analyzing Millie's suggestion. She hadn't really considered a chop shop. It made perfect sense, though, and it also meant there were even more people involved than just the two men who had stolen the Camaro.

Trish chewed on her bottom lip. If they were careful, and followed just long enough to find out where the thieves were taking the car, there was a possibility the whole operation could still be shut down tonight. And it was more than likely that Mrs. Blakely's murderer would be among the sleazebags.

That convinced her. Placing both hands on the steering wheel, she muttered, "Hold on, girls." Then she pressed her foot to the pedal, and her car lurched forward as she raced to catch up to the criminals.

Catching up to the Camaro and the other car had been easy, the occupants evidently not wanting to draw attention to themselves by breaking the speed limit. They had entered the ramp onto Interstate 35 South, cruised past downtown San Antonio, and eventually left the city altogether. Wherever this chop shop was, she hoped they would be able to give good enough directions to the police.

Traffic was light enough to make following the two vehicles easy, yet heavy enough to shield the ladies from detection. Trish kept hoping the bad guys would stop for gas or something, but they just kept traveling steadily forward. So far, the gas in her own car was fine, but she would have killed for a chance to stretch her legs and use the telephone to let somebody know where they were and what they had been doing since they had discovered the battery was dead on Edna's cell phone.

Trish rolled her neck from side to side, trying to loosen muscles that were beginning to tighten painfully. It was time to face facts—they were the most inept *crimestoppers* in the world. Millie had brought a digital camera she didn't know how to use, Edna had brought a cell phone without a battery charger, and she, caught up in the thrill of possibly catching the criminals tonight, had never thought to get her own cell phone from the office. The lioness in her began to meow . . .

"You've been driving for almost two hours now," Edna said. "Do you want me to take over for a little while?"

"Thanks, but I'm fine," Trish said, forcing a lightness to her voice that she didn't feel. Her own anxiety was growing with each passing mile, and she knew it wouldn't take much to send Edna into a panic. Trish had to stay calm and in control for the sake of her friends. Well, for Edna, anyway. Millie was thoroughly enjoying this unexpected road trip as she leaned forward slightly, never taking her eyes off the two cars ahead of them and encouraging her friends by declaring that the chop shop would be just over the next hill.

Of course, there weren't any hills. At least, none that Trish could see in the darkness of the night. Whenever the clouds would shift and allow moonlight to filter through, it appeared that the landscape was made up of flat, desert terrain, rows and rows of citrus orchards, and short, stubby palmetto trees.

From the minute they had left the city limits of San Antonio, Trish and Edna had kept an eye out for a state trooper, or a sheriff, or someone in authority whom they could stop and notify about the stolen car, but so far she hadn't seen a single law officer, a fact that pleased Millie immensely, since her focus was on finding the chop shop.

They had traveled through several small towns where Trish had felt sure the thieves would make a stop, given all the open convenience stores, gas stations, fast-food joints, and motels, but the men hadn't even slowed down.

Where were they heading? And then suddenly it dawned on her. Mexico! Why hadn't she realized it before? The border crossing between Laredo, Texas, and Nuevo Laredo, Mexico, was only about an hour away. Trish sat up straight in her seat. This was not good, not good at all.

Trish became more nervous with each passing mile. They should never have attempted to follow the car thieves, but the excitement of solving the crime had trumped common sense. And Trish knew that she was more to blame than anyone. Well, it was time to put a stop to the madness. As soon as she could, she was going to turn the car around and head home.

Millie would be disappointed, but just because they were calling it quits tonight didn't mean they had to give up the whole plan. The thieves didn't know they had been detected, and now that the ladies knew their grid pattern really worked, they'd schedule another stakeout. And they would make sure Larry came with them.

Trish cleared her throat. "I think I know where they are headed."

"Mexico," Millie said matter-of-factly.

"Oh, dear Lord," Edna groaned.

Nonplussed, Trish glanced at Millie. "How did you know that?"

"I evidently came to the same conclusion you did," Millie said wryly.

"We can't go to Mexico!" Edna said.

"Of course not, but what if they're taking the car to a place right *before* the border?" Millie suggested.

"We are not going anywhere *near* the border!" Trish said. "I don't know much about Mexico, but I do know that Nuevo Laredo has become famous for the Mexican drug wars. There are violent murders and kidnappings, and we're not going to take a chance on becoming a statistic."

"I agree with Trish," Edna said vehemently. "This is much too dangerous. We're not chasing Boy Scouts, you know, and if they are heading toward *friends* this close to the border who are going to help them get rid of the Camaro, then we're in way over our heads. Don't forget, these men very likely murdered an old woman. They probably wouldn't think twice about doing it again, and nobody even knows where we are!"

Millie sat back in her seat and crossed her arms over her chest. "Well, I can see I've been outvoted by members of the chicken farm."

"I'm going to ignore that comment, since it's obvious you're not in your right mind," Trish said through clenched teeth. "We're turning around at the first opportunity, and that's final."

They traveled several more miles in silence, the two cars still ahead of them, moving at a steady pace. Trish searched for a turn-around, anxious to get back to familiar territory and hoping they wouldn't ever have to tell anyone about this episode.

Finally, hazy lights on the horizon appeared. "That has to be Laredo," Edna said.

Trish reached up to rub her right temple, where a monster headache had begun. "I'll turn around at the first overpass."

Millie turned slightly in her seat, as far as the seatbelt would allow, and looked at her friends. Sighing dramatically, she said, "Look, you know I never ask for much, but I need to ask you a big favor."

Trish knew Millie probably couldn't see Trish's open-mouthed surprise at Millie's ironic statement, but regardless, Trish felt better doing it. *Never ask for much?*

"What is it, dear?" Edna asked.

"Well, there are really only two possibilities regarding the stolen car. They're either going to stop in Laredo or they are going to cross the border. Couldn't we follow them just a little bit longer to find out?" she implored.

"Oh, Millie—" Edna began.

"I'm not stupid. I hear the news about the dangers of border towns, but we're so close, girls."

"But—"

"I've been thinking about this," Millie said hurriedly. "If we can determine they are heading for the border, we can get real close, because the bad guys aren't going to suspect three old ladies have followed them from San Antonio. We can take pictures of both cars to give to the police. But if they stop at a butcher shop, we'll have an actual address to give to the police in Laredo, and they can immediately swarm the place."

"Millie, I really—"

"Please?" she asked, her voice pleading.

Edna didn't try to offer any other comments, which meant Millie had played her—and won—again.

Trish sighed. There was a part of her that grudgingly agreed with Millie's idea. They had already traveled two and a half hours; what was another thirty minutes? She'd like to have something to show for their efforts, after all. And really, there was enough traffic on the roads to offer a small sense of security, whether it was real or not.

"It's called a *chop shop*, not a butcher shop," she said.

Millie looked at her and then clapped her hands together. "Thank you, girls. You'll see, this is going to be fun."

Trish had never been to Laredo, and she wasn't quite sure what to expect. Certainly not the small-town feel set in a vibrant metropolis with many of the same familiar landmarks found in San Antonio. Whatever else might happen tonight, at least they wouldn't starve. Her fear slowly started to subside, and she found she was actually enjoying looking at the sights of the city while keeping one eye on the stolen car and its shadow.

"Joe and I used to come to Laredo quite often to do some shopping," Edna said. "That was a long time ago, but we sure had fun. The city has really grown since then."

"I told you there was nothing to worry about," Millie said smugly.

She may have spoken too soon, though. As Trish navigated her way through the city, it wasn't long before signs popped up directing traffic to the border crossing into Mexico.

"Darn," Edna muttered. "I was so hoping they were taking the car somewhere in Laredo, but I think they're going straight to Mexico."

"Step on it, Trish!" Millie demanded as she rifled through the backpack for the camera. "You have to get close to them so I can get good pictures."

Trish felt the tension return in her neck as she changed lanes. They were only a few cars behind the thieves, but they were fast approaching the International Bridge #2. She was pushing the speed limit, afraid that *now* they would garner the attention of a policeman, allowing the bad guys to sail across the border.

Trish pulled in behind the escort car, and Mille clicked the camera several times. Looking as though she was having way too much fun, Millie told Trish to pull alongside the car so Millie could get a picture of the driver. Trish wasn't certain that was such a good idea, but Millie had a good point. The guy would probably think they were tourists just taking general pictures.

Trish did as Millie asked, trying to keep her car even with the other one. She stole a sideways glance. With several overhead street lights, it was easy to make out the features of the driver. Dark hair fell across his forehead and curled on his neck, and as he turned to look at them, she noticed his beady, dark eyes. Edna smiled at him and waved, Millie's camera clicking away madly, capturing the man's angry scowl.

"Now we need to get a picture of the Camaro," Millie said.

Trish took a deep breath and pulled closer to the Camaro. Traffic was starting to slow as the bridge drew near, and Trish knew she wouldn't be able to pull beside the stolen car. But Millie snapped several pictures of the car, and Trish just prayed they would all turn out.

"Okay," Trish breathed, relief and excitement mingling with the dread of having to make the trip home tonight. "We'll give them to Larry in the morning."

"I wonder if you can turn around up here?" Edna said, looking at the many lanes of traffic all heading toward the bridge.

"There should be an exit up here," Trish said. They were so close to the border they could see the Declaration Station, a small steel structure resembling a gas-station canopy. The one thing she didn't see was an exit ramp.

"Go on through, and they'll let us turn around," Millie said.

Trish was getting a little nervous. "Are you sure?"

"Well, I think so. We'll just tell them we're lost."

Pulled to the side of the station were pickup trucks packed full. Mexican army personnel in camouflage uniforms were inspecting them. Most of the cars drove straight through, including the Camaro and its shadow. Trish slowed and pulled over, waving to get the attention of one of the guards.

A stocky man with a moustache and a rifle approached. Trish swallowed. He wasn't smiling, and he didn't look friendly. "Yes, señora?" His voice was deep with a thick accent.

Trish cleared her throat. "I'm so sorry, but we didn't mean to enter the bridge. We need to turn around. Can you help us?"

The man bent down and looked at them, and then, to their dismay, he started walking slowly around the car.

"What's he doing?" Edna whispered.

"He's trying to intimidate us," Millie muttered. She rolled down her window and stuck her head out as the man approached her side of the car.

"Hey!" Millie shouted, and Trish's heart stopped.

"What are you doing?" Millie demanded when the man stopped at her window. "All we did was ask for directions, and you ignored us. You let a stolen car go through, but you treat a bunch of old ladies like criminals! That is not good customer service, young man. I demand to see your supervisor."

"What's this about a stolen car?" he asked, his eyes crinkling at the corners. That could be a good sign or a very bad sign. Trish prayed fervently that the guard had a sense of humor and was as patient with obnoxious old women as their own Grand River police were.

Edna sat frozen in the back seat, a smile on her face as she tried to look as innocent as possible. But it was useless. Trish knew that anyone associated with Millie would never be viewed as innocent.

Millie delved into the story of the stolen car, giving a detailed account that had Trish cringing. Millie even opened the backpack and showed the guard the remainder of their snack food, offering him a Little Debbie cupcake, which he graciously accepted. Finally, the guard shook his head. "I'm sorry, señora, but I feel you will not see the Camaro again. Once a stolen car successfully makes it into Mexico, it is either sold to a buyer or stripped down for parts. You have come all this way for nothing."

"Oh, no, that's where you're wrong, my friend," Millie said, holding up the camera. "We've got evidence now."

The guard nodded, and with a big smile and a slight bow, he said, "I wish you luck, then, señora. Now, if you will follow me, I am going to lead you to a side exit, and you will be back on the main road." He jumped into a green Jeep and waved at them to follow as he led them off the bridge.

Millie turned to look at Edna. "You can relax now."

"I'll relax when we're back at home. I thought for sure you were going to get us arrested."

Trish chuckled and looked at Millie. "I know I'm going to regret telling you this, but you really are amazing."

Millie grinned. "Let's go. We have some evidence to turn over."

"If you guys don't mind, I'd like to stop at a coffeehouse," Edna said. "I could sure use a cup, and I need to call Joe."

Trish nodded. "That's a good idea. I need to stretch my legs, anyway."

"Me too," Millie said with a yawn. "Did either of you recognize those scumbags?"

"Not me," Trish said. "I'm certain I've never seen them before."

"It's a relief to know the thieves aren't someone we know," Edna said. "This means they are not intentionally targeting Michelle or Richard."

Millie shook her head. "Not necessarily. They could have been hired guns, you know. Someone we know could still be pulling the strings."

Trish groaned. *Just like a dog with a bone . . .*

Chapter Eighteen

The ladies sat in Henry's office while he lectured them once again about staying out of police business. Trish endeavored to appear extra attentive and respectful, to make up for Millie's loud yawns, deep sighs, and sarcastic grunts.

Edna, sitting there like the perfect lady she was, kept a serene smile on her face, even after the marathon discussion she said she and Joe had engaged in last night regarding her unplanned trip to Laredo.

Millie made a point of looking at her watch. "Are you through yet, Henry?" she asked. "We do have other things to do today, you know."

"No, I'm not through!" he said sharply, sinking back into his chair. "You three deserve to get a tongue lashing for the risk you took last night. However," he paused, holding up the memory card from Millie's camera, "if these pictures reveal what you say they do, it's going to be a big help in our investigation."

Trish looked at Edna. *Did she just hear what I thought she did?* Apparently so, from the surprised look on her friend's face. "Wow!" she mouthed silently, and Edna grinned.

Millie let out a loud *whoop* and held her hand up for Henry to give her a high five, which, of course, he didn't do.

Instead, he gave her a stern look and continued, "They may not be admissible in a court of law, but regardless, we can use them a lot of different ways in capturing and interrogating the criminals. I'm still upset, mind you," he said when Millie started to interrupt, "but I'm also grateful." Henry coughed into his hand and straightened some papers on his desk. "Thank you," he said without looking up.

Millie shattered the stunned silence that followed Henry's remarks. "You may have the makings of a good lawman yet, Henry," she said with a grin.

"However," he said seriously, completely ignoring Millie's statement, "none of this would have been worth it if you ladies had been hurt last night . . . or worse."

"We appreciate that, Henry," Edna said. "And just so you know, we were very, very careful. We didn't take any undue chances; we just wanted to see if we could get information you could use. We have a personal stake in this, you know, so it's hard to sit back and wait for the normal flow of things to happen. Your concern is well taken, though, and we'll be happy to let the professionals handle it from now on."

"When giraffes do cartwheels!" Millie interjected. "We're in this until the end. Nobody is behind bars, yet, you know."

Just when I thought Millie was behaving herself . . .

The cordial atmosphere had just been effectively destroyed, but, still, Trish thought they had probably broken a record for time spent in Henry's office without being threatened. It would be nice, though, if once, just once, they could leave Henry's office with a friendly handshake and a good-bye instead of scooting out of there under the real possibility of jail time.

"That was totally uncalled for, Millie," Edna admonished as they walked to the car.

Millie shrugged. "I was afraid he was going to get complacent. This thing isn't over with yet, and Michelle and Richard still have to go through an audit. If Henry thinks we're going to stay involved, it might make him more aggressive in his effort to catch the thieves."

"Oh, I'm sure your remarks lit a fire under him," Trish said drily.

Edna hung up the phone. "Joe will be over in a little while," she said, walking to the refrigerator and pulling out lunchmeat, tomatoes, and cheese. "He'll bring cantaloupe and watermelon for dessert."

Fruit for dessert? What happened to the chocolate cake? Trish wondered, stirring a big pot of soup. "That's great." *Gag . . .*

Millie spread mayonnaise and mustard on fresh wheat bread. "I still can't figure out how you managed to get out of trouble with Joe so fast."

"Oh, he was upset," Edna confirmed. "And then I became upset because he had been so worried. It breaks my heart to think of him sitting alone, waiting for me to call, wondering what was going on."

"That had to have been hard for him," Trish sympathized. "How were you able to calm him down?"

Edna raised her eyes. "I asked him what lengths *he* would go to in order to help a friend."

"Oh, that's good." Millie grinned.

Edna nodded. "I explained how careful we were, and I apologized for being so careless as to let the phone battery go dead, and I promised to stop hanging around with friends who get me in trouble."

"I bet that eased his— *wait a minute!* Are you talking about *us*?" Millie demanded.

Edna laughed at Millie's expression, but before she could say anything, the doorbell rang. "Come on in, honey," she called out.

"Well, just for the record, I'm not worried about you leaving us," Millie said. "You'd die of boredom."

Just then, Larry walked into the kitchen. "Thanks, sweetheart."

Edna whirled around as Trish and Millie busted out laughing. "Oh, Larry." Edna grinned, shaking her head. "I thought you were Joe."

Millie snickered and pulled out more bread. "You're just in time for lunch."

"Thank you. I didn't plan on interrupting, though."

"Don't be silly," Trish said. "Have a seat."

"Did your boss tell you we almost cracked the case last night?" Millie asked with a proud tilt to her head.

Larry lowered himself into a chair. "Actually, he did. When I got back in town he filled me in on the amazing job you three did last night. I'm not thrilled you put yourself in such a dangerous situation after I warned you—"

All three women groaned simultaneously.

"—not to go out on your own, but you did provide us with some valuable information."

Trish's eyebrows rose. "Such as?"

Before Larry could answer, Joe came in carrying a large bowl of fruit and a plate that looked—and Trish prayed—like it held several pieces of chocolate cake. He greeted everybody, setting the dishes on the table and giving Edna a kiss on her cheek.

"Hello, Larry. I haven't seen you in a while." He shook Larry's hand and then sat down.

"I know. I wish that meant the girls have been staying out of trouble," he said with a wink, "but it's more likely you and I have just been running in different directions."

Joe laughed. "Yes, that's much more likely."

Millie placed the sandwiches on the table. "You two are very funny. Now, getting back to what you were saying?" she asked, giving Larry a pointed look.

Larry looked at Joe. "I assume you know what the ladies did last night?"

Joe nodded, turning to look at Edna with a knowing smile. Her cheeks turned a soft pink as she sat down next to him and placed her hand over his.

Trish almost started humming the famous theme from *Love Story*, but she didn't want to trivialize the moment. If everyone had the kind of relationship Joe and Edna Radcliff had, the world would be a much better place. A little sappy, perhaps, but a better place, nevertheless.

With an inward smile, she carried the soup to the table. "Dig in, everybody."

Larry picked up the conversation where he had left off. "The driver of the car that followed the stolen Camaro is named Tim Bolton. He has a record a mile long, mainly misdemeanors. We were able to match your pictures of him in our database. The car he was driving is stolen—no surprise there. We couldn't get any information on the other guy, because you weren't able to get close enough to him, but it's just a matter of time before we do."

Joe ladled soup into Edna's bowl, then his own. "Are these men dangerous? I mean, outside of being car thieves?"

Edna's eyes popped open wide. *Uh-oh . . .* they hadn't told Joe about Elaine Blakely.

Quickly, Millie jumped up and grabbed some bowls from the cabinet. "Who's ready for dessert?"

Trish groaned silently as the two men looked down at the meal they had just started. Then Larry looked up and caught her eye. She held her breath, afraid to make any facial expression in case Joe happened to notice. If he did, she'd be changing her tune from *Love Story* to *The Battle Hymn of the Republic.*

"That's one of the reasons I came by, Joe," he said, taking a bite out of his sandwich. "The ladies may have done even more good than they realize. It's possible one, or both, of these men is connected to a murder revolving around one of the stolen cars."

Larry hadn't gotten the reputation of being a great detective from being stupid, and out of gratitude, Trish was going to give him her piece of cake. He had let Joe know the hideous truth without divulging their prior knowledge of it.

Millie gasped. "You're not serious!" she said, placing her hand over her heart as she sat back down. "We had no idea!"

Edna's eyebrows hit her hairline. "Oh my goodness!"

Joe wrapped an arm around her shoulder. "It's okay, dear, don't worry." His face was grim as he looked at Larry. "What happened?"

"We don't know anything for certain at this point," Larry said. "That's why I need to ask for the girls' help one more time."

Everyone's eyes flew to Larry. There was no feigned surprise this time.

"Absolutely not!" Joe said thunderously.

Larry held up his hand. "I'm sorry, that came out wrong. I didn't mean I wanted them to get anywhere near these men. What I need is information on the next likely target for a car theft. I doubt if these guys are going to stop at this point. They have no idea we know who they are."

Joe released a deep breath. "For a minute there, I thought you wanted them to do another stakeout."

Larry shook his head. "No, that's much too dangerous. I'll do this one on my own. As much as I appreciate all you have done," he said, looking at all three women, "I won't allow you to put yourselves in danger again."

Trish tried to smile, but it came off more as a grimace. She'd be eating the cake herself, after all.

Millie was pacing again, complaining to the heavens about how unfair it was that they weren't included in the action tonight. The ladies had played cards, watched an old movie, eaten the rest of the fruit, and watched the clock. Now they were back to discussing the situation. At first, Trish had been extremely upset with Larry, shutting them out like he had. But the more she thought about it, the more she realized that he had done the right thing. He knew what he was dealing with now, and it was going to take all his concentration and dedication to the job to capture these crooks. The last thing he needed to be worrying about was three old ladies tagging along, trying to help.

And, as she told Millie, the sooner he was successful in putting an end to the car thefts, the sooner Michelle and Richard would be off the hook.

"You're right," Millie said and nodded with a sigh. "I'm just so anxious to tell Michelle the nightmare is over."

"Why don't you give her a call and drop a hint?" Edna suggested.

Millie shook her head. "She's probably asleep. I don't want to wake her up for just a hint. She's pretty tired. My grandson's baseball team made the playoffs, and she's been going to the games right after work. Now, if we knew the case was indeed closed, I'd call her in a heartbeat."

"Well, just think," Trish said and smiled. "It's only a matter of time before you can tell both Michelle and Richard."

"Not Richard," Millie said. "Michelle told me he's been at a conference since Thursday. He won't be back until tomorrow afternoon."

"Let's cross our fingers this is solved tonight," Trish said. No sooner had the words left her mouth than a frightening thought entered her mind. If Richard had been gone since Thursday, and Michelle had been at a baseball tournament, then Barbara couldn't have followed either of them to the grocery store yesterday. With a sinking heart, she realized she was the one Barbara had followed. Barbara hadn't shown up at the store at the exact same time she had been there by happenstance. Like Michelle had said, that grocery store wasn't even close to Barbara's neighborhood. Then, why?

Her thoughts were interrupted by the doorbell. She stood and went to the door, her friends right on her heels.

"Who's there?" she called.

"It's me, Trish. You can open the door." Larry walked in with a big smile on his face.

"You got them, didn't you?" Millie whispered.

"I sure did. But it was only one man, not two."

"Come tell us all about it, dear," Edna said. "I'll fix you some coffee."

Larry looked tired, but there was an air of excitement about him. Millie was practically jumping from one foot to the other in anticipation. Larry took a sip of his coffee and then began to tell them the story. "I was only there about an hour when I saw this guy walking down the block. I didn't think too much about it, because I was looking for two men in a car. Well, this guy walks right by, never noticing me in the car. He goes up to the Chevy Suburban, pulls this long tool from his pant leg, and before you know it, he had the door open. I was out of the car and had the man in cuffs before he could blink."

Trish frowned. "I wonder if it's really one of the guys we saw last night. The whole thing is different. It doesn't make sense."

"Oh, it's the same guy," Larry confirmed. "I identified him from your picture."

"Did he say he worked for Tony Matson?" Millie asked eagerly.

Larry grinned and held up his hands. "Sorry, I don't know anything else right now. I dropped him off at the station to get processed. You ladies were instrumental in our being able to catch the guy, and I knew you'd be on pins and needles. You can get a good night's rest now," he said and smiled. "I'm heading back to the station to start the questioning. Unless the guy gets a lawyer, of course, but I'm going to try and convince him to help us in the hopes of a lighter sentence. We know there's still another guy out there."

"Boy, I wish we had been there," Millie said enviously.

Larry laughed. "I'm glad you weren't."

Suddenly Millie jumped up. "We can go to the station with you. I want to hear what the scumbag has to say."

Trish sighed. "They're not going to let us see him, much less talk to him, Millie."

"Trish is right. I'll come back early tomorrow and let you know if anything interesting is said."

"That's not fair—"

"Millie, there's no room for argument," Larry said sternly. "I have work to do, and I have to follow certain procedures. We're not just talking about stealing cars. A woman was murdered, remember? So let me do my job, and you'll find out what happened in the morning. Deal?"

Millie was silent for a few moments, clearly not pleased with this turn of events. Finally, she gave in with a frustrated sigh. "Deal."

When Millie rang the doorbell the next morning, Trish was prepared. She was already dressed and had fresh coffee waiting.

"I forgot to tell you that the window on my car is going to be repaired today. If we do any running around, we'll need to take your car," Millie said.

Trish nodded. "Sure." *Don't we always?*

Millie poured herself a cup of coffee. "I have a plan. After we solve the current case we're on, I think me, you, and Edna should take turns watching the neighborhood at night. We've got to stop all this vandalism going on."

Trish bit her tongue. She didn't think there would be any more pranks, since Barbara knew she'd been busted, but Trish would be talking to Henry regardless, just to make sure.

Half an hour later, Edna and Joe came over. Today could be the day this all ended, the day Millie could tell her daughter the nightmare was over. They all tried to contain their excitement, but it was there just the same, bubbling just below the surface.

"What time do you think Larry will be over?" Millie asked, glancing at the clock for the umpteenth time.

Joe was saved from answering again when they heard a knock on the door. Millie grinned and rushed from the room. "I'll get it!"

Larry entered the kitchen with Millie, her arm linked through his as though he were her favorite person in the world. And right now, he probably was.

Edna placed a fresh cup of coffee in front of him. "Congratulations again," she said with a smile. "We knew you could do it."

"That's nice of you to say, but it wouldn't have happened this quickly if you ladies had not discovered the pattern being used."

Millie agreed. "We're quite a team, aren't we? You should consider leaving Henry and coming to work for us."

Larry chuckled. "I'll remember that if crime suddenly dries up for the Grand River Police Department."

Larry looked as if he hadn't slept all night, but he was smiling, and Trish knew things must have gone well. "I want to hear what happened," she said.

Larry nodded and proceeded to tell them what had occurred. "This guy is so anxious to throw blame on someone else, he's spilling the whole story without even being asked. When you get right down to it, thieves are usually cowards, anyway," he said in disgust.

"According to Tim Bolton, he and a friend, Bob Yates, were contacted by someone named Andy. Tim doesn't know how Andy got their names and phone numbers, but he thinks it was probably from an old friend. Anyway, their job was to steal certain cars selected by Andy. They never knew ahead of time what area of town the car would be in or what type of car they would be stealing. They'd get all that information, along with notification regarding alarm systems, on the day of the theft.

"Two days later, they'd receive two hundred and fifty dollars in a money order sent to a post office box. Plus, they got to keep all the proceeds from selling the cars across the border, or whatever else they wanted to do with the cars. All business is conducted by cell phone. Neither Tim or Bob have ever seen Andy."

Millie's eyes were huge as she hung onto every word. "This was a pretty organized operation, wasn't it?" she commented.

Trish hated to ask, but she wanted to know. "And what about poor Mrs. Blakely? Were they involved in her murder?"

"Yeah." Larry nodded, wrapping his hands around the coffee cup. "Tim said it was all Bob's fault, though. They had been given orders to steal the car. He and Bob were running behind schedule, so they didn't get to the designated house until early in the morning, but were still able to successfully steal it. Then they ran into problems. First of all, the car was almost out of gas. They drove a few miles and stopped to fill it up, but there was a locked cap on the tank. Since they didn't have the keys, they had to break the cap off."

"Serves them right," Edna interrupted him angrily. "I'm glad they had so much trouble with Mrs. Blakely's car. It almost makes it seem as if she went down fighting, doesn't it?"

Trish nodded somberly. It did seem apropos, and she couldn't help but feel glad that Mrs. Blakely's car appeared to have fought against being "kidnapped." There she was again, assigning human emotions to a chunk of steel, but it made her happy to think of it that way.

"So then what happened?" Millie asked. "Why did they end up killing her?"

"According to Tim, Bob was on prescription medication for his blood pressure. He kept the bottle in his shirt pocket, and he noticed it was gone. They searched the stolen car and their own car, and then they searched all over the gas station. The only thing that made sense was that Bob had somehow dropped it at Mrs. Blakely's house. The problem was, the bottle had his name and his doctor's name on it. They had to go back and get it. They left Mrs. Blakely's car at the station and went back to her house." Larry stopped and took a deep breath. "I guess you can figure out what happened next."

"She caught them looking for the medicine, didn't she?" Millie said.

Larry nodded. "Evidently, she had come outside and discovered her car stolen. On her way back into her house to call the police, she found the medicine bottle. She had just re-entered her house when she saw Tim and Bob approach. Tim said she came out screaming, telling them that she had found the bottle and was going to call the police. Bob panicked, grabbed her, and threw her in the car. They drove off in a hurry, and Bob ended up killing her since she could identify them."

Trish shuddered. "How terribly sad."

Edna placed a hand over her mouth. "If that weasel George Drury had offered to help Mrs. Blakely when she told him her car had been stolen instead of just walking away, her murder might have been prevented."

"What?" Larry said, cocking his head. "Who is George Drury?"

Edna waved her hand. "Mrs. Blakely's neighbor. He's not involved in any of this; he's just worthless."

Millie frowned. "How did her body end up at the insurance office?"

Joe raised his eyebrows at that. "The insurance office?"

Edna placed her hand on Joe's arm. "Hush, dear. Let Larry finish the story."

"Supposedly, that was Andy's idea. According to Tim, Andy was furious that Bob had killed someone, but it was too late. They were told where to take the body. They did as ordered and hightailed it out of town."

"I'm learning to hate this Andy person," Trish said.

Millie grimaced. "Me, too. Was anything else said?"

"That's about it." Larry sighed. "Except that the night before last, Bob started complaining about them taking all the risks, and he wanted more money. He called the number Andy had given them and left a message. Tim hasn't seen Bob since, but they already had another job lined up, the one Tim attempted tonight. Tim figured some money was better than no money, so he tried it on his own, thinking Bob would show up. Bob's the one who has the car, so Tim took a bus and walked to the house. That's when I saw him.

"When we locate Bob and this Andy person, they'll both be placed under arrest. Early this morning, Henry and I went to the address Tim gave us to pick up Bob, but there wasn't anybody there. We sent another man there to watch for his return."

"Henry went with you?" Trish asked.

Larry nodded, a twinkle in his eyes. "Of course. Did you think he just sat behind his desk all day?"

Trish grinned and turned her face away. According to Millie, that's all Henry did.

"Anyway, I just wanted to stop by and give you an update. Henry knew you would be anxious, and we wanted to keep you informed."

Edna gave Larry a gentle smile. "Thank you so much, and please thank Henry for us."

"So that's it?" Millie asked.

"Henry is running a trace on the cell phone Andy uses. Once we get that information, we're going to pay him a visit."

"Let's stop talking in code here, Larry," Millie said. "We all know Andy is really Tony. Tony's real name is Anthony. You see? Anthony . . . Andy? He probably hired these thugs."

Larry tilted his head. After a moment he said, "I promise I'll call you if the evidence leads to Tony. I promise."

Chapter Nineteen

It was all over the news. The police in San Antonio were working closely with the local police in Grand River to connect the suspect now in custody to the car thefts recently rocking the city.

Trish frowned and turned off the car radio. "I bet Henry and Larry are livid over this. Now Tim's partner is going to be alerted that Tim has been arrested. He'll skip town for sure."

"Well, let's stick to our original plan," Millie said. "We're just stopping by to see how Michelle is doing. We don't want to say too much and give her the impression this is all over. There are going to be a lot of unanswered questions if Bob Yates and Andy aren't caught, especially since nobody has ever seen this Andy person."

"They're going to be caught," Edna said, her face set in grim determination.

Michelle rose from her chair the minute they entered the insurance office with a hopeful expression on her face that tore at Trish's heart. *She's already heard the news.*

"I've been trying to call you," she said to Millie, her voice no more than a whisper. "Is it true?" The dark circles under Michelle's eyes couldn't hide the obvious yearning for affirmation of what she had heard. "Did they catch the car thief?"

Millie's lips formed a wide smile as she gave her daughter a big hug. "We just heard the same thing, honey."

Trish hoped Michelle didn't notice the strained gruffness in Millie's voice. If pressed, Millie wasn't going to be able to withhold the knowledge she had about the police investigation from her daughter. And right now, that would not be good.

Michelle and Richard both needed to be kept in the dark about any specific details regarding the arrest, the players involved, and where the investigation was heading. Having more information than had been released on the news could be a disaster.

The bell over the door jingled and they all turned to look. Richard walked in, carrying a briefcase and his suit jacket over his arm. He smiled when he saw them. "Hello, ladies. Is this a welcome-home party?" he teased. "I was gone only a couple of days." Richard's face showed signs of strain, the tiny lines at his eyes more pronounced and the furrow between his brows deeper, as if worry had become a constant companion.

"Have you listened to the radio?" Michelle asked.

"No, why?" he asked, placing his briefcase and jacket on the counter.

"One of our clients just called to tell me the car thief had been arrested. Evidently it's all over the news, and Mom just confirmed it."

Richard looked at Michelle, then at Millie and her friends, then back at Michelle. He closed his eyes and drew in a deep breath. "Thank God," he whispered.

In the next instant, Michelle was in his arms, both of them laughing, releasing pent-up stress as the news sunk in. He swung her around in a circle as their laughter filled the room.

Nobody heard the bell ring over the door. "I hope I'm not interrupting anything," Barbara said, her voice so cold the temperature in the room dropped by several degrees.

Trish's eyes widened, but Barbara never looked at Trish. Her gaze was focused solely on Richard and Michelle.

"Hello, Barbara," Richard said. "What brings you by?" He was still smiling, and Trish noticed he hadn't removed his arm from Michelle's waist.

"I wanted to drop off my payment," Barbara said, walking over to the counter and nonchalantly placing her elbows on it. "It seems like I walked in on a celebration, though."

"The police caught the guy who's been on a rampage stealing cars," he said.

"Oh, yes," Barbara said, "I did hear something about that."

She wasn't smiling, and her eyes were hard. "That's very good news."

Trish thought it was a little too convenient that Barbara showed up right after Richard arrived at the office. She obviously wasn't happy, and she wasn't trying to hide the fact. But Trish was happy that while Michelle had tamped down some of her ebullience, Richard was still in full celebratory mode.

"Dinner tonight is on me. You ladies decide where you want to go, and I'll pick you up about seven," he said, giving Michelle a wink. "Now, if you'll all excuse me, I'm going to make a phone call to the home office." He bowed slightly with a smile and turned on his heel. Then he snapped his fingers and looked back over his shoulder. "Barbara, Michelle will help you with that payment." Whistling, he sauntered to his office and closed the door.

Before anyone could say anything, the phone rang. "I'll be right back," Michelle said as she hurried to answer it.

Trish was about to explode. She wanted to jump in the air with both fists pumping and shout, "Yes!" There was no way Barbara could have missed Richard's message. She waited for Barbara to say something about their meeting in the parking lot the other day, or for her to apologize to Millie face to face, but Barbara didn't even seem to be aware they were there. That is, until Millie spoke.

"I think I'll wear my low-cut, strapless black dress tonight," Millie said, crossing her arms and tilting her head as though deep in thought. "You're so good at fashion, Barbara. What do you think?"

Barbara held out a hand and looked at her fingernails, an ugly smirk on her face. "I think that you may be celebrating too soon," she said sardonically.

Trish looked at her. "What do you mean by that?"

"Oh, nothing. I just assume the police have a lot of work to do before they officially settle this, don't you agree?" she said with a sugary smile as she reached in her purse and pulled out a check. "Make sure Michelle gets this, won't you?" She fanned her fingers at them and turned to leave.

"Hey, Barbie," Millie called after her. "You never told me what you thought about my dress."

Barbara stopped and turned back around slowly. She glared at Millie. The *Barbie* thing might have been carrying it a bit far, Trish thought, as a shiver suddenly snaked its way up her spine.

"I think you're a little too full of yourself right now. If I were you, I wouldn't be worrying too much about my wardrobe," Barbara said, her voice deadly quiet. "The police haven't caught the other guy yet."

Millie burst out laughing the minute the door swung shut. "I think we got under her mannequin-style skin." She took a deep breath and wiped a hand over her eyes as her laughter finally subsided. "We can only hope she's out of Richard's life for good now."

Trish stood frozen at the counter, Barbara's check in her hand. "I wouldn't count on it."

"When will he be back?" Trish asked the officer at the front desk.

"I don't know, ma'am," he replied, clearly worried about the lack of blood in her face. "Chief Espinoza left with Larry Thompson about an hour ago, and all he said was they'd be back soon."

Millie's eyes narrowed. "You can reach him by phone, can't you?"

"Well, sure, I suppose so, if it's important."

Edna stepped up. "Young man, this is very important. And *I'm* the one saying that, not the crazy old lady. Please try to reach him."

The officer hesitated, weighing the odds against the chief's irritation at being interrupted and the ladies torturing him. Evidently, the ladies were more of a threat.

"Wait right here."

Moments later, the ladies were on their way home. The officer had contacted Larry, who had promised that he and Henry would come by on their way back to the station.

"I still can't believe it," Edna said. "It just doesn't make sense."

But it made perfect sense. Trish had realized that the moment she had seen Barbara's full name printed on her check: Barbara *Andrea* Ferguson.

Barbara was the infamous *Andy*. Combining that fact with Barbara's comment about catching the other guy, something only the police and the ladies knew, cemented the connection.

Millie sat quietly, presumably trying to come to terms with the fact that Tony Matson wasn't the mastermind behind the car thefts, after all. Tony was still a worm; he just wasn't a criminally insane worm.

Trish turned onto their street as past events flashed through her mind. Barbara hadn't been stalking Richard—she was out to destroy him. Hadn't Michelle told her that Barbara had worked in the office shortly before Richard broke off their relationship? Trish remembered that Michelle had laughed, claiming that Barbara had driven him crazy while she had worked there temporarily. So, if Barbara had sensed Richard's withdrawal from her, she could have easily gained access to the same information that Michelle had printed out for the ladies. That would show forethought, though. A long, detailed plan fueling Barbara's anger and false sense of betrayal.

And Millie . . . Barbara wasn't jealous of Millie's friendship with Richard. No, she must have somehow discovered that Millie was the bulldog who had pushed for an active investigation. Everyone knew that the police didn't have time to chase down stolen cars. They made a report and put the information on a database that authorities could use in the normal course of their work, but they sure didn't have a task force dressed in SWAT gear checking out license tags.

But then Millie became involved, the tigress in her erupting into a powerful force, a steely determination to protect her daughter.

And the aggression against Millie—the mailbox, the surveillance, the brick thrown through the window—all of these incidents had probably been meant to distract Millie, to make her focus on her own series of troubles instead of Michelle's.

Yes, it all made perfect sense, but a major problem remained, Trish thought, pulling into her driveway. As far as she could tell, there was absolutely no way to prove Barbara's involvement in any of this. And if Barbara's goal was to destroy Richard, she had to have had a plan for the finale.

Trish swallowed, a knot of anxiety gripping her as she realized how easy it would be for Barbara to throw overwhelming suspicion onto Michelle and Richard. She was using information only the people in the insurance office would have.

And then a greater fear invaded Trish's thoughts. Barbara had condoned a murder, going so far as to callously suggest where the body should be dumped.

Henry and Larry sat in Trish's kitchen, sipping coffee as they absorbed the information the ladies threw at them in rapid-fire succession. With their expressions stoic, their eyes guarded, they interrupted with a question here and there, but mainly they just listened.

Finally, Trish took a deep breath and looked at them. "What do you think?"

Larry set his cup down and turned to Henry. "Makes sense after what that kid told us."

"What kid?" Millie asked. "Don't tell me there's someone else involved in this!"

Larry grinned, shaking his head. "No. We traced the cell phone to a kid on the north side of San Antonio. He claims that a lady approached him one day after school and offered him quite a bit of money if he would buy, and set up, a cell phone in his name."

"I'm amazed at the lengths Barbara went to," Edna said quietly.

Henry nodded. "Quite a bit of planning went into this. There's still no sign of Bob Yates."

Now was the time for Trish to introduce the idea she had come up with. Clearing her throat, she looked at Henry. "I've been doing some planning of my own. Even if you don't believe Michelle Matson and Richard Kelp are viable suspects any longer, it doesn't mean their home office will feel the same way. At best, they're going to lose their jobs. At worst, they could be charged with fraud. I don't think Barbara has finished playing with Richard yet."

Henry sighed. "You're probably right," he agreed. "But if your theory is correct, then she's going to make a mistake. Crooks always do. And when she does, we'll catch her."

Millie was unusually quiet, sitting with her hands wrapped tightly together, a pensive look on her face. This had to be so difficult for her, knowing there might not be anything anyone could do to salvage the situation, regardless of how much they may have wanted to.

Trish gathered her courage and plunged ahead. "I think I have a plan that will work." Everyone looked at her, waiting for her to continue. "I think you should put a wire on Tim Bolton and have him contact Andy. Barbara probably disguised her voice, because neither Tim nor Bob seemed to realize they were talking to a woman. Barbara's got to be aware of that. Make her think Tim was released on bond and needs money to get out of town immediately. There's no time to go through the usual post office drop; he has to meet with Andy right away."

"Barbara will show up and say something incriminating," Larry finished for her.

"Trish, that's a brilliant idea!" Edna said. "You're getting as good as Millie is at strategic planning."

Larry chuckled while Millie looked at Trish, a small smile playing at her lips. *Why isn't she saying anything?* Trish wondered.

Henry rubbed his chin, a faraway look in his eyes as he pondered the idea. Everyone sat quietly, not wanting to disturb him. He was the one who would make the decision, and Trish found she was holding her breath, waiting for him to speak.

"Henry, please? There isn't time to wait for Barbara to make a mistake. Michelle's life could be ruined by then," Millie said.

Finally, Henry nodded and started to smile. "Actually, I like the idea."

Millie let out a loud *whoop*. "Thank goodness! I was practicing the old-helpless-female thing in case you weren't going to do it."

Henry grinned. "I know."

Trish choked back a laugh as she got up to refresh the coffee cups. Henry and Larry started discussing the particulars of how best to pull the plan off, Larry assuring Henry that Tim would be more than willing to cooperate in lieu of a lighter sentence.

"We could have Tim tell Barbara he wants to meet at that rear picnic area in Stokey's Park. Nobody ever goes there anymore."

"That's good." Millie nodded. "I know right where that is."

Trish grimaced, trying to stretch her back without making any noise. Millie sent her a warning glance, but Trish ignored it. They had been lying on their bellies, hidden under the overgrown shrubs close to the picnic area for an hour, and Trish's body was beginning to protest.

The ladies didn't even know what time the sting was set up for, since Henry and Larry had both adamantly ordered them to stay away from the place. But Millie had heard Henry tell Larry he wanted to do it this afternoon, before Barbara made any further moves.

Edna reached over and plucked a couple of dry leaves from Millie's hair. "You realize we're dead meat if Henry catches us here, don't you?" she whispered.

"Edna, you have a horrible habit of repeating yourself over and over again," Millie muttered in a low voice. "We're not going to get caught. I'm just going to get a picture of Barbara when she's surrounded by the police to give to Michelle and Richard as a wedding present."

Trish's eyes grew round. "I didn't know they were getting married!" she whispered.

Millie grinned. "They don't, either."

Trish stifled a laugh. At least she wasn't the only one Millie practiced her matchmaking skills on.

Suddenly, the three women froze. Barbara appeared from the other edge of the clearing, walking quietly as she looked around before slowly making her way over to the picnic table. She wore jeans and tennis shoes, and a baseball cap covered her hair, but her whole countenance spoke of an underlying tension on the verge of exploding.

Barbara sat on one of the concrete benches, her back to the ladies, as she placed her purse beside her. She looked around again, then reached into her purse and pulled out a gun. She slid it under the folds of her purse and then casually placed her hands in her lap. The women looked at each other. There was no way Henry would know Barbara had brought a gun to the meeting.

Barbara looked up quickly at the sound of approaching footsteps, and Trish saw her take a deep breath right before Tim came into view. *Where are Henry and Larry and the swarm of police officers who are going to help?*

All of a sudden, Millie tapped her and Edna on the arm. Placing a finger to her lips, she gave the camera to Edna, motioning for her to take the pictures. Then, very quietly, Millie slid backward until they couldn't see her anymore. Trish closed her eyes tight and prayed like she never had before. *Please, dear Lord, don't let Millie do something foolish.*

She brought her attention back to the drama unfolding. Tim wasn't a very tall man, Trish noticed as he walked over to the bench, but she had only seen him in the driver's seat of a car. He had a stocky build, but the white button-down shirt he wore still hung loosely on him. Trish wondered if the wire was under his shirt.

"Andy?" Tim asked incredulously. At her slight nod, he started laughing. "I've gotta hand it to you, lady. I never would have thought you were a woman."

"Yes," Barbara said quietly, her voice deadly calm. "Neither did Bob."

That shut Tim up. "Bob? When did you talk to Bob?"

"When he tried to shake me down, just as you're doing now."

"*What?* What are you talking about? I just need some money to get out of town."

"I'm sure you do," Barbara said smoothly, almost conversationally. "But then you'll be back, needing more. And since *I* have no intention of leaving town, I can't give you the ability to identify me later. Blackmail is such an ugly thing, and something I definitely wouldn't put past you. After all, you were willing to stoop to stealing cars."

Uh-oh. This wasn't going like Trish had imagined it would. *Where are the good guys?* she wondered again, sensing that things were going to turn very ugly soon. Barbara had already confessed enough to put her away for a very long time. What where they waiting for? And where in the world was Millie?

"Hey, I did that for you, lady!" Tim said, his face turning red. "You *paid* me to do that."

"So you understand my disappointment now, don't you?" Barbara said. "I paid you and Bob to steal the cars, and then Bob comes back wanting more money, something he didn't live long enough to regret, by the way, and now you're here asking me to pay you so you can leave town."

Trish looked at Edna. Had Barbara just admitted to murder?

Tim looked at Barbara. "What do you mean, Bob didn't live to regret it?"

Barbara sighed. "Believe me, this wasn't how I planned the end of my little charade to turn out. I should be married and enjoying my honeymoon on some tropical island right now. If it wasn't for you and that friend of yours killing that woman, the stupid police would never have gotten involved. Did you know they've had the insurance office under twenty-four-hour surveillance for the past couple of weeks? I couldn't even go by there to see how my plan was working!"

With raised eyebrows, Trish turned her head slightly and looked at Edna. *The police have been watching the insurance office?* How interesting. But she had been wrong about Barbara's motive. Barbara hadn't wanted to destroy Richard. She had wanted to ruin Michelle. That way, she thought, she could wriggle her way back into Richard's life. Millie had been right all along.

"Hey, lady," Tim said, taking a small step back. "I don't know what you're talking about. You're the one who told us to take the body to the insurance company."

Barbara obviously didn't want to admit it, but she had made a critical mistake in ordering her thugs to put Mrs. Blakely's body in front of Security Insurance. At the time, she must have thought it would make things worse for Michelle, which it had, but it also prevented her from doing anything other than drop off payments. She hadn't been able to keep track of how everything was affecting Richard.

"Regardless, you spoiled everything. You and that crazy old lady." As Barbara talked, she paced back and forth next to the picnic table. She didn't appear to be talking to Tim any more. It was as though she were having a conversation with herself. Her voice would rise, and then it would fall so low that Trish had trouble hearing. Thankfully, it was raised now, and Trish heard every word.

"When I overheard her telling her daughter that she and her friends were going to find out who was behind the car thefts, I actually thought for a minute they had some talent. I followed them to the insurance office and to the police station. That's all they ever did! Probably due to my efforts at distracting them," she said and chuckled irrationally. "But when I found out the other day that they knew it was me behind the vandalism, but that they had no idea I was the mastermind engineering the car thefts, I knew I was home free."

Trish groaned to herself. She vividly recalled Barbara's sudden personality change when she had apologized for harassing Millie. Trish could feel her anger building, but she stayed quiet. Any minute now, Henry and Larry would show up and stop Barbara's crazy tirade. And then once Barbara was in handcuffs, Trish planned on giving her a piece of her mind. *That's all they ever did?* If Barbara only knew how wrong she was.

Suddenly, Barbara stopped pacing and looked right at Tim. "That is, I was home free until you were careless and got caught and demanded more money." Barbara turned, and Trish and Edna saw her slip her hand under her purse before she casually walked around the table. Trish held her breath. Barbara was only a few feet away from her now, the hand holding the gun straight down at her side. Tim wouldn't be able to see the gun, but surely he had enough sense to know he was in danger just by the sheer malevolence on Barbara's face.

Barbara turned quickly, bringing the gun up to shoulder height and pointing it directly at Tim.

Edna gasped, but the sound was drowned out by a loud, piercing squeal, followed by a deep, raspy voice reverberating through
the stillness.

"You gotta ask yourself, are you feeling lucky, punk?"

Startled, Barbara whirled around, dropping the gun in the
process. Tim took off running in the direction he had come from
while Barbara tried to regain her balance. Trish did the only
thing she could think of. Screaming like a mad woman to keep
Barbara frightened, she pushed herself off the ground and barreled out of the bushes, crashing into Barbara; they both top-
pled to the ground. Shouting obscenities, Barbara shoved at
Trish, scrambling to free herself.

Suddenly, a familiar voice shouted, "Freeze!"

Trish looked up and saw Henry, his feet planted firmly on
the ground and his gun pointed right at them. She froze.

Larry entered the clearing then, pulling a handcuffed Tim
behind him. Neither Henry nor Larry looked too happy to see
her. The situation might not have gotten any worse, though, if
Edna hadn't stuck her head out from under the bushes exclaim-
ing she had gotten some great pictures, and Millie hadn't strolled
over from behind a large oak tree singing the tune to *Bad Boys*,
her megaphone dangling from her hand.

Millie came over early to wait for Richard and Michelle. Instead
of wearing a black, slinky dress, she looked very attractive in
a rose-colored pantsuit with delicate pearls at her neck.

"How long do you think it will be before Larry speaks to us
again?" Trish asked, pouring Millie a cup of coffee.

Millie waved a hand. "Oh, he'll be fine. The next time we
need him, he'll be there. Don't you worry."

The next time? "Still, I think we ought to bake a cake and
take it over to the station tomorrow and apologize."

Millie shrugged. "Fine with me. But they should be apologizing to *us*. *We* stopped Barbara from shooting Tim, not them.
It's a good thing I remembered I had left my megaphone in
your car."

Trish laughed. "I have to admit, that was some pretty fast
thinking."

There was the sound of a knock on the door, and then Edna and Joe walked in. They were such a handsome couple, Joe in a dark-blue suit and Edna in a red flowing dress. "We're not too early, are we?" Joe asked as they sat at the table.

"No, we've got a few minutes," Trish said, pulling two more cups from the cabinet. "This is going to be fun tonight. I'm looking forward to the Italian restaurant Richard is taking us to."

She had chosen to wear one of the few dresses she owned, one with a swirly pattern of rose and lavender colors, and she was feeling quite festive.

"It's a shame you don't have a date, Trish," Millie said. "We should ask Pat if he'd like to join us. He was in his front yard when I came over here."

"No!" Trish exclaimed. "I don't need a date. Besides, you don't have one, either."

Millie shrugged. "It was just an idea."

Edna laughed. "You can both share my date. By the way, Joe called the station and talked to Larry. With all the evidence against her, Barbara doesn't have a chance of even making bail. But she doesn't seem to care, according to Larry. She even bragged about killing Bob Yates and told them where to find his body."

Joe nodded. "Larry did mention that the court would probably have her undergo psychiatric testing."

"I don't think there's any doubt that woman is loony tunes." Millie shuddered. "Oh, I almost forgot to tell you something. Michelle called me this afternoon. You'll never guess what Tony gave Carol for her birthday."

Trish looked at her. "What?"

"A blue 2010 Acura!"

Trish and Edna both groaned, remembering the note on Tony's notepad.

They heard the light tap of a car horn and they all stood. "Time to go."

"Just a minute," Millie said quickly. "Joe, would you go on out and let Richard and Michelle know we'll be right there?"

"What's wrong?" Edna asked as soon as the door closed behind him.

"Nothing." Millie grinned. "I just wanted to show you both something."

Puzzled, Edna and Trish followed Millie into Trish's office. She walked over to the computer and jerked the mouse, causing the screen to light up. "Open your e-mail, Trish."

Trish sighed. They didn't really have time for this. She sat in her chair, Millie and Edna looking over her shoulder. Trish typed in her password and waited for the program to open.

Then, in a new message from mmorrow007 were the words, *I love you guys. Thank you for standing beside me. BFF!*